Heat
Lightning

Heat
Lightning

Hildegarde Dolson

J. B. Lippincott Company

PHILADELPHIA AND NEW YORK

1970

For Dick

Heat
Lightning

Chapter One

The first earwigs ever to appear in Bevington, Connecticut, came that second week in May. People who turned up early for the meeting of the Civic Affairs and Image Improvement Association told each other the earwigs looked like roaches but seemed to prefer staying outdoors. Mrs. Tyndale, who ran Antique Bibelots and Unpainted Furniture, said darkly, "So far." It was generally agreed the earwigs had come over from England, but nobody said how.

Mrs. Loomite, the wife of the dentist who specialized in gums, tried to wrench the talk away from earwigs with a piece of news she considered more artistic. She was a woman who made quite a to-do about cultivating her mind and only watching Channel 13. In a breathy voice she said, "Guess who's coming to visit Prue Washburn—Alicia Thorne." The others were used to not listening to her, so most of them went right on with earwigs.

Young Cassie Murdoch, who was covering the meeting for her father's paper, and for inflamed reasons of her own, did say, "How exciting. I know Daddy will want to do a story on her." But she said it mostly to be nice, because Mrs. Loomite with her girlish crushes on the Arts and her popping thyroid eyes was somehow pathetic.

A half-dozen hard-core civic reformers came in then, followed by the chairman who had been waylaid by the P.T.A. on an urgent matter.

Chester Humboldt got there a few minutes late, so he missed the alert on earwigs and Alicia Thorne. He wouldn't have cared anyway; his gardener coped with bugs, and he had never heard of Alicia Thorne.

He sat down in the empty back row, on one of those folding chairs unstacked for funerals. It was so inadequate for a tall, well-built man who did push-ups every morning that it made him feel at once uncertain and too big for his britches.

The meeting was in the new wing of the Public Library for reasons that escaped him until he realized some biddy who was against lung cancer must have set it up so that nobody could smoke. He himself had given up smoking at the time of his divorce, in a surge of masochistic healthiness. But now he craved a cigarette so violently he would almost have picked up a stub.

The meeting had been called for the ungodly hour of 7:30 P.M. And because it was, in a sense, the start of a new phase in his life—public service leading, he hoped, to public office —he had expected to feel a buoyancy of high-minded purpose. Instead, he felt lousy.

He had driven up after a sales conference in the New York office, a two-hour drive that took him almost three hours in the rain. He had barely had time to gulp half a Scotch on the rocks and bolt down a chicken thing loaded with lichee nuts, prepared by his housekeeper. The nuts rolled in his stomach like buckshot.

The chairman, Tom Devin, the real-estate man who had sold Chester the old Mortly place that spring, was trying to bring the meeting to order around the edges. By then, the word on earwigs and Alicia Thorne had spiraled to several late-comers. In the final reluctant hush of attention to the chairman, two voices were trapped in action: ". . . been married three times and got the Pulitzer or something". . . "have little pincers on their rear ends."

The chairman waved away these loose ends. He wore a red-jeweled ring on his little finger, and his sports jacket was so tight he looked rather like a sausage encased in madras plaid. "Fellow citizens, the P.T.A. has asked me to make a top-priority announcement. Due to the sudden increase of child molesters, mothers are organizing volunteer watches at all school bus stops. This will continue till summer vacation, June twentieth. Volunteers may call Mrs. Hinck."

"What if the mothers are molested too?" somebody asked.

Mrs. Hinck stood up, or popped up. She looked very flushed and determined. "The mothers will go in pairs and they will be armed—with a paralyzing nerve gas."

"But that stuff is illegal."

"Not this brand," a man said. "It's on sale in the hardware store—doesn't have much effect anyway except maybe make you sneeze." Somebody sneezed but changed it hurriedly to a nose-blow.

"Thank you, Mrs. Hinck," the chairman said. "I'm sure you'll get more volunteers than you can handle."

Mrs. Hinck wasn't ready to sit down. "I called Wes Murdoch, but the *Bugle* had already gone to press for this week, so if you *would* tell everybody you know to keep an eye out."

Chester was making a mental note of the name Murdoch. He must tell his secretary to subscribe to the *Bugle* tomorrow. If she could line up decorators to do his house and employment agencies to service it, she ought to be able to think of a simple, basic thing like subscribing to the local paper. He'd have thought of it himself if he hadn't been up to his neck in problems at the new branch of Pilgrim Mills in Georgia.

Vaguely, he heard a girl's voice: "Daddy had a flyer printed that will be delivered with the *Bugle* tomorrow. And if you're short of volunteers, Mrs. Hinck, I'd love to help even if I'm not a mother."

"I'm sure that can be easily remedied," the chairman said genially. "Uh—I mean—Oliver Yates—uh—June bride."

"He hasn't asked me yet," the voice said gaily, "But maybe I can shame him into it."

Brazen kid, Chester thought. Probably gobbled the Pill like candy.

Mrs. Hinck said she needed more volunteers for the 8 A.M. shift. "Most of the mothers think nothing could happen to their children so early in the morning, but we can't count on that with a sex fiend."

When she left the room two youngish women followed her, either to sign up for the 8 A.M. shift or to get more details.

". . . main item on the agenda tonight," the chairman was saying, "is whether Bevington will heed the call of progress and adopt a floating zone code. As you know, we need new businesses in our community, and the only way we can get them is to give them what they want."

A babble of voices erupted. They sounded to Chester mostly angry.

"Fellow citizens—fellow citizens—*Folks!* PLEASE! One at a time. Let's keep an open mind till we hear both sides."

"Everybody knows which side you're on, Tom Devin." The speaker looked like a turkey festooned with beads. "You want everything floating loose so you can sell land to that TV parts plant to build spang in the middle of a residential area. This is a beautiful, historic community which my ancestors helped settle in seventeen twenty-eight and. . . ."

Chester Humboldt listened uneasily. His own ancestors had come over, belatedly, in steerage. His grandfather had been a scutcher in the same New England mill Chester now owned, which currently did an annual gross of around nine million, give or take a few tax write-offs. Chester had been too busy turning a creaky Pilgrim Mills into a going concern—matching sets of bedspreads, curtains (called "drapes"), towels, even toilet-seat covers (called "commoders")—to do much delving into New England's historic past. The closest he'd come was to develop the current American Eagle line, an eagle-with-stars design copied from an 18th-century mirror in the Fogg Museum, but with a little something added: two small white doves, one cuddled under each wing of the eagle. It was the hottest seller in years.

Once that would have made him exultantly happy. But recently he had felt more and more that it wasn't enough to be a millionaire; one must be a *reform* millionaire, with the spirit that had sent Christians into lions' dens. He had watched at first incredulously, then thoughtfully, as other millionaires his age abandoned their corporations to run for governor or senator or something. And he had picked Bevington as his community, after his aides had shopped around quietly, because it seemed ideal as background and springboard. It was very old, Republican in a democratic way, and very photogenic. His accountant who lived in the next county had put him onto the old Mortly place because it was going cheap. And it *was* a good buy, if anybody wanted forty-seven acres with a fourteen-room mansion, guest house, tennis court, and God knows what else. He hadn't had time to walk around his estate as he'd pictured himself walking, in a hand-loomed country-squire jacket, with bounding dog.

The argument over a floating zone code had been amplified into a shouting match, having to do mostly with septic tanks. "No sanitary engineer in his right mind" . . . "we pay more school taxes so they can move in here tax-free and dump their sewage problem right in our laps . . . desecration of historic landmarks" . . . "I don't care if they put Paul Revere's steeple on top, the exterior elevations still stink" . . . "can't stop progress" . . . "bull-dozer over my dead body. . . ."

The voices battered against Chester's head. He wished he were home watching an old movie on his color set with hand-volume control. Why hadn't somebody invented a hand-volume control for politicians in meetings? The voices were getting louder and madder.

"MR. CHAIRMAN! MR. CHAIRMAN! Before we get more involved in a knock-down DRAG-out that goes on half the night—and you know what time we got out of here at our last meeting—twenty minutes of ONE—I MUST make an announcement on the courses at the Community Center which will start in June." The woman was very tall and gave the impression of having four elbows. She also had a mouthful of

13

capital letters which she took out like pins to jab here and there . . . "GREAT deal of interest in the DOG OBEDIENCE course and JAPANESE flower ARRANGING . . . SIX lectures on HALLUCINOGENIC drugs, their DISGUISES, such as SUGAR, their DANGERS for TEEN-agers . . . only RESIDENTS may register for this series, and by residents we include SUMMER PEOPLE provided they OWN or RENT. . . ."

Like anybody who read or swallowed news capsules, Chester knew teen-age addicts in well-off communities were a problem, but the knowledge didn't arouse any civic do-good in him, it simply made him sore. If those brats had had to work the way he'd had to work, never even a Saturday afternoon off, earn their own tuition and not have everything handed them on a silver spoon. . . . As the speaker went on—lessons in chair CANING . . . Yoga to HIGHER health of MIND and BODY—he kept his head in chin-up listening formation while he focused a professional eye on the curtains at the side right window behind the chairman. Skipping twill in a dull monochromatic—wouldn't clean too well—ought to have one of his washable synthetics . . . offer the library two or three pairs—might make some decorating committee mad at him—send them anonymously, in a plain wrapper, no fingerprints. . . .

Directly across from the offending curtains, a half-open door led to the stacks; he remembered how the word "stacks" had put him off, in his freshman year at the University, conjuring up high, endless stacks of books he must somehow get on top of. He had learned what he needed, although he'd learned a hell of a lot more working at the mill, but did he know enough to be in government? Did anybody know enough to be in government now? Did anybody in their right mind *want* to be in government now?

These thoughts, combined with the undigested lichee nuts, made his stomach churn. He groped in the jacket pocket of his three-hundred-dollar suit to find a TUMS to suck. No TUMS,

14

only a hole in the lining . . . damn valet service in his New York hotel should have taken care of it . . . or his house-keeper, but she was too busy reading about Zen Buddha and the guys who sat around bare-ass contemplating their navels. A fat lot of good *that* did humanity. He wriggled his finger down through the hole in his pocket, convinced he could feel something round and hard. He was absorbed in this explora-tion when a woman sat down beside him and spread her possessions over two other chairs as if she were opening a market stall. She whispered cosily, "Terrible night, isn't it?"

Chester freed his finger unostentatiously, poked back the pocket lining, and nodded agreement. She went on, "I had to wait till my house guest arrived . . . I did hate to leave her but I had to come because I'm president of"—it sounded to Chester as if she said—"of the Hysterical Association." What she said next seemed to bear this out rather forcibly: "We have to plan ahead for the revolution."

She didn't look like an advocate of revolution—black, red, or even white. She looked more like the kind of woman who would clap for Tinkerbell. She was built like a bean pot, but a soft, melted-down bean pot, with short legs and a flattish lid sprouting gray frizzled hair. She was beaming at Chester so nicely, with such a ladylike air, he decided she was merely barmy. One of those barmy old maids of good family that New England overproduced. But the last thing he wanted was to get mixed up with any crackpots, however harmless. His new public relations man had warned him on that. He turned away and made a show of listening to Four Elbows' windup: ". . . six lessons in teen-age POISE—or conversa-tional RUSSIAN made EASY." She folded her elbows to sub-side.

The fixed-versus-floating-zone belligerents were still mutter-ing when the chairman called eagerly, "Ah, Miss Washburn, there you are, just in time." He didn't add, "to create a diversion," but the thought hung in the air.

"I'm terribly sorry to be late," Bean Pot said. "But I had to give poor Alicia dinner in bed on a tray because the Saw Mill River Parkway was absolutely *flooded* with rain, and she was exhausted after the drive from New York."

"I understand from Mrs. Loomite," the chairman said, "that your friend Miss Thorne is a very distinguished celebrity. We're honored to have her in our midst. And as long as you have such a good excuse for tardiness—ha-ha—we'll forgive you. Folks, the Historical Association feels—and I think they're right—that we ought to join forces way ahead and start planning now for our bicentennial celebration of the War of Independence."

That Revolution. Chester looked up at Miss Washburn standing dumpily beside him, and smiled his best rumpled-boyish smile. He certainly didn't want to be known as a man who was against the only all-American Revolution of the lot. He vibrated encouragement—I'm-with-you-all-the-way. Miss Washburn beamed back at him trustingly. "Of course we do have a few more years till the actual date. But as I was saying to Mr. Devin this morning, if you recall the Civil War celebration, just about everybody jumped the gun way ahead, and we don't want to be scooped by Ridgefield or Guilford or any of the towns around that aren't nearly as historic as Bevington."

There was a murmurous ground swell of local pride, or the surge of competition. Miss Washburn sat down looking pleased. Her coat had slid off the seat, and Chester helped her retrieve it and adjust it around her shoulders. Automatically he noticed the label—Saks-Fifth-Avenue—and was a bit surprised. Miss Washburn looked like one of those little women who buy their clothes at a bake sale.

A short, pot-bellied man with the jolly red aura of a Santa Claus got up: "A guy from Georgia I met at a hardware convention was telling me that by the time his town started getting a move on for the Civil War shindig, most of the Confederate uniforms and muskets had been bought up by fast-thinking types in another county. So I say we get off our tails and get the ball rolling—the sooner the better."

A baldish man sitting in front of Chester said, "Publishers fought the Civil War five, six years ahead. By Centennial year you couldn't even give the books away with green stamps."

Chester was already dictating more memos to himself: "Get the art department onto this Revolutionary kick tomorrow. . . . Facsimile map of Bunker Hill, done in good strong reds on beige linen? . . . Might look too much like blood trickles. Better plug the positive angle—*Give Me Liberty* written in script—all-over repeat pattern—clear medium blue on white? . . . *The British Are Coming.* . . . Needs a twist—*The British Are Coming and Going.* . . ."

The atmosphere wasn't angry now, or restive. Even Turkey Wattles, who had been throwing her ancestors into the breach, seemed gratified when the chairman asked her to head a committee to line up descendants of early settlers "who fought the good fight, starting with your own illustruss Maulridge branch."

After correcting the chairman on "branch"—"This was the main family tree, in Bevington"—Miss Maulridge said graciously, "We might line up some descendants of governors and one or two eminent historians."

Devin cut in: "Now you're on target. What we want are some big names—say, for an advisory committee."

Chester began to feel he'd come to the right place. Too bad the Revolution—the main show—couldn't be shoved up a few years. His new public relations man had stressed the importance of selling a man's name to the voters before selling the man. "They know Pilgrim Mills, but we can't change your name to Pilgrim. It's not like you're a movie stud. See what I mean?" Chester had seen.

If he were to serve on a committee for a cause as safe and solid as celebrating the Revolution, it would be a gilt-edged way to establish himself and get his name around.

The pot-bellied hardware man said, "And how about we line up some top TV stars—get us nation-wide publicity?"

Prudence Washburn put her hand on Chester's arm anxiously, confidingly. "But TV entertainers aren't really old New England. And most of them are so—well—*you* know." Chester was unaccountably flattered.

"I do wish we could get my friend Alicia to stay a while and help us. New England's history is bred in her bones."

Chester had a swift picture of a woman bony as a hatrack draped in old parchment.

". . . one of her ancestors came over with Justice Holmes' forbears on the *Angel Gabriel*."

This latter reference baffled him. The only Angel Gabriel he had heard of was the one who blew trumpet in heaven. But he remembered belatedly that Miss Washburn's guest was—what had Devin called her?—a "distinguished celebrity." He roused to Miss Washburn's prattle with the special leaning-forward interest of a man who may run for something.

". . . Sir Walter Raleigh's ship, before his Virginia tobacco period, I believe. Alicia could tell us exactly. When we roomed together in school, she used to tell us such delightful stories. Her great-grandfather was a close friend of Mr. Emerson's—of course that's not really connected with the Revolution, but I think it's so interesting, don't you?"

Chester did. He hadn't read more than a few bits of Emerson's, but the essay on Self-Reliance had turned him on hard, in high school. If Alicia Whosis had inherited some good family anecdotes on Emerson, Mister Self-Reliant himself, and Chester told the stories in speeches or maybe to magazine interviewers—"Alicia Whosis was telling me the other night about the time her great-grandfather and Mr. Emerson. . . ." He must find out what Alicia Whosis was famous for, and what her last name was. He turned to bestow another, even more warmly boyish, smile on Miss Washburn, but it was wasted on the back of her head. "Oh, there's Oliver."

A young man came in the side door as if blown by ill winds from behind. His raincoat was splotched and dribbling; his shoes squeaked wetly as he started down the center aisle, peering.

A young girl stood up near the front, waving a notebook

like a banner. What struck Chester instantly about the girl was not that she was pretty—he'd seen prettier—but that she didn't have straight hair dangling down her cheeks like curtains. This girl's was short, and springy as a wire-haired terrier. Since his divorce, he had taken out quite a few youngish girls; only the week before he had taken one to a new discotheque, the Magnum Carte. Later on, he had left her to go to the men's room, and when he came back all the girls in the room looked so much alike—dangled straight hair, dangled white faces—that he hadn't the foggiest notion which was his. Partly, this may have been due to three drinks, one above his usual quota. By a process of geographic determination, he had soon rejoined the right female. But the experience had shaken him oddly. And as he looked at the girl waving the notebook, he thought how easy she'd be to pick out. It wasn't that he lusted after her; she was too short for his taste and her legs were a bit on the solid side. His new friend Miss Washburn said, "That's Cassie Murdoch—Wes Murdoch's daughter. And that's her young man."

The girl deserved better, Chester thought, here again quite impersonally. The young man looked as if he belonged with a danky-locks type. "She's applied for the Peace Corps," Miss Washburn went on, "but now I think she might just get married instead."

The girl was tucking the young man into a seat beside her, and even helped him off with his mildewed raincoat.

"Glad you finally made it, Yates," Devin said. "Looks like you had to swim over from the school."

"My car broke down halfway here."

Chester decided Yates was the sort whose car would always break down. Yates himself had a reedy, breakable look.

"We were just talking about our bicentennial of the Revolution, and I'd like you to hear this, Yates. The pitch is, we want to stir up advance publicity—get the young people and the schools involved early—maybe train a drummer-boys corps to drum up interest, ha-ha. Say we work up some stuff, sort of preview—for our Fourth of July celebration this year. Do you think your music department could help us with that?"

"I'll ask Dr. Talladay," Yates said, without enthusiasm.

Chester disliked the voice. It went with limp handshakes.

"The Talladay School might put on a concert of old marching songs," Miss Maulridge said. "I have some very valuable sheet music of the period, Oliver, which you may examine."

"Thanks," Yates said, in a swallowed tone.

"I hardly think Oliver would be interested in marching songs," Mrs. Loomite said, with a languorous bulging-eyed look at Yates. "After all, they are not what he or I would regard as music."

Miss Maulridge's wattles were rising again. The chairman said hastily, "Yes, Al, you wanted to say something?"

The pot-bellied hardware man, Al Farwell, said, "Kids are crazy about guns, and the quickest way you'd get 'em hooked on this Revolution shindig is to form rival musket teams."

Mrs. Loomite leaped from her aisle seat so violently her chair turned over. "So they can practice being killed? And go off to kill helpless little people in some backward country—innocent peasants—who only want rice and peace?"

"Now, Mrs. Loomite," Devin said. "Nobody wants our boys killed. But if we're going to stop the Communists—say, that's an angle we could use for our bicentennial. The boys of 'seventy-six fought to make us free—now we fight to make the world free."

"Let's not confuse ourselves with the Birch Society," the mild-voiced man in the row in front of Chester said. "I suggest we get back to the zoning code and that survey on septic tanks."

"I think peace is more vital than septic tanks," Mrs. Loomite said passionately. "If we blow each other up, what good are septic tanks?"

"If we don't have septic tanks, we might as well blow each other up." Mild man again.

Mrs. Loomite surged on. "Don't we have enough war already, without glorifying it like a great holy cause, in a huge, phony celebration?"

20

Miss Maulridge was flaying the air with her beak. "The Revolution *was* a great holy cause—the most glorious moment in our history—the shot heard round the world."

"I do think this country was *meant* to be a democracy," Miss Washburn said to Chester. "But I sometimes wonder about the others—I mean in Asia and Africa and all."

Everybody in the room was talking at once. War or peace, floating fixed zoning code—it was impossible to tell, in the melee, who was for what.

"*Folks! Folks!*" The chairman shouted. "Let's get down to business. The Fourth of July is Coming."

This startling news brought relative quiet.

"Bevington has always put on a bang-up parade. And as you know, our fireworks display brings crowds from all over the county. But that takes *coordination*. And due to some civic disturbances which I won't go into, we are behind in our planning. Whaddya say we all pull together and nominate our committees for the glorious Fourth? And we can throw in some teasers for our Revolutionary bicentennial—kill two birds with one stone. Do I hear a motion?"

"Listen—please, listen first." The girl who didn't have straight hair had jumped up. Chester saw her young man— Yates—twitch at her arm, trying to pull her down. Chester ordinarily detested women getting up on soapboxes ranting, but he was perversely pleased that Yates couldn't keep the girl in hand.

"I promise not to take long, but there's something I just have to say."

She turned to face Chester and the others, flinging out her arms. "This was such a wonderful village in the old days. People helped each other—ground each other's flour—harvested each other's crops—and worked together and loved each other." She glanced down briefly, tenderly, at the young man, who was staring at his knees. "They even made their own *soap*." Nobody laughed. But quite a few people smiled, as one smiles at the antics of children.

"Oliver—Mr. Yates—and I have been reading some old

histories of Bevington. Sort of research—because Oliver wants to write some ballads based on early New England. He's a very fine composer."

I'll bet, Chester thought. If he's so great, why is he teaching music in some crummy school?

"Our people were good and kind then. They didn't care about materialistic trappings; they were proud of the right things—and that's what made them free. *That's* what was glorious—what we ought to celebrate. So instead of the same corny Fourth of July speeches and the same floats and the same old "Star-Spangled Banner" gargle, why don't we have a liberty-pole festival? We thought of that name—I mean Mr. Yates thought of it—because we read that several years before the Revolution people in this village put up liberty poles."

Chester felt a creepy tingle of excitement—the same sort of tingle that had come on him when he saw the American-eagle-sitting-on-stars design and saw how it cried out for doves. Liberty pole—do it like a Maypole. Peppermint-striped poles with varicolored streamers. . . .

"Every time the British knocked one down, people would sneak out at night and put up a new liberty pole and paint it —yellow or green or orange or blue but never redcoat. Don't you love thinking of it?"

Chester, for one, did. His mind was racing. He could already see the layout for the ads.

Everybody in the room except the chairman seemed to be listening quite amiably, or at least tolerantly. Devin was fidgeting and fingering some papers as if he'd even reopen the septic-tank fight to end this foolishness. But when the daughter of the local newspaper publisher is speaking, it's awkward to say, "Cut the cackle."

". . . could put up our own poles and have ballad singers —and square dances and fiddlers—and ancestors' family portraits and old millstones and things . . . a display of instruments of the period like a dulcimer . . . and maybe a folk play with music. . . ."

Music seemed to play rather a large part in her plans.

22

Devin said, "Honey, I hate to tell you, but if you're thinking of—like—a music festival, forget it. Either they go in the red or they bring out the weirdies and drunks and homos and you end up calling the riot squad. Look at Newport."

"But we aren't Newport." She flung out her arms again. "All of you know so much more about Bevington's history than I do. And if you'd all pitch in and help—I know seven weeks isn't much time to get ready, but. . . ."

The "seven weeks isn't much time" hit Chester as a bucket of cold water hits a drunk. Never have the merchandise ready for a tie-in.

". . . instead of politicians sounding off with blabby clichés," the girl was saying ardently, "Oh, if you knew how reporters hate covering Fourth of July speeches and clambakes—Daddy called them talking clams—but this would be *fresh*. We'd be written up all over the place."

Chester's mind did a double flip-flop. Fresh! No flag-waving blabby clichés. What other millionaire had vaulted from a liberty pole into public life? None. His scalp tingled again; his antennae, with sharpened awareness, picked up the shift among listeners. The girl was putting it across. Quite a few of the women were already hooked . . . the pop-eyed dame who'd sounded off on peace . . . the men were going along for the moment, maybe because they liked the girl.

"So many of my generation don't know who they are," she was saying. Her young voice trembled with feeling: "We're trying desperately to find out." Chester had read that line *ad nauseam* in news stories, and it had always made him wonder what the hell these kids thought life was—a chase-your-tail and smash the world to find True Self in the rubble? But now he was rather moved. He wanted this festival for sensible reasons, but in a more formless way, he also wanted it for this kid.

". . . and as a country, I think we've forgotten what we are, what we came from and stood for. We have to find out again. Instead of celebrating shooting and killing, we'd be honoring the lovely, good, simple things in our past—the true spirit of people who loved *all* freedoms. Please, please, at least think about it." She sat down.

Prudence Washburn said to Chester, "Alicia would absolutely love this."

"We could sell advertising to our local merchants," the hardware-store man said. "Get their names on the liberty pole."

Mild-voice said, "Like a combination totem pole and kiosk." Chester noticed this time that the man's bald spot was precisely the size of a tennis ball.

"We can NOT have advertising on the pole," Mrs. Loomite half shrieked. "That would vulgarize the whole idea. I see a liberty pole rising brightly on the Village Green—a symbol of peace and freedom—and small dancers circling around it—children of all creeds and colors."

"No trespassing on the Village Green," the chairman said. "Especially kids. Cost us a wad of dough to reseed it after the —er—incident this spring. You can't hold a festival there anyway. It's a traffic island."

"No man is an island," Mild-voice said, "but now everybody's a traffic island. Ask not for whom the horn honksh. . . ." He was beginning to sound rather potted.

"Let's think of places we *could* have the festival," Cassie Murdoch said. Chester had already thought of one. "The high-school stadium is pretty bare, but we might put down artificial green sod. . . ."

"Stadium's out. Soccer, Little League, and Dog Obedience right through the summer."

"How about getting somebody with a big estate. . . ." the girl began.

You've got him, Chester said silently.

The gavel pounded. "Folks, this is all very interesting, but it's not getting us anywhere. Let's face it—a festival costs too much dough."

"So do fireworks," Cassie said hotly.

"Not as much as a festival. Al Farwell gets us a forty percent discount."

24

"Forty-five," the hardware man said, with modesty.

"And a Fourth of July parade and fireworks are sure-fire entertainment. More festivals flop than you can shake a stick at."

"Moneywise, I'd say we can't touch it."

"We've raised money for the new wing of the library," Cassie said, "and for an integrated swimming pool, and we could raise money for this—I know we could."

"No time," Devin said. "I tell you what, honey, let's think about it as a possibility for next year."

"But we need this kind of thing *now*. Who knows where any of us will be next year?" "Who knows if the world will even *be*, by then? We can't afford to wait."

Chester stood up. "Mr. Chairman, I'm new here and I hope you people who are much more experienced will forgive my butting in. But I think this is too good an idea to let go down the drain, because it fits Bevington. And to start the ball rolling—or to raise the liberty pole—I'd like to pledge ten thousand right now."

There was a stunned silence, then a cricking of necks and clicking of tongues.

Cassie Murdoch said, "You're an angel. Isn't he, Oliver?"

"A feet-on-the-ground angel," Chester said modestly. "Would you consider using my place—that is, the old Mortly place—for your festival?"

His neighbor, Miss Washburn, started the clapping, and soon it sounded like a claque.

Chapter
Two

Prudence Washburn's house was small and old, circa 1800, sturdily planted with its back to a hill. The roof still had most of the original cypress shingles, hand-rived. The front room had the hand-hewn, rock-maple beams, and wide old floorboards. Alicia Thorne was pacing up and down this room like a caged Amazon queen when Prudence unlatched the front door.

"This damn house shrinks when it's wet," Alicia said. "Where in God's name have you been all night?"

"But it's only a little after ten."

"You've been gone for hours. Just when I needed you most. I've been so hideously low. How could you leave me alone in this state?"

"But you weren't in a state when I left. You said you felt deliciously unwound and you had a new book—oh, I'm dripping on it." She squatted to pick up a book from the floor near the hearth. "What a shame. I got the cover all messy."

Her guest laughed rather wildly. "The better to match what's inside. I meant to throw it in the fire but I missed."

Prudence, with one arm out of her sopping coat, stood as if turned to wet salt. "Lishy! You were going to burn a *book*? What's come over you?"

"Ask what's come over the world," Alicia said. "We seem to be buried in sewage. A new kind of Pompeii."

"They were fussing about sewage tonight at the Civic Affairs meeting. You should have come with me. It was so exciting."

"Civic affairs are not my idea of excitement." She walked—or trailed—over in her velvet robe, picked up the book fastidiously by one corner like a dead rat, and dropped it into a pink wastebasket painted with forget-me-nots. "How the critics could hail that minicreature as a 'powerful new voice—penetrating as a madman's scream in the murk' "—She shuddered.

"But why should anybody want to pay five ninety-five to hear a madman's scream in the murk?" Prudence's round face shone with the need for enlightenment. "I think that was meant to be a bad review."

Alicia's mouth, with the exquisitely chiseled upper lip, pulled down at the corners. "It's a rave, I assure you."

"Then the critic is raving mad, and that's why he likes to hear other madmen scream in the murk. It makes him feel safer." She rattled the fire tongs triumphantly.

"Will you stop brandishing and listen? I had a shattering experience tonight with that book. I saw I'd outlived my prime. I should have died at my peak."

"You're still resting on it." Prudence stirred the fire to a comfortable liveliness and turned to face her friend. "You reached your peak in your twenties and you've been sitting there ever since."

"You make me sound like a flagpole sitter," Alicia complained. "Hanging on grimly to save my neck." She raised her head so that her white, curving throat showed to advantage. "My sagging old neck."

"Don't be a goony." Prudence liked to trot out the words they'd used in school. "You're as beautiful as ever. You look at least ten years younger than your age." Noticing the frown, she revised hurriedly, "Twenty years younger, really. You look about twenty-seven."

"Oh, Prue, Prue-blue, you do mean it, don't you? I felt so desolate and depressed here, alone."

"All the more reason you should have come with me. People at the meeting were so disappointed. They're longing to see you. Wait till I tell you what happened. Wes Murdoch's daughter—"

"Wes Murdoch! I hadn't thought of him in years. Remember when you and I visited your aunt here, and Wes followed me around like a dog? A spotty dog with short legs." She chucked herself gaily under one breast. "He came up to about here on me."

"I remember," Prue said. Her face looked so drained suddenly that her freckles stood out. "Let's have a cup of tea."

"I had enough tea those years with Harley to turn me to tannic acid. You know, the English boil tea like an old shoe. You can actually taste the leather. I was leathery inside and out."

A good many men, and some fair-minded women, had described Alicia Thorne's skin as *translucent*. One besotted scholarly sort had even used the word *hyaline*, but translucent was more generally favored. Her skin hadn't the milky opaqueness of most redheads'—it shimmered.

"Leathery like pigskin," Alicia went on. "Weathered and worn."

Prudence made clucking sounds of reassurance, the sort she'd been making to her friend for over twenty-five years. She may have sounded less vehement than usual, because Alicia became more dramatic. "God, what I went through. Harley was such a niggler."

Harley was husband before last; it seemed odd to have him cropping up again as a whipping boy.

"All critics are nigglers when you're married to them. I'd thought he was the most generous man on earth when he reviewed my first book. But they save all their best adjectives to spend in public. And in private they're carping mean hoarders. Harley insisted on sending money to his ex-wife even if I had to wear rags." Her lovely long fingers twitched at a fold in her velvet robe. "And when the bills came in he'd keep saying, 'I need hardly point out'—and then point and point till I nearly went mad. Where are you going? Stop bouncing around like a yo-yo."

Prudence said she wanted to get out of her damp clothes and make some tea.

"Prue! What a selfish beast I am. You're shivering and dank. Let me run you a bath. I'll scatter iris leaves in it. I've carried a little bag of dried iris leaves for my bath ever since Japan. Wait till I find which case they're in." She was girlishly eager, opening bags, making a chiffony clutter, wanting to serve her friend.

Prudence had followed her into the guest room saying doggedly she didn't want a bath, not even with dried iris leaves. "I had a shower before dinner. All I want is tea."

Alicia insisted on making the tea herself. "With my very own Lapsang souchong. Oh, those lovely little porcelain cups on the rack up there—perfect."

She was tall enough to reach the cups in one fluid snatch. Prudence herself always had to use the stepladder at spring and fall cleaning time. She never allowed her cleaning woman to wash the heirloom china. Luckily, the cups had had their semiannual sudsing the month before. And the teapot, too, pleased Alicia's sensibilities.

By the time Prue was wadded into her navy flannel robe, her guest had the kitchenware drawer turned upside down on the counter. "I can't find a silver tea caddy," she said in a frantic, accusing tone. Her hostess produced a dime-store strainer. Alicia's dark eyebrows, which tended to wing up at the outer ends, winged even higher, but she took the strainer. "This is the most inconvenient house to work in, like one of those antique doll houses some fool collects and gives to a hapless museum."

Prudence cut lemon in silence. For revenge, however unconscious, she cut the slices too thick.

29

"Not that it isn't a beautiful job of restoring. Even those hinges on the cupboards. You were exactly the right person to inherit this house. You've had so little else, poor lamb. And you pour out kindnesses and comfort. The least I can do is settle you sweetly by the fire and bring you tea in style."

She led Prue to a high-backed, bony-spindled Brewster rocker in the room which still smacked a bit of antimacassared parlor. "And a footstool for your pretty little feet—just so. There!"

Prudence's legs were too short to get a grip on the needle-point footstool; when the rocker lurched backward, she had to grope with curled toes. And the tea was awfully weak amber. She would have liked a stiffer brew, the kind she made for herself with Flo-thru teabags, but she knew better than to say so. With Alicia, tea had always been a ritual; she had written ecstatically from London, when she and Harley first went there to live till his wife gave him a divorce, about the delights of hot scones for tea, and nightingales for lovers. Her face, even her manner, as she poured now, was classically serene, Portrait of a Lady. "And we must have a slug of brandy in it."

This was a new touch; Alicia had never drunk much. One perfectly made martini before dinner, an occasional glass of wine, but she could be wildly intoxicated on gaiety, especially her own.

"Where's the brandy?" There was none. In the cherry hutch with authentic wormholes and doweled pegs, which served as a liquor closet, the only liquors were crème de menthe, apricot cordial, and the cloudy dregs of benedictine. "You always did love sickeningly sweet things, pet. And you never minded gaining weight, which must be so restful. I watch every ounce now."

When she came back across the room carrying a bottle of rum, she walked with a delicately overdone sway that showed off her hips.

"Yo-ho-ho and a dollop of rum." She poured a lavish dollop. "To the spirit of my sea-captain ancestors. Down the hatch."

Prudence, after a first ladylike sip, drank, amost slurped the tea with pleasure. "What a good idea. I think I'll serve it this way the next time our Historical Association meets here. What I started to tell you—"

"Don't tell me about New England history, you prairie lamb. We Thornes flowered in its heyday."

"But that's just why I wanted to—"

Alicia was deaf to any interruptions but her own. "Historians write so endlessly about the Puritan strain in New Englanders and forget all the sea captains roiling in our blood, mixing strange spices. They didn't sail to the Orient to make money; they could have made fortunes as ship builders with burgomaster tummies. But they hungered for adventure. Not to be adventurers—oh, no!—they always came home every year or two to sell off a cargo, deposit the gold, beget a legitimate child. They'd go in tandem to church, make respectful gestures to God the Puritan father, but their real gods always reclaimed them." Prue's eyes shut dozily; she jerked to attention as Alicia's voice heralded a climax: "I know so well how they felt; they wanted both worlds, the safe, solid world and the gloriously reckless explorings. But finally they had to come home to stay, inert as rock. How did they learn to accept that? Maybe they never did. Will I ever accept it?"

"You don't have to settle anything tonight," Prudence said. "It's like overloading your stomach at bedtime. We'll sleep late and go for a walk in the woods behind the old Mortly place." Approaching her objective a new, longer way round, she said cunningly, "I met the new owner—we can walk there any time. It's only a mile up the road."

"With you, I always feel as if there's a sensible solution for everything. The only trouble is that when I get close to a sensible solution and look it in the face, I shy like a runaway horse. But I'm so tired of running—and it's such heaven to be with you."

"Stay longer," Prudence said. "Stay at least a month."

"Pet, I promised the Dilmans in Stockbridge I'd come next week and stay in their guest house all summer. I can't really str-r-r-r-etch here." She stretched luxuriously, admiring her arms in front of her. "I need space and aloneness to work."

"The old Mortly place is forty acres," Prudence said. "It's so refreshing when somebody actually buys one of these big old estates to live in now. They always seem to be sold for a funeral home or a camp for difficult chidren. There's a guest house behind the main house, not too close. Maybe Mr. Humboldt would let you use it—at least till the Fourth of July."

"What a curious deadline. Am I supposed to go off then like a firecracker? Not that I'd dream of accepting a house from a Mr. Humburg."

"Humboldt," Prudence said, almost sternly. Alicia's small flare-ups of anti-Semitism had always bothered her, and sometimes she'd said so. But this wasn't the moment to take a chance. One never knew, with Alicia, whether criticism would make her rage like a tiger or crumple like a slapped child.

"He looks Scandinavian and he's rangy and quite attractive. He owns Pilgrim Mills."

"What do they turn out—pilgrims? Everything's so *made* now—why not synthetic pilgrims to trudge after some guru or other?"

"You know very well Pilgrim Mills has always made sheets and things. Even when we were children."

"Were we ever children?" Alicia said somberly. "My father should never have married my mother."

This was a subject Alicia could ride for hours; Prudence grabbed the reins instantly, with unusual firmness. "Mr. Humboldt told me after the meeting he's been down in Georgia opening a new plant there, but he plans to spend much more time here this summer. He's asked us all there for drinks Saturday and. . . ."

"We are not going," Alicia said. "I refuse to be used by some pushy little Jew manufacturer."

"He's not little and he's not pushy and he is *not* Jewish— he's blond." Hearing herself in a kind of delayed echo, she flushed. "Not that it would make any difference. He's *nice*. And he's very generous."

"Jews can be the most generous people alive," Alicia said. "Maybe I should marry one sometime. Such good, faithful family men, such good providers. Why don't I ever fall in love with that sort?"

"Geoffrey was—" Prue broke off and gulped her tea.

"Say it. Go on, say it. Geoff was faithful—Geoff was a family man—Geoff was a good provider. He even provided me with a baby on the honeymoon."

Prue, intent on distraction, wriggled out of the rocker: "I forgot to show you the borning room. It used to be the sewing room—remember? I had it restored just exactly the way it used to be. Come see."

Like a small tug nudging a majestic liner, she manipulated Alicia into the little room behind the kitchen. It was cold and rather bare, with only a ladder-back chair, a narrow four-poster bed carved with pineapples, and a pile of old copies of *American Heritage*. The fireplace had a huge iron pot suspended from a hook, hanging over the grate. "That's one of the original kettles used to heat water when the baby was being born."

"What did they do—boil the baby in it? No wonder new babies always looked so red and squally. Mine did. As if it had caught the way I felt for those nine awful months before."

Prudence tried to chatter brightly about the search she'd had for the kettle; Alicia was having none of it. "This place smells like a delivery room. Let's get out of here."

Prudence followed her guest silently back to the front room. Alicia was talking for two. "I know I wasn't a good mother," she said. "But even as a child I loathed dolls bleating 'Ma-ma, Ma-ma.' I'd lock myself in father's study and read. And then Geoff gave me a baby doll that screamed all night. Did I ever tell you I saw her once, five or six years ago? Geoff's family didn't know. I went to her school all starry with mother love. I pictured her looking like me. But she was ugly. She wore braces and turned in her toes and had spots. Spots! A pox of spots. My own child, all spotty. She should have been Wes Murdoch's daughter. I never had a spot in my life. And I will say for Geoff, at least he was beautiful to look at. But oh, so deadly heavy to live with. He kept talking about debentures. What are debentures? They always sounded to me like bent dentures. And he was obsessed with his boat. Yar, yar, yar— lower the fo'c'sle—batten the boom. . . ."

Prudence couldn't help giggling.

Alicia, playing up happily, acted out the way her first husband had tried to teach her to tie a square knot. Prudence beeped at intervals, to keep Alicia in a good humor.

"This is such fun. Put another log on, will you, lambie?"

Her hostess bit back a yawn and put another log on the fire, but a smallish one. From long experience, she knew Alicia had something much meatier on her mind, and it was bound to come out eventually; so far, they'd only had a fancy first course and the fish. To speed up the process, she said, "How's Barnes?"

Either Alicia was deaf or she didn't recognize the name of her current husband. "This sofa feels as if it's stuffed with old telephone books and rocks. The Puritan notion that it's sinful to be too comfortable—I've never quite got over it. I can't even loll and lie back after love-making. I have to leap up and sit in a straight chair and do something worthwhile. Working till five A.M., or reading something I have to chew on. 'My body is tired to death of my mischievous brain.'"

Prudence said without malice, "I should think your brain would be tired of your mischievous body."

"Oh, it often is. That's the most hellish conflict of the lot." She started to raise her cup, then held it broodingly in mid-air. "But the body can't go on making mischief much longer."

"Will Barnes be able to get away this summer and join you?"

A blast of thunder drowned her out. Alicia rushed to the one large window. "How I love New England storms. Somehow they're clearer here—sharper—harsher. My silly mother was so terrified of storms on the Cape. She didn't mind them in Boston; she was too busy giving parties to notice. Father and I loved walking even in the foulest weather. Once we had to take shelter at a farmer's during a storm and Pa was late for my mother's dinner party and they had a smashing fight right in front of the guests. Pa said, 'I didn't ask these people here and if they want to leave it's all right with me.' He could be wickedly rude." She turned from the window, face alight with the pleasures of storm and remembered rudeness. "I take after him in that."

"I don't think it's anything to brag about," Prudence said.

"I'm not bragging. I'm just being factual. But sometimes I take after my mother, when I'm trivial, spoiled—and then I can't bear myself till I exorcise the little bitcheries."

Lightning shot across the sky and cracked close; the little house seemed to quiver under the onslaught. Alicia flung open the front door to exult closer to: " 'Broad lightnings glare, long thunders roll.' "

"You'll get drenched." Prue bravely didn't add that her prized *gros point* rug, another heirloom, would be drenched too.

"Damn, this velvet spots horribly. I must get this robe to the cleaner tomorrow. Would you take it in for me, pet? I want to get it back Monday before I leave. I'm too old to rush out tilting at storms, but how I love them. That's not womanly, is it? I'm not afraid of lightning or mice or snakes. The only thing I'm terrified of is getting old. Cheeks sunken in . . . runny hips . . . neck like a sagging chicken's. . . ."

"Chickens don't sag. They run back and forth, whichever side of the road they aren't on looks greener."

"I get the metaphor," Alicia said. "However scrambled the hen. And I know why you're asking so solicitiously about Barnes. Yes, I've left him. I went to Italy with another man. And to save you asking where the other man is now, I sent him back to his wife."

Her hostess said, with rum-flavored candor, "That's a switch."

"I know people say I've broken up three marriages—"

"Really six marriages, counting your own. It's odd that people don't count that way."

35

Alicia looked startled, then burst out laughing. "You have the purest illogic I ever met up with. Remember when we went to have our fortunes told and I wanted to leave because the woman had a dirty neck and you said, 'If she's really clairvoyant she wouldn't bother scrubbing herself.' You made me stay, and take first turn so I wouldn't run away."

Prudence had a sudden, too-vivid memory of the fortune-teller's back room, crowded with enormous rubber plants fetid as a hothouse, and of the woman clutching her hand greasily, saying, "You have a longer life line than your friend. And you'll come into money but you won't get a husband. She's got a jumpy way to go—a pack of trouble—mind, I didn't tell her that. I told her what she wanted to hear, but it leaves a bad taste in my mouth—and I'm telling you the truth."

"What was my fortune?" Alicia said now, greedy as a child who wants to hear a fairy tale again.

"You were going to be famous and make a good marriage."

"That old slut was looking at my face, not my brains. Not that writing takes brains. What was Harley's line when he reviewed my first collection of stories?—'the crazy, blazing northern lights of genius.' And now I suppose he'll join the parade for that lump of prose in the wastebasket. Fetch it out, will you, lamb? I must show you her picture on the back."

Prudence hauled out the book. "Doesn't she look like one of those creatures who have to be operated on in Sweden to turn into women? I think in her case that halfway through the operation the power went off and nobody could locate a candle. Pour us more tea while you're up."

Prue poured, handling the tea strainer clumsily from tiredness.

"Look! Tea leaves in my cup. Let's tell our fortunes. You tell mine first."

Prudence peered into the cup with what, for her, was a sly smile. "You're going to have a change of plans and postpone a trip and meet a tall blond man and do something exciting."

"As a seeress, you're about as inscrutable as cheesecloth. I will not go to cocktails at Mr. Synthetic Pilgrim's." In a half-mocking, half-fond tone she said, " 'Upstart wealth's overted gaze.' Pa loved that poem of Emerson's. Anyway, you know I never fall for millionaires."

"It's odd, when you spend so much money."

Alicia laughed. "I do owe Saks a whale of a bill. You think I'm due for a millionaire? But not a manufacturer of mattress covers and ghastly tufty bedspreads."

Prue said she didn't even know if Mr. Humboldt was married. "I never saw him till the meeting tonight. I was sitting beside him when Cassie Murdoch—"

"Do tell me about Wes's daughter," Alicia said. "Is she short-legged with spots too? And doggedly devoted to the unattainable?"

Prudence put down her cup with a reckless bang. "She's a darling. One of the dearest, most natural—"

"With short legs and spots, obviously. You're dodging the question."

"She's *very* attractive. And the fact that she's my godchild has nothing to do with my saying that. Plenty of other people think so."

"I'll bet she's athletic as all get out. Hockey?"

"Tennis," Prue said, slamming it over the net.

Alicia was enjoying the game. "I knew it. She races around the court on her bunchy short legs and looks like this." She held up the book teasingly, waving it back and forth to flaunt the photograph.

"Cassie is much, much prettier." In her vehemence, Prudence forgot a basic rule of friendship with Alicia, didn't even notice her guest's mouth pull in ominously. "She's engaged to a composer." This was overdoing the story, but there are times when the plain truth is much too plain. "He's enormously talented—he's already had one opera done in New York, and they're probably going to be married this summer." The "probably" salved her conscience.

"And live spottily ever after." Alicia uncoiled from the sofa. "I think I'll drop in and see Wes sometime tomorrow." She went into the guest room, opened the largest suitcase, and pulled out several dresses, humming tunelessly as she slid them onto hangers and hooked all three over the closet door. Then she examined them like still lifes, her head on one side, hand on cheek, totally absorbed. Prudence, looking through the open door, recognized the stance of old, even the humming accompaniment. It meant that Alicia was assembling her equipment to go forth and conquer another mountain. Although to be quite fair about it, any mountain, when Alicia strolled by, turned into a molehill waiting to be conquered.

"The Pucci print, I think," Alicia murmured. "Those colors like a Mandarin orange freshly picked. My God! Wes is color-blind. What a good joke on me." She came back into the living room. "I remember because he said, 'I may be color-blind but you can't carry a tune. That's the one thing the Fates left out of you. When you try to sing, you're the princess-into-frog.' Wes was quite a delightful man, if you could close your eyes and just listen, and not look at him."

"His wife isn't really at all pretty," Prue said, trying to repair the damage. "She's nice but she doesn't have too many brains. Cassie is more like Wes."

"Poor spotted calf," Alicia said, so amiably that Prudence rushed on: "She has the most original idea for the Fourth of July celebration this year—a festival. That's why I wanted you to come to Mr. Humboldt's with me, to advise us. You'd be such a wonderful help."

"There've been only ninety thousand or so festivals of the arts scheduled for this summer," Alicia said. "I've been invited to dozens of them. I didn't even bother answering most of the letters. I'm in no mood for that sort of phony hoopla."

"But this one's different." Prue explained, rather confusedly, about the Liberty Pole Festival.

Alicia was regally indifferent. "Just another country fair, and they're all disgustingly commercial now. This whole country is like a giant medicine show, a television commercial that never shuts off. Painting, writing, theater—noisy, chaotic vulgarity. Topless waitresses—topless art, if it has shock value, Americans will buy it. They don't know any other values."

"But this Festival will remind people that—oh, if only you'd heard Cassie tell about it. She was so young and—and believing. To have somebody believe that much in love and goodness and the nicest things in the past—it was enough to lift your heart."

"Not my heart, thank you." Alicia's voice shrilled up like a cockatoo's. "Don't tell me about the young. As unformed as blobs in a womb, all unkempt and greedy and witless. Love, the arts—what the hell do they know of love, of creating? The real creating—not popping a baby, but the dredging and soaring to create a work of art. Not 'The Arts.'" She smiled rather wryly. As Barnes would say, 'Down with the Capital A.'"

"I wish you'd go back to Barnes. You seemed so right together."

"A match lit in heaven? Lamb, you're a Gothic romantic. I told Barnes one time your parents must have conceived you in a lending library under the shelf marked GOTHIC ROMANCE. He loved that line—he used it in a lecture—without giving me credit."

"That's no excuse for leaving him."

This time, Alicia's laugh verged on the hysterical. "The joke is—he left me."

"He couldn't have. You said yourself you went to Italy with another man."

"That was a spur-of-the-moment thing, when I was bored and cross with Barnes. The man turned out to be a name-dropper. And he let a manicurist in Palermo put *polish* on his nails. I cabled Barnes I was coming back. But he'd already gone. He wants a divorce."

Prudence let out a small, involuntary whimper of distress.

"I couldn't bear to tell you. Not right away. He went off with a twenty-year-old—a squash-nosed, thick-ankled twenty-year-old."

"Lishy, I can't believe it."

"He left me a note. He said living with me was like having to stand on tiptoe the whole time. He said the calves of his legs ached." She smiled sadly, tiredly. "He was putting it as chivalrously as he could—the goddess no mortal could possess. But I know the real reason. That girl he went off with was young—young—it was the only thing she had. And I'll never have it again." Tears rolled down her cheeks. "I'm terrified."

"All you have to do is look in a mirror and you'll feel better."

This at least had the effect of making Alicia blow her nose and stop crying. "I even know the name of what I've got—I heard a psychiatrist at a party talking about the disease of middle age: *Torschlusspanik.*"

Prue said, "Well, I've never heard of it, so it can't be anything fatal."

Alicia went on as if she were talking to herself: "The perfect name for it—closing-gate panic. Like people in the old walled cities—frantic they'd be late getting in at night before the gates clanged shut. Crowding in too much. Running scared. And once you run scared, everything's changed. Not just the old night fears. The nightmares creep deeper into the day. The wrinkles show more in daylight."

"Show me a single wrinkle."

"Not even to you. I can hide them—maybe I can even hide them for another few years. But I'll know they're inching, crawling, eating me like a malignancy."

"Lots of women have their faces lifted. Not that you're anywhere near ready, but it's something to keep in mind—like carrying an umbrella so it won't rain."

Her guest jumped up and began pacing. "For Alicia Thorne to wear a false face—I'd rather die."

"But it's not a false face; it's just taking up the slack or something. A woman in Bevington is supposed to have had it done and the district nurse told me all you can see is two teensy scars in front of her ears."

"How about the scars on her heart?" Alicia clutched her velvet-swathed bosom. "I tell you, I'd rather die. I've been thinking so longingly of death. I'm not afraid of it. All I dread is living to an overripe old age. Smelly, rotting—"

"All you smell of is that perfume that costs the moon. You're simply overtired, and you've worked yourself into a terrible state."

"Because you left me all alone when I needed you."

"You told me you weren't coming till tomorrow afternoon, so I promised the chairman of the Historical Association I'd go to this meeting because she had to go into the hospital for a gall bladder."

"A gall bladder! Some stupid little technical thing that can be fixed in ten minutes. You dare to sit there and say you're more concerned with some pudgy clubwomen's gall bladder than what's happening to me? Granted I might have left Barnes anyway, but don't you realize what agony it is for a woman to know she'll lose her looks?"

Prudence tried to bite back another yawn, but this time it broke loose from exhausted muscles and gave the effect rather of lockjaw. In her hurry to cover up and get words out, she said, "It's something all of us have to learn to accept."

Alicia whirled to attack. "As if you'd know what I'm talking about. You never had any looks to lose."

This time, Prudence set her cup down very gently. "I'm going to bed, Alicia."

"Don't leave me. You can't leave me. It's been years since we had a good talk."

"It will wait till tomorrow." As she stood in the doorway, the layers of soft chin looked tucked in, almost taut.

"You're mad at me. Prue, I couldn't bear it if you were mad at me. You, of all people. You've always stood up for me. Even when my father acted as if I were a monster to leave my child —you were the one who loaned me plane fare. I did pay you back, didn't I? You had to cash bonds. . . ." Prudence nodded silently. "What I said to you was absolutely beastly, about your not having any looks to lose. You have a dear, good face, a loving face, and I thought so the minute I saw you in our room in Fox Hall." She was talking feverishly fast. "But first I saw the pink blotter—remember? You were already unpacked, so tidily, and you'd put a huge pink blotter on the desk, and I said, Oh, *no!* Not pink—it's ghastly with my red hair. And you looked at me and said so seriously, 'But your hair isn't red—it's bronze. I can't imagine any color being wrong on you.' In those days, *I could* wear any color, couldn't I?"

"I'm sure you still can," Prudence said. "Good night."

Alicia grabbed at the navy flannel sleeve. "Prue, Prue-blue." A desolate wail. "I beg you, forgive your bad, sad old Alicia."

"There's nothing to forgive. You're quite right. I never had any looks to lose. I was never any competition for you."

"You got a higher mark in Biology than I did." Appealing, childish pout. "And Physical Ed."

"Fat lot of good it's done me."

"Darling, you are *loved.* You are loved by so many people. By me most of all. I'll show you. I'll prove it. I'll go to Mr. Whosis' with you for cocktails and be utterly charming and helpful. I'll think up brilliant ideas for their Festival. I'll make it the biggest smash hit since 'seventy-six. But I can't help if you don't give me more background. Sit down here and start at the beginning."

"Well. . . ." Prudence said.

An hour and two rummed-up cups of tea later, Alicia said, "But why should Humboldt give ten thousand dollars right off the bat? Is he buying his way into something?" Prue said sleepily, a bit rummily, "I think maybe because he was taken with Cassie. He kept looking at her."

Alicia looked, not at all sleepily, at the dresses still hanging on the guest-room door.

Chapter
Three

The Talladay School allowed its unmarried instructors to have
what it wishfully referred to as "Friendly visits by members of
the opposite sex." The ruling carried an old-fashioned sting in
the tail: "Visits must terminate by midnight."

In Oliver's room on the second floor of the staff's quarters,
Cassie kicked off her wet shoes. "What time is it?" She was
looking straight at the electric wall clock in the kitchenette
end of the room. "Ahead or behind?"

Oliver always set the clock by some mysterious reckoning of
his own, depending on whether he wanted to feel rushed or
lulled into lateness. He glanced at his wrist watch. "Ten
thirty-one."

"An hour and twenty-nine minutes to celebrate in!" She
flung herself down on the couch bed, rosy and expectant, but
Oliver wasn't feeling snuggly. His sensitive, bony face was
closed, rather tense. The high forehead, what showed of it
under a trailing forelock, was riffled with frown lines. "I'll
make some coffee." He said it flatly, almost disapprovingly, in
the tone one might use to a drunken acquaintance who'd
zigzagged in reeking of spirits.

"When did the garage say your car would be ready?"

"Not before Monday. If they can fix it at all."

"But the choke is the only thing the matter. It's probably just flooded."

Oliver was in no mood for simple solutions. "If it costs too much to fix, I may sell it for junk. I can do without a car—I've done without one before."

"But you can't now," Cassie wailed. "You'll need it for rehearsals and everything. You can use mine. You're a thousand times more important to the Festival than I am. You're more important than all the rest of us put together."

"I'll be giving up time I could spend on my opera—God knows I have little enough time for my serious work anyway. And I'll have to look for a new libretto for the opera besides." He slammed the teakettle onto a burner. "That witch story I tried to get the dramatic rights to—I had a snotty letter from the author's agent today saying they'd want five hundred a month for an option, and the author prefers a 'name' composer. Which puts me right back where I started."

Cassie was suitably scornful of fools and Philistines who cared for money and big names. "You'll have a free hand in the Festival, and you can do the sort of thing you've been longing to do. You know, the way you told me Bartok absorbed the Hungarian folk songs and built around them. Your ballads will make people feel nourished by the past and strengthened and full of new hope. And it's so right—it's just what our country needs now."

Oliver was exasperated at Cassie for taking him at his word. He had talked high on a few beers, and now she had conjured up a Festival and dumped it into his lap and the thing weighed like a stone.

"I merely said that *sometime* I wanted to do ballads. With a decent grant from a foundation so I could give up this bloody teaching."

"You only have to teach fifteen hours a week here. That's not so much."

"That's like saying somebody on a chain gang only has to wear chains on his ankles."

"Well, Mozart managed."

44

Oliver's sulkiness deepened. Did she think he, Oliver, should play a wheezy church organ and have a dozen or so children and a runny-nosed marriage like Mozart?

"Isn't it lovely we got so much money for the Festival right off the bat? I thought I was hearing voices."

Oliver said rather unpleasantly that she'd better not count on much. "You never saw the guy before. And even if he's rich, he may change his mind by tomorrow."

"But he can't. Not when he's offered us the old Mortly place for the Festival. Anyway, he looks so sort of clear-eyed and feet-on-the-ground."

"So do good con men," Oliver muttered.

". . . and he really *cares* about doing something like this. While you were off getting the car, he told me he thinks New England is the logical place to start, to rediscover the old virtues."

The teakettle screeched in protest. Oliver loped over to grab it and pour boiling water into the Chemex pot. He seemed so absorbed in this operation, standing by the stove watching the water dribble through, that Cassie said a bit wistfully, "Instant coffee is quicker."

"It tastes like *Reader's Digest* boiled." But when he saw her settle back resignedly, he said, "I have a surprise for you— fresh doughnuts. I wangled some from the cook in Scurvy Hall after lunch."

She sat up as greedily pleased as a child. "Throw me one. I'm starved."

He disliked her way of rushing things. He went on arranging the powdery doughnuts on a plate, pyramiding them with his long, dextrous fingers, as precisely as a balancing act, then put the heaped plate down on a small, teetery wicker table. "That moronic maid. Every time I prop up the leg"—he folded a match-packet and knelt down to jam it under— "Fiera takes it away to show she's a thorough cleaner. And if I'm working in the studio, she comes in to dust the piano and drapes herself with what she calls her 'fall' swishing my neck. It feels like a noose."

"You need me to protect you. Mrs. Loomite was mooning over you tonight."

He laughed rather sheepishly. "Mrs. Loomite just wants to dabble her feet in the Arts—she thinks I'm part of the surge. And Fiera practices on everything above and below the age of consent. She pops her breasts like bubble gum."

Cassie didn't pop her breasts as she leaned forward; she didn't have to. For a small girl, she was decidedly well endowed. "Do men have to be the age of consent?"

Oliver ducked that one. "Fiera even practices on Lo. Did I tell you?—he saw a television documentary called *The Third Sex* and he was indignant because it sounded like the third rail."

"I wish he'd been at the meeting tonight."

"If he condescends to do the costumes, he'll dress the early settlers in the style of Prince Albert on Carnaby Street. He's very mod this month."

"Isn't the coffee through yet?"

Oliver said he'd made a big pot so he'd have enough left for breakfast. "It'll be ready in a minute." He went into the bathroom he shared with Lo Bender, who taught Costume Design, and came back with a bath towel. "Here. You'd better dry your hair or you'll get a cold." Chronic bronchitis had kept him out of the draft, but he was subject to seizures of hypochondria, even vicariously.

"I never get colds." But she took a few brisk swipes at her short damp hair, before she put down the towel. "Ugh. Look at this." She held up Pilgrim Mills' hottest-selling item: "Doesn't the eagle look like a vulture with a squab under each wing? 'The better to eat you.' What's the name of the disease you get from parrots?"

"Psittacosis." He liked telling Cassie things she ought to know. It wasn't that she was stupid, but there were stunning gaps in her knowledge. Sometimes he pictured her going through college like a small mountain goat, leaping from peak to peak, occasionally scrambling up or down some interesting incline, but mostly preferring to jump. "From the Greek word for parrot—*psittakos*." He had come across this when he was

46

looking up "psaltery," and he was pleased to be able to use it.

"Well, I think eagle-osis is worse. Screaming and flapping and swooping like a vulture, all in the name of democracy."

"Have a doughnut," Oliver said. He wanted to head her off before she got to the situation in Southeast Asia. "One lump?"

Cassie held out for two. She drank two cups of coffee with two lumps each and ate three doughnuts and said she'd been absolutely longing for homemade doughnuts all day and how uncanny of Oliver always to know what she felt like most.

Her vivid pleasures and appreciations, like her appetite, were rather catching. Oliver, well stuffed and warmed, leaned back beside her contentedly, smoking a triple-filter brand while she explained why his melodic line was finer than Leonard Bernstein's and why his talent would be the greatest contribution to the Festival. "Compared to your music, ten thousand dollars is just green paper with pictures of dead presidents on it."

His smile made his whole face charmingly open, alive, much younger. "I'd like to roll in some of that hay."

"With me crackling beside you. I do crackle for you, don't I?"

Oliver said she crackled.

"I used to feel so unglamorously wholesome. Oh, but I hated being short. When I was in seventh or eighth grade a new girl moved here from Troy, New York—I've always remembered where she came from because it fitted."

"You mean her name was Helen?"

"It was Linda. But she was tall and curvy and all the boys in dancing school stampeded like buffalo to get to her. The worst thing was, she played a terrific game of tennis, and she wore a pale pink tennis dress with a little teeny pleated skirt, and her legs were so long and divine—I felt like a blob beside her. I'd read in a magazine my brother Davy took—you know, the kind that shows how you too may have bulging biceps—anyway, this thing I read told how you could 'gain inches in stature' with some sort of rope and pulley exerciser. Davy and I rigged up our own exerciser—we cut up a brand new nylon clothesline—and then I lay on the bed and Davy tied me to the bedposts, with loops on my ankles and wrists. He was supposed to pull the ropes so I'd be stretched out like taffy. But he yanked so hard my arms nearly came out of the sockets. I was sore for a week afterwards, and furious because I'd suffered for nothing. I looked exactly the same. I've hardly grown since."

"You still look about thirteen years old," Oliver said, in a slightly husky tone. "Except here—and here—and here."

"Eee, not there—I'm ticklish."

They were pleasantly engaged in finding places Cassie wasn't ticklish when a kind of soprano bellow pulled them upright. "Are you decent?" This was followed by a banging of bathroom pipes. "Ready or not, here I come. *Ein, zwei, drei, vier,* fimpf. . . ."

"It's Lo," Oliver said unnecessarily. "I forgot to lock the door on this side." He raised his voice. "I'm busy."

"Don't be carnal. I saw Cassie's car outside. I have to talk to you about the *Festival.*"

Cassie pulled down her skirt. "We'd better let him in. If he gets peeved, he won't do the costumes."

"I don't give a damn if he does the costumes." But Oliver was already tidying his hair and more intimate parts. He grabbed a notebook from the desk and put on the tight-lipped expression of a man in the grip of his intellect.

Lo made an entrance from the bathroom carrying a bottle, and with a hand towel draped over his arm like a waiter's napkin. He was wearing a swallow-tailed frock coat, vintage pre-World War I, with very tight pants that required more a wiggle than walk. "Compliments of Pilgrim Mills," he said, unfolding the towel, eaglet size, and whipping it around the bottle. "Or Pilgrims' millions. And the grape is my own humble offering." He tossed his head so that his shiny black hair fell into ringlets. This made him look like a plump ex-faun dressed as a Mack Sennett waiter. Cassie exclaimed tactfully over the effect and accepted a glass of the domestic brandy with every appearance of delight. She even managed not to shudder over the taste. "What a lovely way to celebrate.

We've been itching to tell you the news, haven't we, Oliver?"

Oliver, who had refused the brandy after one look at the label, sipped cold coffee and grunted.

"How did you hear?"

"I ran into Popsy Eyeballs in the pub, or was it at the chemist's? La Loomite luminescent. She told me Oliver had thought of an idea for a Festival that was the greatest expression of the rights of man since the Magna Carta."

"It was Cassie's idea," Oliver mumbled.

Cassie denied this fondly.

Lo plumped down on the floor at her feet, dunked a doughnut in his brandy, and gobbled. He had tucked the towel into his wing collar to protect his sartorial splendor. "But how did you latch onto Pilgrim Mills?" he said thickly through doughnut. "You have struck the mother lode."

When he saw from their baffled looks that he knew something they didn't, he jounced on his buttocks in anticipation. Lo adored being the first to bring news, even if he had to make it up himself. "Your angel Humboldt owns Pilgrim Mills to the tune of a billion per annum. When he bought the Mortly place, he wrote out a check for the full amount—two hundred thousand—just like that."

Oliver knew Lo's capacity for exaggeration. Like his hunger for dressing up in wild costumes, Lo would try on any story for size or color, and parade in it for an hour, a day, a week, convinced of its beauty and rightness.

"Tom Devin invited me to Humboldt's place Saturday for what he calls the spark session. How we will spark, ducks. We'll get Humboldt to underwrite a Broadway production in no time. Oliver will do the music and I'll do the costumes and Cassie will clap hands on opening night. Cassie is a claque unto herself."

"But first we'll concentrate on the Festival," Cassie said. "We only have seven weeks."

"What *is* a liberty pole? Loomite tried to tell me, but I got tangled up in the ribbons."

Cassie began to explain.

"Frankly, I think it was a mistake for us ever to break off from England."

"Lo! You can't be serious." Cassie was off. ". . . and taxation without representation."

"Taxes are much higher now," Lo said. "And I don't feel that Congress really represents me."

"But think of the tyranny of George the Second."

"George the Third," Oliver said.

"George needn't have lasted long," Lo said sunnily. "We could have encouraged them to behead him. That's the sort of thing the C.I.A. does quite well."

Oliver laughed. Cassie was so agitated her brandy glass tilted perilously. "But we'd have been under the thumb of a colonial power."

"I think that's better than *being* a colonial power. All that codswollop about the sun never setting on the British Empire —now the sun never sets on Uncle Sammy, and the heat is ghastly. A mad noonday glare night and day."

"When we founded the New England colonies. . . ."

"Old England founded the colonies as a nice, big green place to send younger sons and religious nuts. . . ."

Oliver was making squiggly quarter notes in his notebook. Lo went on talking in counterpoint to Cassie, faster and higher . . . "We could have pooled all our gold in Fort Knoxingham-on-Thames. And Fifth Avenue would be Savile Row the Second. Why don't we use that as the theme for the Festival—Hail Anglamerica? We could have some delicious costumes."

Cassie, trying to sound calm, explained in more detail what the Liberty Pole Festival stood for.

"Ducks, I adore you and I'll do what I can, but I think the poles will look prettier than the people. The seventeen hundreds were a dreadfully dreary period over here—linsey-woolsey and the sort of hats and shoes one wears in the stocks."

"You can have a few Tories," Cassie said generously. "We'll borrow some red coats from the Hunt Club."

"Pink coats."

"When Tories wear them, they're red."

"I adored the parade last Fourth of July, when Paul Revere fell off his horse. Couldn't we do that again? It got the biggest laugh of the day."

Cassie said sternly that the Festival was not for laughs. "But we needn't be too fussy about the exact period, on costumes. We can get some marvelous stuff from people's attics. You'll have fun going through old trunks."

"You know, I've never been in an attic." Lo licked the powdered sugar from a finger. "It might be amusing. Florida is so frightfully one-story. And New York may have a few attics left, but not among people one knows. Will I find skeletons and old love letters?"

Cassie promised recklessly he could have any skeletons and read any love letters he found in Prue Washburn's attic, for one.

"La Loomite said Alicia Thorne is staying there."

Oliver's head jerked up. "Alicia Thorne! Why would she be staying in Prue Washburn's attic?"

"Well, she is," Lo said. "When I drove by tonight I happened to glance up at the attic window and there was a tatty old face pressed against the glass, framed in cobwebs."

Oliver snorted in disgust. "I should have known. I'm sick of your adolescent fibs. Alicia Thorne's the author I've been trying to get the dramatic rights from—her witch story. And I'm in no mood for your panty-waist make-believe."

Lo's full lips were quivering, almost blubbery. He flung his towel-bib on the floor.

"Oliver! Alicia Thorne *is* here at Prue's." Cassie said. "I heard it tonight."

"And you didn't tell me?"

"If you'd told him, he'd have called you an adolescent fibber."

"I can believe what *she* says."

"It's not your fault you have such a pedestrian mind; I've run across it before in musicians."

A muscle in Oliver's cheek twitched. "Just because I prefer facts to fairy tales—"

"Stop it, both of you," Cassie said. "Or you'll spoil our celebration. Lo, I'm so glad you remembered to tell us about Alicia Thorne. If she's staying all weekend, I can ask Prue to let Oliver come meet her."

"She'll be at Humboldt's Saturday. Miss Washburn told La Loomite so. Of course if you'd prefer a notarized statement—"

"But how marvelous. What could be better?"

Oliver was still brooding. "You can play her some of your music."

"Like *Young at Heart*," Lo said. His grievances seldom lasted longer than a commercial. "I saw it last week on the Late Show. Sinatra plays some of his music for Ethel Barrymore. She's the girl's grandmother, very autocratic crust but underneath madly responsive and anti-Establishment. She secretly loathes the rich boy her granddaughter's engaged to and she's excited about Sinatra's symphony. . . ." Lo was becoming rather flushed with excitement himself, as he touched up the plot. "And she helps him get a production at Lincoln Center and elope with the girl."

"There, you see, darling. It's all going to work out beautifully."

It wasn't really Oliver's fault that he pictured a dignified white-haired Ethel Barrymore type of lady author, her patrician features alight with appreciation of his talent.

"I think she's lived abroad a lot, but she comes from some old, old New England clan."

Lo, wanting to make clear who was the fount of real news on the lady, said off the top of his head, "She absolutely flipped over the idea of the Festival. Popsy Loomite said that's why she's coming Saturday."

Cassie made happy noises; Oliver moved his Ethel Barrymore vision over to the Saturday spark session, where she listened radiantly as he played the opening number.

Lo yawned, wide and open, showing what looked like baby teeth. "For breakfast," he said, "I am going to pour brandy

52

over crunchy-wunchy Triscuit. Unless you'd like me to leave you the bottle, to anoint Oliver's brow."

Cassie, who had hidden her barely touched glass behind a goose-necked student lamp, assured him she'd had enough. "I'm already floating. It's been a lovely party."

"You two may continue where you left off."

Cassie giggled. Oliver said, "I think I'll go right over to the studio now and work. I have an idea for a liberty-pole thing that might. . . ." His voice trailed away. He made another squiggle in his notebook.

It was clear from Cassie's face (1) that she felt short-circuited and (2) that she would put the Festival before fleshly love. "I'll drop you off on my way home."

Oliver said not to bother, he'd walk.

"It's raining too hard. I'll just go to the john and then we'll be off." She shut the bathroom door with a small bang to show she was hurrying. Oliver turned on the faucet to rinse the coffee cups.

"Are you really going to let her go into the Peace Corps?" Lo asked.

Oliver said it wasn't any of his business.

"Of course it's your business. If you married her, she'd stay home."

Oliver's face was closed again, tightly resentful. "I'm in no position to marry. I can barely support myself."

"You heterosexuals are always so budget-minded. Anyway, Cassie would get a job. Of course, she's the sort who'd want children. She'll have babies in a row like hot biscuits. Then you can have your own little family choral group. Like the Trapps, la-la-la."

Oliver said stiffly he wasn't even considering marriage.

"You mean you'd rather let her go off to some dungheap in Africa and get amoebic dysentery?"

"Who has amoebic dysentery?" Cassie said, reappearing.

"A dear friend of mine." Lo's voice was sorrowfully hushed. "She was bitten by a tsetse fly too. They think she may never recover. And she's still very young."

"I don't think that's funny," Oliver said harshly.

"Oliver! Of course it's not funny." She kissed Lo on his round pink cheek. He wasn't much taller than she was. "Bless you for being so nice about the Festival." She started for the door. "Oh, I forgot my shoes."

The studio was almost a half mile from the instructors' quarters, on a narrow dirt road that was mucky in the rain. Cassie, inching and bouncing her small Volks through, said, "When you were little, did you make mud pies?"

Oliver made a negative sound. He had told Cassie a great deal about his childhood in Rochester; in his version, no childish pleasures had peeped through the endless gloom of life with a widowed-young mother and a grandmother who did all the cooking, cleaning, and laundry and quoted from mean parts of the Bible. Although he'd never had the slightest desire to make mud pies, a self-pitying twang came into his voice: "I didn't dare even spill anything. Once I got raspberry stains on my Sunday shirt—I'd snitched some out of the icebox after church—and my grandmother said God would send the lightning to strike me dead. That was her favorite threat."

"What a horrible old witch. Wasn't she *ever* nice to you?"

She had made him cookies every week and bought him his first matching coat and pants, but he saw no reason to go into that. He disliked her even dead. She had sneered at his mother, who had developed operatic leanings in a normal-school choral group, married a sickly dentist who played the violin, and pumped her dreams into Oliver from the time he could reach the piano keys. On his ninth birthday, his mother had given him *Lives of Great Composers,* and they had read it together and agreed Verdi was the one for Oliver to emulate. "Stop making the boy think he's another genius," his grandmother had said. "Folks don't need symphonies and operas— they need teeth, real or false. If he gets through dental school like his father, he'll be lucky. Whosoever puts himself up with the mighty shall be smitten by the Lord God."

With his mother's conniving and passionate encouragement,

he had held onto the thing he cared most about. But by the time he was in the Eastman School of Music on a fellowship, her fierce ambition for him had come to feel like a steel corset. He had longed at times to take it off, but love and fear had kept him encased till her death, and perhaps after.

Cassie was prattling on. "Once when Davy and I made mud pies we put our initials on them with pebbles and baked them in the Toastmaster, and a new cleaning woman actually bit into one. She thought it was gingerbread."

Cassie often told him tidbits like that, as if her own happy childhood could rub off on him, or work like an antidote for snake bite. Sometimes he was amused; this wasn't one of the times.

"You won't forget to call Miss Washburn in the morning?" he said. "Make sure Alicia Thorne will be there Saturday. I still don't trust Lo's word for it. But don't tell her why you want to know."

"I'll be devious as a cat."

"You're about as devious as a ruler." After she stopped the car in front of the studio, he was overcome, suddenly, with a surge of affection and gratefulness, so much that he nearly asked her in. But she gave him a copy of the *Bugle* to put over his head as an umbrella and said, "Work well, darling."

He had the key of the studio in his hand, and was making a dash for the door, clutching the *Bugle* over his head, when the lightning flashed. He tripped over the step onto the little porch and fell heavily.

Cassie was out of the car so fast she had her arms around him before he knew what had hit him. Although he had long since stopped believing that God sent lightning expressly to strike Oliver Yates dead, he was so shaken by the fall he reverted to the old mindless terror. As the lightning stabbed closed and thunderbolts roared, he clung to Cassie, and she crooned and rocked him like a baby.

Even after the storm let up, he wanted her there. She bathed his bruised cheek with cold water and laved his manly ego, and, eventually, comforted him in the best possible way.

Afterward they lay naked together on the couch, legs still entangled in drowsy fulfillment. At such times, with Cassie, Oliver could feel free of constrictions. It wasn't that he felt less consciously ambitious; he simply felt a lazy, contented sense of success at hand, as if he could do anything he wanted to, all in good time. In the back of his mind, the notes of a melody had arranged themselves clear and black as starlings perched on a telephone wire. Knowing they were there, sitting tight, he could afford to ignore them for now. He and Cassie talked, now and then, in the lovers' patois that doesn't need subject, predicate or active verbs. Cassie's social conscience was lying deliciously dormant. In the six months Oliver had known her, he had learned that her concern for mankind could appear at the most unexpected moments, like a hedgehog popping up in bed. But tonight, or at least for this hour of tonight, she was brandishing no cause.

"I'm glad now that Lo interrupted us," she murmured. "We just worked up more appetite."

When she said, eventually, that she had to leave, Oliver protested sleepily. "Stay all night."

Cassie said she couldn't. "Even if you had a phone here, I couldn't call Mother at this hour. Once when Davy had a puncture he called her at 3 A.M. and she was so frightened she grabbed too far for the phone by her bed and fell out and broke her collarbone. So I really have to go."

Heaven chose that moment to let loose with a few new storm bolts. Oliver clutched Cassie, who was sitting on the edge of the day bed, and pulled her down again. "If I make a lot of money, we could get married." He was surprised, but not too alarmed, to hear what he was saying.

And Cassie's response was so passionately affirmative—just weepy enough—that he felt very masterful.

Again he saw the white-haired Ethel Barrymore type, Alicia Thorne, smiling as he sat at the piano, but this time she seemed to be smiling at both Cassie and himself, with a Bless-you-my-children benevolence.

Chapter
Four

Chester Humboldt was in bed by eleven, dialing 212 for New York. Ordinarily he liked to sit bolt upright when he made business calls, but he had bummed a cigarette from Tom Devin after the meeting and had sneaked it home and upstairs so he could celebrate in private. His housekeeper, Mrs. Gifford, lived in a back wing connected with the kitchen, within sniffing distance of what Chester called his office and the interior decorator called his think-pit. It wasn't that he was afraid Mrs. Gifford would come barging into the office and say, "What are you *doing*, you naughty boy—*smoking?*" But she had commented very favorably on his self-denial, with a quotation from some Hindu sage: "One cannot ascend to Nirvana on the frayed rope of nervous habit."

He was torn between smoking the cigarette instantly, or after he made the first call, to the musical director of Pilgrim Mills' television show. He decided to wait until after, to prolong the delicious, guilty anticipation.

He was lying in a vast, low-slung bed the decorator had considered suitable for a millionaire's nocturnal thrashings-about, but which made Chester feel at times as if he were laid out on the lone prairie. He put the cigarette, a longer-than-king-size, on his bedside table, arranging it beside a huge ceramic ash tray, a silver table lighter and the phone like the central piece in a still life. But once he had dialed, he was crisply direct in his questions.

"Yes, I've heard of Yates," the musical director said. "Yeah, I've heard some of his stuff . . . folk opera about two years ago off Broadway. Crummy little theater and a libretto like moldy swiss cheese, but the music came through. He isn't one of the boys who thinks melody is for the birds. I don't say you can whistle all his tunes, but these days who whistles? Anyway, he's got it—he's good."

In some perverse way, Chester was sorry to hear this. As the musical director went on weaving laurels for Yates, describing specific numbers, his listener absently lit the cigarette and just as absently smoked it. Afterward, staring at the teensy butt, he felt wistful and cheated.

He would have liked to have the moral support of a cigarette savored full millimeter before he made his next call. He had never called his new public relations man, Ross Trumbine, at home before. When the easy voice answered after a half-dozen rings and said, "Just got out of the shower. Hold it a second, fella," Chester held on meekly.

Trumbine was seven or eight years younger than Chester, probably not much more than thirty, but he was one of the no-age breed of Ivy Leaguers who are so effortlessly well tailored, well coifed and compact they made Chester think of a good packaging job. It was impossible to imagine Trumbine coming out of a shower except fully clothed, combed, dry behind the ears, as unshakably sure as ever. He was credited with electing five senators, three governors, and part of a president. "Now what can I do for you, fella?"

Chester explained, not without pride, about his part in the Liberty Pole Festival. When Trumbine listened, he was like a vacuum cleaner sucking in facts; no piece was too small for him to catch. One could almost hear him emptying the bag and sorting the contents. "Hmmm . . . hmmm . . . yeah . . . yeah. . . ." At the end, he said, "It has a great potential. The point is, fella, you can't afford to be mixed up with a flop. If you let a bunch of amateurs loose. . . ."

Chester found himself in the unwelcome job of touting Oliver Yates as a talent, quoting the musical director. Trumbine *hmmmed* and said Yates would probably be O.K. for a few folk songs. "But none of the two-piano bit with girlish soprano lead and the school choir. We're going to want some big classy numbers, something the pic boys can go to town on, and for that we'll need professionals . . . use the singers and dancers from the Pilgrim TV show . . . choreographers . . ."

Chester cut in to say uneasily that the girl—uh, the people who'd thought of the idea had pictured it as a community affair.

"And if the first selectman's daughter wants to yodel a ballad or do a Puritan fling and she's turned down because she stinks, guess who papa would be sore at. He wouldn't even help you run for skunk-catcher."

Chester said he'd thought that everybody who went into politics had to make some enemies.

"That comes later. When you're learning the game, you have to play footsie right and left and aim your pecker in the middle. By the way, that ten-thousand-bucks donation was exactly the right amount. We'll spend more like two hundred thousand on the show, but any more dough at the start might have made them suspect something. You can do a good bit of hidden financing by using your TV people and charging it off to business. This has to be big-time stuff."

Remembering the Murdoch girl's impassioned little speech at the meeting, Chester said, "But the whole idea is to remind people of the simple virtues in our past—the, uh, pioneer simplicities."

Trumbine said coldly, "Amateurs can never do anything simple."

For Chester, it was at once a disturbing and buoying conversation. Trumbine knew the Governor's left-hand man (they had worked on the Harvard *Crimson* together) and would guarantee to deliver not only the Governor of Connecticut but possibly the Attorney General for opening night. "You'll give an intimate little dinner before the show, with all the wire services covering. We get you linked with top politicos. And from now on, we'll forget the Chester. It's too dated—Chester A. Arthur, Tippecanoe and all that barnacle bilge. We've come up with a great little nickname for you—'Hum.' "

At first, Chester thought Trumbine was simply saying "Hmmm" again, and it took him a while to understand his new name.

"You make things *hum*. Hum—bold. . . . Sure, stress the olden-time virtues. It's a natural for feature stories. I'll get Research onto it pronto. They can dig up a lot of early-settler stuff . . . examples of rugged individualism . . . spirit that made America and raised the liberty pole. But we gotta get a groovier word than 'Festival.' We'll work on that. I'll let you know what we come up with."

Trumbine said he wouldn't appear at the first planning session. "You can let them think it's all their idea. You know the pitch—the old Greek dodge: elicit spontaneity without being spontaneous." He suggested a half-dozen ways to make the locals feel involved. "The sense of involvement is a must, as long as they can't get their hands on the buttons that run the real show."

Having sat through one meeting of the Bevington Civic Affairs and Image Improvement Association, Chester knew Trumbine was probably right. And the ideas he rattled off as a starter, for making the locals feel involved, were mostly sound. As a manufacturer who had to know what would catch the public fancy, Chester knew instantly which ideas he could promote Saturday to hook the pop-eyed dame, the ancestor-worshiper, the wheeler-dealer Devin. But he still couldn't help feeling uneasy about Miss Murdoch. Would she be happy?

Trumbine was still talking ". . . picked yourself an absolutely great theme there, Hum . . . sensational timing . . . get headlines all over the country. I just thought of a slogan we can use: 'Let's make America safe for democracy—again.' I wouldn't be surprised if dozens of communities pick up the liberty-pole idea. In fact, I'd be damned surprised if they didn't, because we'll give them a goosing. You're really doing something constructive for your country."

Chester's spirit expanded till he seemed to fill the vast bed and steer it like a ship of state.

Later he remembered he'd forgotten to mention Alicia Whosis to Trumbine. Thorne. Alicia Thorne. He had made a point of asking Miss Washburn, and urging her to bring Miss Thorne Saturday. He hadn't mentioned the girl, Miss Murdoch, to Trumbine either, but that hadn't been forgetfulness. More an odd instinct of protectiveness.

Trumbine had approved the idea of a small group as a nucleus. "Friendly little party—that's the atmosphere. Plenty of liquor—no bartender. Let them see you're a nice, modest guy who mixes a vodka martini like anybody else and waits on guests with his own two hands."

But by three-thirty Saturday afternoon, soon before the guests were due, Chester was as nervous as a bride. This was the first time he had entertained, except in restaurants, since his divorce. Looking around the big, long living room, so newly, expensively decorated, he tried to figure what was missing. Somehow the place looked untouched by human hands. The bar in the front end of the room, to the right of the doorway, was already set up and well stocked, with its automatic ice-maker clinking hospitably. The sofas and chairs were arranged in what should have been inviting clumps. But something was off. Chester ran through the last-minute things his ex-wife had done before a party; he poked several cushions with a tentative finger, then moved a lamp and ash tray closer together on a Danish teak table, trying for a matey effect; the surface still looked bare, blank. *Flowers!* Where were the bouquets? He had told the housekeeper to tell the gardener. . . . He was so rattled by this eleventh-hour discovery he shouted for Mrs. Gifford, who ignored it. She disliked being summoned by overt sound. He found his housekeeper in the kitchen, contemplating several trays of hors d'oeuvres with an expression of intense suffering. A local caterer had supplied the hors d'oeuvres, so Chester was damned if he knew why Mrs. Gifford should take it so hard. She was a thin, fiftyish woman who gave an impression of being held together by picture-frame wire; if you touched her, you might get a fuzzy little steel sliver in your finger. Chester had never put this to the test and he didn't now. He worded his question carefully: "Did I forget to ask you? . . ."

Mrs. Gifford said loftily she had discussed the matter with the gardener, who had said there was nothing suitable ready in the cutting garden. A frost had killed off the last of the tulips and daffodils; the iris would come along in their time. "We should learn from Nature, Mr. Humboldt."

"We already have," Chester muttered.

Mrs. Gifford said she was referring to Nature's eternal cycle: "Motion and rest, motion and rest—to lie dormant until one is ready. We cannot push ourselves into doing at the expense of being. . . ."

There was more in this vein. Chester escaped through the back door—the service entrance—and walked morosely around in the unusually balmy spring sunshine. The only flowers he saw were three dandelions between the guest house and the tennis court. He took the driveway around to the front, kicking childishly at pebbles, and nearly missed seeing the big lilac bush at the far corner of the lawn; it was loaded. Lilacs are flowers; the thought came to him like a bursting revelation. Within two minutes he was whacking away with clippers from the tool shed. It gave him a good destructive feeling, and was such a healthy outlet for hostility he cut more than he'd intended. He had just gathered up a giant double armful when a small bottle-green Volks stopped at the door with its snub nose aimed right at him. His first impulse was to climb a tree or become invisible. There was something so shamefully unmanly about being caught picking flowers. He could only advance, so burdened he looked like a lilac bush coming to Birnam Wood.

"Hi. Do you mind my being early?" It was Miss Murdoch,

and for some reason, alone. Chester mouthed the usual hostly platitudes and silently cursed eager beavers. "I wanted to ask you something before the others come. What marvelous lilacs. Can't I help you fix them in water?"

She wore a dirndl skirt that made her look rather bunchy around the middle. He noticed this, and regretted it for her, before he noticed, as she came over to smell the lilacs, that her eyes were the color known in the trade as Mountain Lake Blue; Pilgrim Mills was promoting it in summer bedspreads. And her lashes were as long and thick as the kind glued on. He didn't ask himself how he knew Miss Murdoch's eyelashes were not glued on. He just knew.

There was a sink in the butler's pantry. While he dumped the lilacs on the counter, Miss Murdoch opened cupboards, with that atavistic instinct some women have for finding the proper receptacle. She had a tendency to shove the lilacs into vases, like a child with posies, but she was fast and intent. When they ran out of vases, she thrust the last bunch into a lacquered Bonnier wastebasket. "Do you think they'd look better on the hearth or over in a corner by the back window?" They decided congenially on the corner by the back window.

It was a mammoth window that took up the entire back wall of the living room. Standing there looking out, she seemed to be stretching on tiptoe. "What a view—with the hills and that hawthorne tree and the big ash. You know, you've arranged it so the view really decorates the room."

He had never really had time to look at the view head on, but he felt enormously pleased by his cleverness, as if he'd told the decorator, "Remember, no clutter. I want the view to decorate the room."

He found himself telling her why he'd been whacking at bushes, and that this was the first time he'd entertained since his divorce.

"It must be so terrible," she said. "Like having a leg cut off and learning to walk all over again."

He had never heard divorce described in just that way. But the simile clicked in him like a key. He thought of the months he had gone along, steady enough at the plant but lurching after dark, off-balance. . . . He was surprised to hear himself babbling that his wife had walked out and just left a note. "It was a lot my fault. I was working so hard I left her alone too much." Then, afraid he'd sounded corny, he said, "The great American success story."

"Can't you get her back?"

"She's already married again."

Miss Murdoch looked at him solemnly, appraisingly. "You will be too," she said. "You're very attractive. But you have a piece of lilac in your hair." He pawed to locate the offending blossom. "Behind your left ear—there. You know, I honestly think the Festival will do you good. And I'm glad, because you're doing so much for it."

Chester had been unwinding so pleasantly he had almost forgotten why she was there.

"What I wanted to ask you—would you ask Oliver to play some of his things? He's been working like mad on an opening number—he's still at the Talladay studio now. We could all go over there with him afterward, if you don't have a piano here."

"It's across the hall." He had never known quite why he'd bought the thing; Tom Devin, showing him the house, had said expansively, "And this is the music room." Chester had looked at the grand piano sitting alone in the empty room, abandoned, massively graceful, mute. "The Mortly heirs want to sell it with the house. Got a great tone." Devin had jabbed with a pudgy finger to demonstrate. After his brassy voice, the piano had sounded low and rich and lovely.

"A Bechstein!" She had rushed in ahead of him. The room also contained Chester's largest color television set, a stereo phonograph, and a Toulouse-Lautrec called *Intermission at the Opera*. She ignored these to stroke the piano. "It's fabulous. Oliver will be out of his mind. You will ask him to play some things, won't you? He's too shy to push himself. And then Miss Thorne can—" She broke off and changed tack.

64

"But even more, I want you to hear him. I do hope you'll like his music."

She looked so young, so blue-eyed and anxious, that Chester's nicer self responded even while his lower self compared Yates's chicken-liver guts—too shy to push himself—with Chester's own two-fisted drive to the top. He quoted Pilgrim Mills' musical director on Yates, this time quite unselfishly. The girl was so radiant, listening to praise of her love, that he kept heaping more on her plate for the bittersweet pleasure of watching her eat it up.

But when Yates arrived, as if on cue, long and limp in a tan-striped seersucker suit, Chester disliked him all over again. Not that Yates was making any effort to be liked. He wandered into the piano as soon as Cassie, joyfully, pointed it out. And he stayed crouched over it, playing the same dum-dee-dah over and over. Or at least it sounded to Chester like the same dum-dee-dah. Cassie said, "He's changing the middle part."

She introduced the odd little fat-cheeked character who had brought Oliver as "Louis Bender. He's going to do the costumes."

In a pig's eye, Chester thought, making courteous sounds. He and Trumbine had discussed this possible threat in one of their half-dozen phone conferences. "Keep hitting on how short a time we've got to mount the show," Trumbine had said. "And that a community like Bevington wouldn't be happy with less than the best. And you'll be so grateful blah-blah for the advice of the locals, without which etcetera. . . ."

". . . mostly britches and aprons," Bender was saying. "The mobcaps are quite piquant, but I still think the Boxer Rebellion would be a more amusing period to costume."

Chester didn't hear any more of this, because he was awash in an influx of guests. Some of them he hadn't seen before. A large, solid-footed man who carried his stomach before him gave his name as Pickett. "Some name for a lawyer, eh? Devin

65

told me what you're doing and I think it's an admirable thing. I came along to say if you need free legal help, like you step on somebody's ancestor's toes. . . ."

Chester thanked him.

"Say, I was thinking, the earliest patent the U. S. Government ever granted was to a Connecticut inventor. That's something we could use to show Yankee ingenuity in the Festival. And Connecticut still has more patents granted than any other state in the union. Doesn't hurt to blow our own horn, eh?" Chester decided Pickett must be a patent lawyer and was repelled by the man's wanting to use the Festival for self-advertisement until he remembered he was in no position to throw stony thoughts. He said heartily he'd like to hear more about that sometime. He was retreating fast when he ran smack into a musket pointed carelessly at his loins. Al Farwell, the hardware-store man, chuckled. "Scared yuh, dinnint I? See, this is the powder horn that goes with it. You pour the powder into the priming pan. . . ."

Chester cut that off nicely by saying he had to make drinks and needed somebody to give him a hand. Farwell, still beaming his Santa Claus beam, propped his musket against the bar. "You name it—I'll make it."

Mrs. Tyndale, Antique Bibelots and Unpainted Furniture, had brought a tattered pile of old books and prints, "to inspire us," but after the second round of drinks, nobody bothered to glance at them. Even the teetotallers were floating high on inspirations of their own. Mrs. Loomite thought they should have geese wandering on the Village Green "as in olden times." Miss Maulridge said her dear father had collected epitaphs from old New England tombstones, and she did hope the Festival could capture that "quaint flavor. I remember one we always laughed over together." In a cracked voice somewhat like a turkey cackle, she recited:

> "Here lies the silent clay
> Of Miss Arabella Young
> Who on the twenty-first of May
> Began to hold her tongue."

"But it's divine," Lo Bender said, bouncing up and down. "We'll have a tombstone chorus—in stone-gray costumes, cardboard-stiffened, oblong—some leaning sideways or moss-grown—and they sing their own epitaphs."

Just for a second, Chester had a pang of doubt, almost guilt. Left to their own crazy devices, the locals might have come up with something quite fresh and charming—if they could ever agree. Trumbine had suggested placating the natives by letting them handle what he called the artsy-craftsy end—"exhibits, contests, old games, the best johnnycake recipe handed down in a family—and collections of their Wistar glass and hand-painted china and Great-great-aunt Sarah's cross-stitch sampler—it will keep them occupied and out of trouble."

But would it? Lo was saying to Miss Maulridge, "You marvelous fount, tell me more."

Miss Maulridge looked quite tipsy with pleasure, as if the tonic water had fizzed to her head. She recited one about rising to heaven, "Where armless spirits dwell." Cassie gave her seat beside Miss Maulridge to Lo. "You two make notes and I'll tell Oliver what you're working on."

Oliver had appeared in the doorway, looked around, and was just withdrawing, presumably back to his dum-dee-dah, when Cassie called, "Prue told me they might be late. We'd better go ahead and start planning."

She turned to Chester trustingly. "Will you sort of get things underway?"

Now that she'd led him right up to the hurdle, he cleared it without visible effort. "You've all heard by now about the Liberty Pole Festival," he began. "I for one feel excited and privileged to be a part of it." (Trumbine had had a speech written out and rushed up by courier pouch so that Chester would have time to memorize the main points and fill in details. He had also sent up several alternative names for "Festival"—one was "Bee" as in husking bee, another was "Bounce"—but Chester had discarded the lot). "We have a tremendous amount of work and not too much time to do it. I hope and think we'll show a profit, enough to help out on some civic projects—maybe a new recreation area with jogging track and a public golf course . . . restore more historical landmarks, say a one-room schoolhouse and a tavern . . . bring more top lecturers and art exhibits to our community center. . . ." He went on pandering gracefully, not too concretely, to special interests. He even improvised a new one: "And perhaps someday a museum showing models of early Connecticut inventors, Yankee ingenuity at its best, when man ran machines instead of letting machines run him ragged." When he paused, the sounds of approval were like a chorus of peepers.

"Now to immediate details," Chester said. "A friend of mine, a business colleague, is so enthusiastic about what you're doing with this Festival he has offered to furnish a music tent that seats a thousand."

At the word "music," Cassie Murdoch salivated like a Pavlov dog. She blew a kiss at Oliver, who permitted himself to smile very slightly.

Chester went smoothly on, ". . . with sound amplifiers and lighting equipment, and of course the technicians to run them." (He was being deliberately matter-of-fact, skipping such items on Trumbine's list as the thirty-piece orchestra . . . saturation spot announcements on TV and radio . . . a top folk-singer group called the Illegitimate Mamas—all that could come later.) ". . . stalls for exhibits . . . posters and programs . . ." As far as he could see, everybody was listening raptly, or at least passively, to his giveaway spiel. He had been a little worried some of them might object, but Trumbine had said, "Not unless you hand out hundred-dollar bills. For some reason, that makes people nervous. But if you just promise them a ten-billion-dollar program, or a subsidy for whatever they want, they'll buy it every time."

"We ought to appoint some chairmen of committees. First, Finance." He paused delicately. Tom Devin, waving his glass of twelve-year-old Scotch, moved that Chester Humboldt be appointed Chairman of Finance.

"Look, I don't want you to feel that just because you let me make a contribution, you have to—" He was nominated by acclamation. Even Yates, who was now sitting with Cassie and Bender, applauded in a limp-wristed manner. Chester accepted the chairmanship modestly, with a boyish grin. "I'll try not to waste any of our money. Personally, I feel we shouldn't pinch nickels when it comes to the music. We're asking a highly talented young composer to work under pressure with too little time, and the least we can do is provide him with whatever he needs to do the job." He was standing near the bar facing the dozen people in the room, and he sensed there was at least one pocket of dissent among his listeners—Devin and Al Farwell were whispering together— but he didn't give it time to erupt. Jumping ahead on the script, he asked Tom Devin to be in charge of Festival promotion among local merchants. "If anybody can sell them on the idea, it's you. I ought to know—you sold me a place ten times bigger than I needed." (*Wait for laughs here,* the script said. Chester waited; Tom Devin laughed hardest of all.)

"And you, musketeer." He couldn't remember Farwell's name, but it was simple enough to point to the only man in the room with a musket, "Will you be head consultant on erecting liberty poles?"

"Like mebbe aluminum flagpoles?" Farwell said. "These I can handle, and the paints. You can have 'em at cost. But where you gonna put up the poles?"

Chester said, "It seems to me any businessman or homeowner who allows a liberty pole to go up on his property should have his name inscribed on it on a small, dignified plaque."

Mrs. Loomite was half out of her chair, foaming protests, but Chester raised his voice and hurried on to discuss "a key chairmanship—committee on Early American Art and Crafts. This job requires a very special knowledge and taste." At least five people spoke at once, out of the kindness of their hearts, to nominate Mrs. Loomite. In a rush of gratitude, her eyeballs glistening, Mrs. Loomite said she would make a point of including "authentic artifacts, to give the olden-time primitive charm. The simplest household objects—uh, pewter plates, brass warming pans—"

A new voice interrupted gaily, from the doorway: "And don't forget Black Jack mugs and Hopkins Elixir and bosom bottles."

Everybody in the room turned to look—rather, gape—at the speaker. Chester thought it was somebody who'd come to the wrong party until he saw Prudence Washburn beside her, dowdily insignificant and yet significant as identification. Miss Thorne! It had to be Miss Thorne. Somehow he had thought of all lady authors as wearing glasses and sensible shoes. Especially a lady author who had roomed with Miss Washburn in college. But this woman was beautiful, red-haired and stacked, in an elegant ladylike way. As she came toward her host in a lovely flow of motion, the jaws of every man in the room hung slack.

"You're Chester Humboldt," she said.

This was undeniably true. He was Chester Humboldt. Beyond that, he was suddenly not too sure of anything.

Chapter Five

Nobody was talking about earwigs, or even the Festival, much.

"Wow, she's terrific-looking," Cassie said. "For anybody that old. She's old enough to be my mother. Let's go over and meet her."

Oliver scrunched lower in his chair. He felt as if he'd reached for a doorknob and got a violent electric shock. His instinct was to sit tight until he stopped tingling.

Lo Bender's hips were already swaying in the breeze around Alicia Thorne. "You are a mirage. In a Pucci print, of course."

"Of course," she said. "What else would you expect a mirage to wear? But I'm a thirsty mirage. Won't somebody get me a drink?"

"Look, they're buzzing around her like fruit flies," Cassie said. "Come on. You've been dying to meet her. We'll finagle her in to the piano."

"You can't just barge over and say, 'Go sit on the piano,'" Oliver muttered.

"Silly, I hadn't planned to. Mr. Humboldt already said he'd arrange it. Aren't they handsome together? I haven't had a chance to tell you—his wife left him for somebody else and he's been terribly lonely. Wouldn't it be nice if they fell for each other?"

"Who?" Oliver said.

"Mr. Humboldt and Miss Thorne. But I think she's already married. The fourth or fifth time."

"The fourth or fifth time what?"

Cassie said, with fond exasperation, "When you're thinking about work, you don't even know which end is up."

Oliver, who wasn't thinking about work at the moment, knew which end was up. An instinctive male caution kept him from saying so.

Cassie patted his seersuckered arm. "I'll go pave the way."

Chester, claiming the rights of host, had separated Alicia from her admirers on the pretext of showing her the view, and had taken her out to the back terrace. And it wasn't entirely pretext. He wanted to show off; he was as eager as a small boy emptying his pockets to display his treasures. Cassie Murdoch had made him feel the view was his own special triumph; he waited confidently for this more important praise. Alicia Thorne said, "Oh, aren't the hills magnificent! I can't understand people who say Nature makes them feel small and humble. It makes me feel swaggering tall."

This wasn't quite the reaction he'd expected; it seemed to credit God rather than Chester, and he wanted to get the conversation on a twosier level. He said, "You're just tall enough." She was, too. Her nose came to his chin. Her other measurements were equally satisfactory. "I'll tell you a joke on me. I'd intended to pick your brains for anecdotes about Emerson. He was sort of a hero of mine. But when I saw you —I can't even remember now who Emerson is."

Her reaction rather dumbfounded him. She moved in so fast, and so close, she might have been about to bite him. She said intensely, "Don't you get furious at the way the better mousetrappers have taken him over? They've tried to make him sound like one of those dreadful columnists who're syndicated in a hundred and thirty-nine papers and lay a Nugget Thought a day: 'Be self-reliant . . . the one good in life is

72

concentration.' . . . But he was no homey philosopher. He felt empathy with the fox, the centipede, the wild night wind music. He loved the *Chanson de Roland* that Taillefer sang riding to battle, and the ways of the wandering minstrels. . . ."

By the time she'd got to transcendentalism, Chester was sorry he'd brought up Emerson at all. He had nothing against brainy women, but he disliked having them spatter their brains all over him. She was standing so close he couldn't help seeing that her neck was beginning to show the slightest signs of wear, front center; there was a tiny, very tiny, line on each side of the beautiful mouth. She was gesturing, as she talked, with the hands a half-dozen painters and sculptors had sweated to catch on canvas, in bronze. She stopped talking so suddenly he was caught in the midst of his critical inventory. He adjusted his expression fast, as much out of chivalry as anything, but not fast enough. She lifted her throat, all pure line now. "I'm so tiresome when I get on my family. And Emerson has always seemed like family, because my great-grandfather—my great-great-grandfather, that is—knew him so well. They were devoted friends. Tell me about your family, Mr. Humboldt? Did they start in New England as peddlers? Is that why you're backing the Festival—like buying a family crest? Bevington does rather care about family."

After the first sickening impact, he felt quite cool and wary. He even recognized the switchover; sometimes he'd gone into business meetings hazy after a late night—till he'd run head on into trouble; it always cleared the cobwebs.

"My grandfather was a scutcher in the mill," he said. "My father never went beyond tenth grade. He was a dropout for quite a dull reason—his mother and three younger brothers had to eat. And I waited on tables to get through college— that's how I learned which fork to use. It's come in very handy. As for why I'm backing the Festival, I happen to love New England. I don't want to buy it—I want to pay back." He must remember to give Trumbine that last line.

"Forgive me. What I said was cruel. And tasteless." The

73

second sin was obviously the worse of the two. "But when I meet a very strong, attractive, successful man like you, I have a dreadful impulse to lash out. Maybe it's not so dreadful—maybe it's just a healthy instinct of self-preservation." She smiled at him with such dazzling femaleness he felt the heat rise even while he knew he'd been rendered immune.

"You see, I've heard nothing but giant praise of you ever since I came. Prue is so carried away she tried to ram you down my throat. And I'd made up my mind not to like you. But I'm not sure I can help myself. Will you put on a fright wig and make nasty faces and do something disgustingly vulgar to stiffen my resolve? I must repeat to myself fifty times 'I will *not* find him so attractive—I am hostile to millionaires.' Please help me remember."

He couldn't help being flattered and amused. "Request denied. After all, I'm not hostile to beautiful women. But if I don't return you to the party, all Bevington will be hostile to one millionaire."

Cassie Murdoch was waiting for them just inside the door. "I knew you were getting Miss Thorne's advice about the Festival and I didn't want to interrupt, but I have a message for her from Daddy. I'm Wesley Murdoch's daughter and I've been hearing about you ever since I was a little girl."

Oh-oh, Chester thought. He said too heartily, "That must have been all of five years ago. It couldn't be more—impossible on the face of it."

His attention was momentarily distracted by a tray thrust under his nose and a nasal voice saying, "Would you care for a horse derve?"

The speaker was in maid's uniform, with the somewhat unusual addition of a flower in her streaming hair. Mrs. Gifford had mentioned that the gardener's daughter Fiera, who was a maid at the Talladay School, would "serve" that afternoon. She was serving, all right. She seemed to be offering her breasts on the tray, along with horse derve. "Don't this caviar look like black ants?" she said in a cosy hiss. He waved away her offered goodies.

Cassie was saying ". . . and Daddy is so sorry to miss you. It's a convention of newspaper publishers in San Francisco. Mummy thought he ought to go for a rest, so she said she'd go too and then they'll fly on to Hawaii. They just decided last night."

Just as Chester shooed Fiera away, Prudence Washburn nabbed him to ask if a tour of the oldest Landmark houses might be included as a feature of the Festival. "We could charge four dollars for a tour of six houses, upstairs and down. Last year I was the only one to show my upstairs and somebody swiped an antique pin tray and a Sheffield silver buttonhook. But next time we're going to rope the rooms off so they can have a peek but no pinching. All the ladies love to look around other peoples' bedrooms. . . ."

Chester listened with less than half an ear; all his nerve ganglia or antennae were directed toward Cassie's confident young voice: "I know you and Daddy were great friends when you were young."

The almost invisible lines around Alicia Thorne's mouth were decidedly visible now, grooved as the corners turned down.

"You don't look at all the way I expected," Cassie went on.

"You mean I'm remarkable for my age?" Something about her reminded Chester of a tiger purring.

"When I was in junior high, we had a story of yours in a textbook and it was already considered a classic."

"Perhaps I should be put out to pasture," Alicia said. "Like a spavined race horse."

"Oh, no! You're still a *great* writer. I have a friend who just worships your stuff. He's right over there." She waved in Oliver's direction, possessively, proudly.

"He's the young man I told you about, Lishy," Prudence said. "The composer—remember?"

"I remember," Alicia said thoughtfully. "He has an interesting face. There's a bust of Shelley in the Yale library with those same heavy-lidded eyes. Looking asleep when they're most aware."

75

. "He's longing to meet you, but he's sort of shy, and anyway he's in awe of you."

"We must do something about that!" Her eyes sparkled, golden flecks in amber. She shone with kindness and good humor. Watching her, Chester felt even more uneasy.

Cassie looked at him and waggled a message, pointing across the hall to the music room. He got the message—a child of two would have got the message—but his instinct was to stall. Let Thorne cool down first. Get her surrounded. This was a cinch. Devin and the patent lawyer had crowded in close, breathing heavy compliments and whisky fumes. Al Farwell, propped beside his musket against the bar, was studying Miss Thorne's lower anatomical structure openly, beamishly. He had perhaps never heard Plutarch's line, "The bright splendor of her thighs," but the thought was there, printed in block capitals on his round red face. Lo Bender had squatted at Alicia's feet, close enough to lick the Ferragamo pumps, which matched a color note of her dress. "You and Pucci have managed to achieve the exact orange of a lizard's balloon," he said. "Those tiny green Florida lizards that suddenly shoot out a balloon. . . ." He puffed his plump cheeks and stuck out his tongue to demonstrate. "But it's really more from their Adam's apple. I've never been sure whether they do it to start a fight or to make love."

"Both," Alicia said. "It's so much the same thing. I must tell Pucci about the balloon. He'd adore that."

Chester saw her glance over at Oliver once or twice, but she was in no rush. She went on being charming, blossoming on the attention, even the soggiest compliments. Devin said, "Fiera Young asked me if you're a movie star. I told her, you oughta be."

"I should," Alicia said, twinkling at him. "It pays so much better. Will you be my manager?"

She was even delightful to ladies; Mrs. Tyndale asked her about bosom bottles and Alicia showed, with pretty gestures, how a bosom bottle was attached to a stayhook in the bodice "with a few teaspoons of water to keep a nosegay fresh. *Do*

76

have some on sale at the Festival. I must put in my order right now."

Mrs. Loomite said, "May we call it the Alicia Thorne bouquet bottle?"

Permission was gaily granted. "But bosom's more fun."

"I thought at first you meant Hopkins Elixir was kept in the bosom bottles."

"Why didn't *they* think of that—all those ladylike tipplers! Oh, and the Black Jack mugs. They're another thing you should have. Made of leather and edged with silver or copper. Like drinking out of a boot! Men were supermen in those days." But her smiles around the group signaled that she still thought well of mens' potency. And Pickett swore he'd drink to her out of a boot.

Cassie had gone to fetch Oliver to join the star turn, but Mrs. Loomite had had the same thought earlier, and he had escaped again to the music room. Cassie looked at Chester imploringly. He didn't want to go back on his promise—he would have to ask Yates to play—but he didn't want Alicia Thorne involved. He wasn't even sure exactly why. He pretended to be busy at the bar, although by then things were so convivial guests were making their own drinks. Cassie cornered him there, to say it was about six and couldn't he get everybody in to the piano.

"Why don't you and I go in and have the audition by ourselves?"

"But he especially wanted Miss Thorne," she blurted.

"If she goes in there everybody will trail after her and the music will get lost in the shuffle. That wouldn't be fair to Yates."

Cassie ran her fingers through her hair till it stood out springily, expressing agitated thought.

"I know. And Oliver hates people yakking when he's playing. But Prue doesn't have a piano. And Miss Thorne's leaving Monday, so this is his only chance." She explained about Oliver wanting operatic rights to a story of Alicia's. "Just between us, he's not as good on straight opera as he is on the

77

folk kinds. But he has his heart absolutely set on doing this."
And he wants you to get everything set up for him the way you did at the meeting. He thought of a fresh excuse. "Yates will have his hands full with the Festival. Couldn't the other wait?"

"But he may never see her again."

Chester said silently, That's what I hope. "Why don't I get her back here quietly without the others, tomorrow?" Tomorrow seemed safer—one of those tomorrows that needn't come. He heard the piano start up again.

"Oh, that would be so marvelous. You always know how to fix everything." She clutched his hand in an excess of gratitude.

Now he'd have to go through with it. He'd get Thorne Sunday if he had to lasso her. And he'd run interference—he'd make a big ploy. . . . "Tomorrow it is." He kept her hand, which was small, tanned, and not at all soft, but somehow felt very pleasant in his. It reminded him of the paw of a Scotch terrier he'd loved as a boy. His parents had refused to let the dog stay indoors at night; he'd had to sneak it into his room from the roof and hide it under the covers and pat it to keep it from barking. He patted her hand, as if to keep her from barking. "Tomorrow," she said.

But it turned out to be sooner.

He had just relinquished her paw when there was a crash and a shot. Fiera Young, carrying a fresh load of horse derve, had tripped over the musket propped by the bar, and it had gone off. The musket ball, luckily, had hit only the ceiling. A small amount of plaster fell on Fiera, who was lying on the floor screaming, "I'm shot."

Cassie moved to the rescue so fast she seemed to leap over the bar. She slapped the screaming, sobbing Fiera efficiently on both cheeks; the screams ebbed to sniffles and moans. "I'll take her upstairs," she told Chester. "We don't want to spoil your beautiful party."

Al Farwell was cradling his musket, saying over and over,

"Gee, I didn't mean to load it. I only put a few sprinkles in here and. . . ."

Chester disengaged him from his weapon, tactfully, and assured him the ceiling could be patched. "Let's just be thankful no one was hurt." Mrs. Loomite, the other victim, wasn't exactly hurt, but the contents of Fiera's spilled tray had hurtled down her front and she was a mess of egg and anchovy tidbit. Chester had to take her out to Mrs. Gifford for emergency repairs.

As soon as he returned, Cassie rushed at him with bulletins: "Fiera's O.K., I gave her a sedative—I found some phenobarb in your medicine chest. She's resting on your bed. Oliver and I will take her home when he's finished. He's in there playing for Miss Thorne! She wouldn't let anybody else come in because she wanted to concentrate on the music. Isn't that thoughtful?"

Chester said it was very thoughtful.

Chapter Six

Oliver, lost in the key of A flat, had honestly forgotten about Alicia Thorne and, in fact, the whole party. When he heard what sounded like a shot from across the hall, his ears registered the sound but as background noise, incidental to the chords he was pounding on the piano. It was at least three or four minutes later, when he stopped dum-dee-dahing long enough to light a cigarette, that he realized he'd heard something odd. He got up, rather reluctantly, to go and find out if Cassie was all right.

He couldn't see her among the clumps of guests. "Where's Cassie?" he asked Lo.

"She took Fiera upstairs to dress her wounds." Lo gave a vividly overdone account of the incident. "Look at the ceiling —the whole place is pock-marked with bullets."

He cut off Oliver's "But a musket doesn't—" with "We're working on a graveyard chorus."

"You mean somebody got killed?" Oliver almost shouted. "Who?"

"I didn't say anybody got killed—not yet. But I'm collecting the most divine epitaphs for a Festival number—we've been telling Miss Thorne about it, and she said they used to have coffin pies shaped exactly like little coffins, with very tough

80

crusts. Talk about black humor! We'll have hawkers calling, 'Get your coffin at intermission.' I think mincemeat loaded with brandy. . . ."

Oliver's attention had strayed, as it often did from Lo, but this time with more reason. Alicia Thorne, on second viewing, was like lightning hitting back. She was sitting on an olive-green love seat, with her bronze hair and that incredibly white skin, her face upturned smiling as she listened to Mrs. Loomite's dentist husband. What the hell could a gum-care man have to say that delighted her?

"Isn't she fabulous?" Lo said. "Wouldn't you like to hang her over your mantel like a painting and light candles? Come on, I'll introduce you. She and I are already bloody good friends."

Oliver said, "I think I'll go see how Cassie's doing." Although he often ignored Cassie when she was around, her not being around when she was supposed to be made a frightening void, a hole he might drop through into he knew not what. He intended to skirt it cautiously, and bring her back to re-establish solid ground.

"You may as well marry the gel." Lo was being even more British than usual, or usual that month. "You don't even gnaw at the leash. Run get her permission."

Oliver said resentfully he didn't need anybody's permission to meet Miss Thorne. And he let himself be led like a lamb.

Alicia Thorne took his hand in both of hers and said very simply, "I've been wanting very much to meet you. Sit here beside me." Her voice was like fresh silk wrapping around him. "Prue told me you'd done an opera. I've been so out of touch—tell me, where was it done?"

Oliver was about to name, with some embarrassment, the little East Village theater when Lo said, "Lincoln Center."

After that, it would have seemed boorish for Oliver to tell her right then.

"Of course you know my friend Willy Latham."

William Latham was one of the heads of Lincoln Center.

Oliver might have said, "I've talked to his secretary at least

ten times on the phone. He's always in conference or Europe."
He shook his head, then remembered that if his opera had
actually been done at Lincoln Center, he should have met
Latham.

Alicia Thorne didn't notice, or didn't choose to notice, the
discrepancy.

"You must meet him. I'd be doing him a favor. He's often
told me how hard it is to find really talented young composers."

Oliver felt like asking, Where did he look—under bushel
baskets? He cleared his throat noncommittally.

Miss Maulridge, who had been sitting in a happy trance on
the edge of a Danish modern chair, searching her dusty mind
for more epitaphs, roused to say, "We owe Oliver a great deal
for thinking up the Liberty Pole Festival."

"It was Cassie's idea," Lo said. On the rare occasions when
he came out with the naked truth, it was apt to seem awfully
naked.

"The little girl with the sturdy legs?" Alicia said, with gentle
amusement. "Frankly, I'd have thought it seemed much more
like you." She looked at Oliver very directly; he swam around
dizzily in her gaze. "Confess—wasn't it really your idea?"

"Cassie helped me with the research." He was already half
persuaded this was so.

"She's a sweet, helpful child. If you could have seen her
giving that maid first aid—like a brownie scout who's passed
her test for treating hysterics." She pudged her jaw in carica-
ture and made a few slaps in the air. Her laughter bubbled
up. "It was so delicious to watch. You'd have loved it." Oliver
couldn't help laughing disloyally. In a few gestures, she had
caught Cassie at her do-goodiest.

"I thought you'd already left by then and I was so disappointed." She dropped her voice. "You were the person I most
wanted to meet."

Oliver mumbled that he'd been across the hall working on a
song for the Festival.

She clasped her lovely hands together. "When may I hear
it?"

It was as easy as that.

He could hardly believe he was sitting down at the piano about to play for Miss Thorne as audience, beautiful, eager audience of one. She had refused, prettily, to let even Lo tag along. "Because I want to keep a pure stream of listening."

If she'd said that in connection with anything else than his music, Oliver would have thought she was sounding rather precious. But as it was, when she appealed to him, "Do you think I'm right or am I just being selfish?" there was only one possible answer.

He told her the number was still in the rough stage, but he didn't make it an apology. Once at a piano, he was very much his own man. The feel of the hard ivory keys was like a talisman, a charm that made him invincible. Like most composers, he had no real voice, but he could project: "Raise a liberty pole," he bellowed. "Summer, winter, spring or fall— Raise our freedom standard tall. . . ."

At the end Alicia Thorne said she was utterly thrilled. "It has a *driving* beauty—a wonderful upbeat swing. . . ." He realized it was even better than he'd thought.

In a different tone, rather brisk and businesslike, she said, "But the lyrics aren't right. It should be 'Grow a liberty pole.'"

He had the creative artist's mulish instant reflex to any suggestion for change in his masterpiece. And to strengthen his resistance, Miss Thorne was singing "Grow a liberty pole" painfully out of tune. To drown her out, he pounded the melody line with one finger. But as he pounded, he found himself crooning, 'Grow a liberty pole.' It sang better.

Alicia was so excited she hitched her chair right up to the piano. "You make it sound so right!" It was right; he had to admit this. "The chorus comes on with little stumpy sticks— then as they sing the poles grow—keep stretching up and up and up. 'No Tory frost or British fire . . . Can dah-dee-dumdah in the mire.'"

Neither of them liked "mire." Being against something together was even more stimulating than being united *for* something. "Tell George the Third we're not for hire . . . We grow our freedom whole . . . High as a liberty pole."

"There'll be a ballet—the British soldiers slash down the poles but they keep growing again. . . ."

"And the kids have a dance—each couple grips a pole between them and wrestles it."

" 'The Liberty Pole-ka.' " That was Alicia's. "Don't you adore it?"

"Doesn't come off. It would just sound like 'polka'—moldy fig."

She got white around the mouth, although she didn't actually foam; her eyes turned greenish. " 'Moldy fig!' "

"Old hat—shush, I've almost got it. . . ." Dum-dee-dah-*dah*-dat—" 'The Liberty Pole Polecat.' "

"It couldn't be sillier," she said crossly. "In case you're too ignorant to know, a polecat is a skunk."

"Tories were skunks." He was rather apolitical himself, but he was ready to defend to the death his own idea for a song title.

"Some of the most brilliant, cultivated, charming men in the entire colonies were Tories."

"You sound like Lo. He says we should have stayed a colony." He gave her a few highlights. "Cassie nearly hit him."

A small snort of laughter escaped her. "I can imagine how that child would react. She was preaching to me about how we've forgotten what we came from—and that most of her generation don't know who they are. But I've always known who I am and I'm sure you have too."

Oliver couldn't deny this.

"People with our talent have our own liberty poles, like an axis, and the world turns around us."

He was a little taken aback to hear anybody refer to herself, in effect, as the center of the universe. Especially a woman. But since she was including him bang in the middle, beside her, he was inclined to accept what she said, and be generous in return: "When I first read your story about the witch trial, it sang like music. I was so excited I paced. I couldn't sleep all night—I wanted to talk to you about it for hours." In the shared glow of two great talents, it seemed natural to tell her about trying to get the operatic rights. He had barely started

"Your agent. . . ." when Lo burst in like a grape popping out of its skin: "I didn't hear the piano, so I knew you'd finished. Ducks, wait till you hear. My costumes for the Festival will blaze a trail backward in men's fashions—*knee* buckles and gorgets—and long hair tied in queues. Stab my vitals! I think they should carry liberty poles as canes."

Alicia said that sounded a bit Bo Peepish. "Let's not be quaint."

Lo's plump cheeks sagged; she couldn't have chosen a filthier epithet. "The canes would really be swordsticks."

"Run away, sweetie," Alicia said carelessly. Oliver had drifted back to his dum-dee. "And will you tell Prue she needn't wait for me if she's in a rush to start dinner. Tell her I'm working on something."

Lo went, quivering, but when he turned at the door she blew him a kiss. And after a second's poutish hesitation, he blew one back.

Oliver, who had been smoothing a few rough edges, played "Grow a Liberty Pole" again, with more authority, and sang their new lyrics straight through. He and Alicia were so set up it was like an artistic orgasm.

Her eyes shone goldenly. "I've thought of another song—exactly that same period—the trimmers."

Oliver looked blank.

"They took one side and then the other—Tory, Loyalist—whichever seemed safer—trimming their sails with the wind."

Oliver nodded; from his far-out expression, he might have been on a trip. He played a rather tiresome number of dum-dee-dum-dahs in various keys. Alicia took out her compact and glanced in its mirror and smiled; but she slipped it back in her purse as Oliver sang suddenly, loudly, "Him's a trimmer."

In the kitchen, the housekeeper and Mrs. Loomite were having a good talk on the evil of guns. Mrs. Loomite was wearing a dress of Mrs. Gifford's because her own had been too mucked with egg and anchovy to respond to cleaning fluid. "They should be outlawed entirely," Mrs. Gifford said.

"Even for police. If men went back to primitive ways, serenely at one with Nature. . . ."

Mrs. Loomite agreed warmly. "You know, in Westchester County hunters are only allowed to shoot deer with bows and arrows."

Mrs. Gifford looked faintly worried, as if she were thinking that was hard on the deer. But the conversation was flowering too nicely to nip it right then. "I myself have taken up archery although I wouldn't dream of killing. I don't even aim."

Now it was Mrs. Loomite who looked worried.

"Part of my exercises in Knowing and Being," Mrs. Gifford went on. "I follow Herrigel's theory—you just let go with the quiver and shoot, without conscious aim. The real target is yourself. You must hit the core of the unconscious."

Mrs. Loomite, whose unconscious had been giving her trouble at night, said, "What a marvelous thought. It's just occurred to me that the Far Eastern mystics have much in common with our early settlers."

The thought didn't seem to have occurred to Mrs. Gifford, but she put on an interested look.

"The oneness with Nature—the simplicity of mind and body."

Mrs. Gifford was sold: "We become so involved, so frenzied. We must learn again to disattach. There's a beautiful old Chinese saying: 'A man can't prevent the birds from flying over his head, but he can keep them from nesting in his hair.' "

Mrs. Loomite was so struck with this she asked Mrs. Gifford to write it down; Mrs. Gifford wrote it on the pad she used for grocery orders.

Mrs. Gifford was eager to know more about the Festival, now that it somehow related to Far Eastern mystics. Mrs. Loomite was eager to tell her: ". . . used vegetable and berry dyes for their paints, so I plan an exhibit of home-dyed art, as one facet."

Mrs. Gifford said what a welcome relief from what passed for art nowadays.

Mrs. Loomite expanded on her idea a few minutes later to a

small, culture-bent group of Lo, Miss Maulridge, and Mrs. Tyndale. "We'll use the same berries and vegetables they used, and the artists will squeeze their own dyes."

"You should call it 'home-squeezed art,'" Lo said. "Be more provocative for the posters."

A man who'd come in from the golf club with Mrs. Loomite's husband waylaid Chester, who didn't recognize him at first. "Decided to tell you I checked up on you after the meeting. Wanted to make sure you weren't pulling a fast one."

The mild, amused, slightly fuddled voice was somehow familiar, but as he turned to wave at Pickett, Chester recognized him from the bald spot: tennis ball, sat in front of me. "Is my credit rating O.K.?" They grinned at each other.

"Satishfactory." He introduced himself. "Name's Wood— ex-magazine editor." He named one of the most massive mass-market media. "Got my arm caught in a merger. And I know all about you, from a pal who edits *Textile Talk*. What I can't figure is how you moved into town without the grapevine tripping you up to get all the vital statistics. The women's phones have been buzzing hot and loud all day, to make up for lost time."

Chester explained why he'd had to be away since he bought the Mortly place. "But I plan to spend a good bit of time here this summer."

Wood said he was glad to hear it. "This liberty-pole thing might be quite a shot in the arm. I can raise four or five thousand bucks more around here, in backing, not much more. But I gather you're not worried about that. This could have a national angle. Who's handling your publicity?"

Chester told him.

"Ross Trumbine! Well, well—that answers the big question. You might get my vote." They grinned at each other again, man to man. "I thought maybe you wanted to get in good so you could move a plant in here with a sneaky deal on taxes. By the way, keep both eyes on Devin. I don't say he's crooked —he just bends. And politically, he's a twig off the old birch."

Chester said thanks.

"Hear Alicia Thorne's around. Never met her myself, but when Klepp published her there was a rumor in the trade he'd flay young authors and use their hides to make her special bindings in calfskin. I gather she's what they used to call imperious."

"That reminds me," Chester said, "I have to check on some things with Miss Murdoch." If it sounded like a *non sequitur,* it wasn't.

"Now *she* doesn't bend, that Cassie. She rides into action on a white charger—a white pony. Last month the town council cut the education budget to vote fifteen hundred bucks for a ladies' room for the rifle range, and boy, did Cassie draw a bead. Raised such a healthy stink—and Wes backed her up in the *Bugle*—that the rifle lobby had to—there she is now, sliding down the bannisters."

Cassie wasn't quite sliding down the bannisters, but she looked as if she might. Chester met her at the bottom of the stairs. "Fiera's sleeping peacefully. I won't wake her till the last minute. I'm so pleased that Miss Thorne is giving Oliver all this time." As they went past the closed door of the music room, she said, "Oh, he's playing something brand-new for her. Even I haven't heard it before. I'll bet he's improvising for her on the witches."

Chester thought it more probable that a witch was improvising on Oliver.

The only problem Cassie was concerned with was the Festival. "There's a class in square dancing and one in the bougaloo at the Community Center. I thought we could get our dancers from there, but Oliver says if we mix squares and bougaloos and throw in the Yogi ballet group, we're inciting to riot."

Chester began to have a higher opinion of Yates's mentality.

"He can rehearse singers and do simple arrangements for two pianos or the dulcimer, fiddle and whatever, but I guess we'd be safer without dancers."

Chester said he'd just had a brainstorm. "Look, I pay all these performers anyway, for the television show. And we've got this thirty-piece orchestra. . . ." He talked rather fast and he hoped convincingly. To have her accept the whole caboodle so instantly, so joyfully, should have been a relief. Instead, it was somehow a letdown. He reflected sourly that the young who ranted most against money and materialistic trappings were the ones who'd always had it and expected more of the same. To give them a handout was like giving candy to a baby. But as she poured out her gratefulness, laving him with appreciative looks of mountain-lake blue, the sourness washed away. She was so little, so good, so unselfish. After all, she didn't want any of this for herself. He felt tender and broad-shouldered. ". . . just have to tell you a secret," she was saying. "If the Festival's a big success, and Oliver gets some commissions for jobs, we're going to be married right away."

Chester said all the suitable things and thought gray thoughts.

"Of course we've been sleeping together for months," Cassie said sunnily. "But I don't think it's fair to have children till . . ." His stomach began to hurt. He wished people would go home. The Festival was off to a fast start, better than he and Trumbine had hoped. And it was nothing to him if this kid wanted to marry a noodle.

"Before I forget," Cassie said, "I ought to go up and check on—"

Chester lost the rest.

"Hear ye, hear ye," Alicia Thorne chanted. She was standing beside the bar holding a very full glass, looking luminously lovely. "All you dear people, I'm staying on for the Festival. Oliver's persuaded me."

In the excitement, nobody thought of Fiera Young. The gardener called Mrs. Gifford around nine, to ask when the party would be over and whether he should pick up his daughter. And since the party had been over for two hours, Mrs. Gifford knocked on the study door to ask Chester if he knew where Fiera had been taken.

"Good Lord, she must still be up in my bed."

It took a bit of explaining.

By midnight, Chester was smoking like a chimney.

Chapter
Seven

When Cassie walked into the Talladay studio, she seemed to Oliver oddly foreshortened. "The little girl with sturdy legs" —Alicia Thorne's phrase skidded across his mind.

"I cooked chicken livers for Davy and they were marvelous. I put dry vermouth in the sauce. And apricot mousse. You should have eaten with us."

Instantly, he felt aggrieved. He had refused her invitation because he had somehow assumed he and Alicia would go on working, a delicious shared nibble and song-fest. But the attorney Pickett, after the party, had raced off with Alicia in a bright red Ferrari, the damn show-off. She had called to Oliver, "Will you finish 'Him's a Trimmer' by tomorrow? I can hardly wait."

He had dined in the studio on some tired crackers and a diet cola that was an ominous brownish purple, or burple. By the time the song was finished, he had needed somebody to tell him how great it was. Prudence Washburn, when he phoned, said Alicia wasn't back yet. And to Oliver's overdetailed explanation of why he'd wanted to get in touch with her house guest, Prudence said, "I doubt if Lishy'd be much help. She can't even carry a tune. When she used to try to sing, she sounded like a grasshopper rubbing its legs together."

Frustrated old maid, old bitch, trampling sour grapes. Prodding and poking: "Why don't you get Cassie? She has Wes's ear."

Oliver said Cassie wanted to spoon-feed Davy his dinner.

Prudence made fond clucking sounds: "What a darling that girl is. And a good cook since she was twelve." Not exactly saying, "She'll make somebody a wonderful wife." But making clear who that somebody was: "You look as if you needed fattening up." For the kill.

It exasperated him so much he decided not to call Cassie at all. He had held off till 10:45.

When she went over to sit in the soggy big chair she always sat in for listening, a bit to the right of the piano, he noticed with annoyance how she tucked her legs up under her. In the past, he had found this habit of hers charming and childlike. Tonight she looked squatty, and he resented it as a personal affront. He had been honestly unaware of looking at Alicia Thorne's legs while he played that afternoon, but the after-image struck now: long, silken, slender yet so beautifully curved, the delicately boned ankles, sleek orange pumps . . . Cassie was wearing sneakers. And a wholesome shiny-nosed air. Her nose was small and pretty; even without make-up her face had a reaching-out vividness. But what Oliver noted at the moment, compiling his list of debits, was a peeling fleck of sunburned skin on her firm, round chin. "I'm a mess," she said comfortably. "But I didn't want to keep you waiting."

To punish her for being so precipitate, he shifted his papers around on the music rack, made picayune changes on the lead sheet, and tried out the opening chord in three different keys.

Cassie was totally still. She had very little technical knowledge of music, but she did have an inspired ignorance, an instinct she rode like a broomstick to light on whatever was good. Even in his discontented state, Oliver counted on that. He played "Him's a Trimmer" first, and in spite of his professionalism, his voice almost smirked as he sang his favorite lines. There were some rhymes he enunciated with special bellowing clarity:

"shifts faster than a weathercock . . .
a tricky tickin' two-time clock. . . ."

Cassie smiled, but not enough, so he did a reprise to wow her. Even then she wasn't exactly laughing-girl ecstatic. She said it was clever. "But it seems to have too many words. I think the idea is stronger than the lyrics. After all, she's new at this, and you haven't had time to polish her stuff yet. When you've cut down the words and brought up the melody so the lyrics and music are more—well, married . . ."

Obviously she was so marriage-crazy it distorted everything she heard or said. She didn't know the meaning of personal freedom. Alicia did: "People like us have our own liberty pole, like an axis, and the world turns around us."

He played "Grow a Liberty Pole" in almost a fury, an incitement to himself, a throwing-off of yokes.

Cassie uncurled her legs and beat time with her sneakered feet. "It's a thousand times better this way. The lyrics even make the music grow." He thought that was going too far; the music, in his opinion, had reached considerable heights on its own. But he admitted that "Grow" brought out what the music was saying.

"Now Miss Thorne has to stay, no matter. Prue's acting so funny all of a sudden. She said when we left the party, 'Lishy can be very difficult—she blows hot and cold—she has to be humored.' So we'll humor her. Don't you think it's worth it?"

Oliver, with remarkable restraint, said he supposed so.

"You'll be able to handle her," Cassie went on confidently. "Older women always flip for you. Like La Loomite and poor Miss Maulridge and the cook at Scurvy Hall and my mother."

He was so infuriated at this comparison he teetered on the verge—the dangerous verge—of repeating the things Alicia had said to him that very afternoon. In a way, Cassie did it for him: "I have a hunch she's staying because she realizes how good you are."

Put that way, Oliver could afford to deprecate his role: "She really wants to help."

92

"Oh, I *know*. Now that I've heard the opening number I can tell she has a terrific feeling for what we're trying to do. I already told Prue Miss Thorne could stay in our guest room." He opened and closed his mouth like a fish tossed onto dry land.

"Because Prue's decided it's too much for her to have Miss Thorne for seven weeks. She says it would be bad for her blood pressure. And I'm sure mother and daddy wouldn't mind. They'll be away at least a month. Prue said it would solve a lot of things."

Oliver felt as if the walls were pushing in, flattening him out, making him stand straight and narrow.

When Cassie said, "Let's go get a hamburger. Aren't you starved?" he shook his head moodily, denying all animal instincts. But then he was afraid she might stay on, to arouse alternative appetites, and he wasn't hungry for that either. Food seemed the safer way out.

They went off in Cassie's car to the Stick Shift, a drive-in with adjoining beer *boîte*, a hangout for those unpolluted by age and soft automatic thinking. As Cassie's little green Volks nosed its way in, the noise rushed out to greet them, howling jukebox and ocean roar of voices; even the neon glare seemed to be part of the decibel content. To habitués, anything less would have seemed creepy.

"I forgot to bring any money," Cassie said. "I'll settle with you tomorrow."

Oliver counted his available assets. Paychecks were due after the weekend. "We can have two hamburgers apiece. Or one hamburger and beer."

"There's Lo's car." She pointed to a Saab with a large rear-end placard: I AM AN OPSIST—BEWARE. "If we want more, we can borrow from him."

They debated whether they were hungry enough to take on Lo. It turned out to be an academic discussion because Lo burst out of the beer *boîte* flailing his short plump arms: "Gail says come on in—she's buying. She sold a painting today to Dr. Talladay's accountant."

Inside, a voice from the jukebox moaned: "Speed me, Mama, down to Heaven below." The fug was as thick as a blanket; because of some vagary of interior lighting, the faces clumped around tables seemed to float in a greenish light, like heads of St. John the Baptist only more hairy.

Lo bounced ahead, leading the way to Gail. Oliver and Cassie had almost caught up, and were within greeting range of their hostess, when they were blocked by an occupied chair. An intensely bearded youth had shoved back from the table next to Gail's to achieve more room for expression. He was saying loudly, "I agree with Che Guevara's blueprint. Let's have more wars, more killings, more horror, to enrage more people and make the climate riper for revolution." He seemed to be spitting through a thicket of hair. "Oh, hi, Cassie. Is Davy around?"

Cassie said her brother had gone to bed early. "We're playing tennis at seven."

"Tennis!" he sneered. "Nero fiddled and Davy plays tennis."

"And you look at pornographic pictures," she said, in a tolerant, sisterly tone. "Davy showed me that book you loaned him."

The youth lowered his beard in some embarrassment. "I didn't mean him to show it to you."

"Oh, it didn't shock *me*. I've often seen—"

Oliver, who found her candor terrifying in public and sometimes even in private, fled to the men's room.

The bearded boy revolutionary hurriedly moved his chair to let Cassie pass. She patted him on the shoulder. "You'll outgrow it. We went through that Che Guevara bit with Davy last year. I could have killed him. Now he's a Buddhist."

As she reached the table, Lo said in his highest-pitched tone, "I've just been telling Gail a divinely bummer bit about Alicia the Beautiful. Did you know she ran away with a married man?"

"Good for her," Cassie said. "If she loved him, I'm all on her side."

"But she—" Lo began, even more shrilly.

94

"Shush, everybody can hear you."

"They're too busy plotting a revolution. And all I'm doing is repeating a simple bit of dirt Wood told me."

"I know how you repeat things, Louis. You're an artist. Have a cracker." She grabbed a cracker from a wicker basket on the table and rammed it into his mouth. "Gail, I'd much rather hear about the painting you sold."

Gail Scott was a sinewy girl with chopped-off black hair and a nervous way of ducking her head when somebody spoke right at her. "Did an optic-reality job," she muttered. She was a strange combination of diffidence and truculence; Oliver once said her earlier paintings looked as if they were done with clenched fists. Gail herself often had the clenched look of somebody braced for unfriendliness. Tonight, instead of her usual costume of stained blue jeans and shirt hanging out, she wore quite a handsome tie-silk dress. But when she got up to find another ash tray, she moved in a cautious, stiff-legged way as if the looseness of skirts might cause her to skid.

Lo, recovering lubrication of speech, took over telling Cassie about the painting: "She attached one of those toy adding machines to a canvas—"

"Recessed," Gail explained. "For optic withdrawal. It's a new way of fighting dimension."

Oliver came back in time to hear: ". . . and around the adding machine she pasted clippings from the *Times* stock-market page, and a cow with horns made out of ivory toothpicks. She got twenty-five hundred bucks."

"Fifteen hundred," Gail said.

Cassie said she thought it was wonderful. Oliver, who knew her taste in painting was of the nice, no-nonsense school, the "I know what I don't like so don't even show me" sort, listened half amused, half annoyed, as she rejoiced for Gail. He thought, I never got fifteen hundred for anything in my life. And I'm at least four years older than Gail. At twenty-nine, he had begun to feel the bitterness of seeing the young ones rush past him. Several of the younger ex-students at the Eastman

School of Music had already copped fat commissions for electronic works. And at times he felt as if he were racing down the runway after a plane that had already taken off. The lucky ones were settled on board, peering down, waving, and he had to wave back, smiling. "Have a good trip—just came to see you off. . . ." Only last month one of the fledglings had had an electronic symphony, *Pneumatic Drill Protest*, done at Lincoln Center. Oliver had tried some of the total-dissonance stuff, but it made him feel tentative, foundering, as if he'd lost his interior compass. He had tried head music too—the rambling-with-a-message stuff that was selling by the millions on records. But he didn't have any message to communicate. All he wanted to do was write music that was so much a part of him it was like a sixth sense. Cassie had encouraged him to stick to this. "Good music always gets heard, eventually." But who could afford to wait for eventually? He felt, meanly, that it was somehow Cassie's fault he hadn't crashed through to success on the dodecaphony of dissonance, of electric machines. *Pneumatic Drill Protest*—for Christ's sake! At Lincoln Center! Damn William Latham. He remembered suddenly that Alicia wanted him to meet her dear friend Willy, and he un-damned the man, began even to like him. Alicia might get their Festival songs done at the Center. They might be commissioned to do an opera together. But how could they even talk about anything, at the Murdochs', with Cassie breathing down their necks? Part of him knew this was unfair—Cassie wasn't a neck-breather-downer—but the other part went right on thinking it anyway.

"Hey, are you having onions on your hamburger?" Cassie said. "I won't if you aren't."

He said coolly he wasn't having onions but he didn't care what she did.

"Oh, if you're going to go right back to work. Onions on mine, Jilly. How's your baby?"

The waitress, a hulking, hairy maiden, said, "Doin' fine now, Cassie. He's kicked the penicillin drag. That stuff costs more a shot than a trip on acid."

When she brought their orders, Cassie decided she wanted a chocolate float too. "I'll have to work up a sweat and take off pounds tomorrow. We're playing on Mr. Humboldt's court."

"You may call him Chester," Lo said. "Or Angel Sucker."

"He's not a sucker. He simply wants to do some good."

"If he wanted to do me some good," Gail said, "he could loan me that other house of his behind the tennis court. I was taking a walk on the old Mortly place and I peeked in the window."

"Oh, you mean the guest house," Cassie said.

Oliver stopped fingering the catsup bottle.

"A living room two stories high, and north light—all one wall glass. What a studio! All he has to say is, 'Be my guest,' and I'll pack my gear and come running."

"Why don't I ask him tomorrow?" Cassie said.

Oliver waggled signals with his eyebrows. "I thought you'd promised Prudence Washburn to find a place for Miss Thorne."

"But I already—" She caught a stronger waggle. "Oh!"

"Property is theft," one of the hairy boys roared. "Proudhon is right."

"So just break a window and move in," Lo said to Gail. "It's simple anarchist logic. Humboldt trampled the poor to make millions." He looked wistful. "I wish I could trample the poor. But they never lie still long enough. And the stench would offend me. Anyway, it's more amusing to trample the rich. I trample them on tippety-toe."

Cassie said, "Chester Humboldt would never trample on anybody. He was poor himself. He had to work day and night and he lost his wife in the process."

"Let him buy another," Lo said. "Let him eat concubines."

Cassie was looking tenderly at Oliver. "No matter how hard you worked or how much money you made, I'd never leave you."

Oliver chewed uncomfortably. He found it difficult to swallow.

"Gail, I'm terribly sorry. I forgot Miss Thorne will have to stay in the guest house till after the Fourth. She and Oliver have so much work to do. But as soon as she leaves. . . ."

As Cassie was driving Oliver home, she said, "That was an absolute brainstorm. It wouldn't have occurred to me in a million years, putting her in his guest house."

Oliver said modestly it had seemed like a sensible solution.

"Better than that—it will throw them together. Of course he's younger than she is, but a few years wouldn't matter. At least they could have an affair."

"Do you ever think of anything besides mating?"

"It was your idea."

"Until you twisted it around. I simply wanted a place for us to work without Davy and his crazy friends racing in and out."

"But what's so twisted about wanting people to sleep together and be happy?"

There was really no answer to this. Or at least, no safe answer.

Chapter
Eight

Chester Humboldt paced to the window and stood there looking straight ahead, being careful not to look down.

Pilgrim Mills' main office and display rooms spread expansively over the thirty-seventh floor of one of the newer glass slabs on Madison Avenue. An even higher glass slab was going up across the street, with workmen crawling, z-z-z-z-z-z-ing their feelers like crazy bugs. The noise didn't bother Chester, or the threat of being overshadowed. His office was soundproof, temperature-controlled, lit by push-button sunlight. What bothered him was the height; he was one of those people who can't look down without feeling dizzy, scared silly of toppling. His ex-wife had joked about it one night at a party on a penthouse terrace: "Look at Chet back away from the edge. He has hydrophobia—fear of high places." The silly remark had upset him out of all proportion, as if she'd disclosed some shameful disease. He had never once mentioned his phobia to associates since they'd moved up two years before. And he had trained himself not to look down.

But as he stared across at the coming glass slab, one of the workmen knelt on the rim of a girder and leaned way over, no hands. Chester's insides lurched in violent, vicarious reaction. He was so dizzy he had to back off and sit down.

On the pickled oak desk in front of him was a list—a précis —of nine possible businesses Pilgrim Mills might acquire, including a paper towel plant, a Swedish textile firm, a television station and a peanut factory. (This was known as diversification, an increasingly popular way of not putting all your eggs in one balance sheet). He read it over a second time and got up to walk around again and make decisions. He preferred to think standing up; it seemed to make his blood rush uphill to his brain in a clear stream that swept away minor obstructions. Besides, he didn't smoke so much standing up. This time, he stayed away from the window.

The inner walls were covered in a warm beige piña cloth that made an attractive background for the prints and paintings. Some of the prints were a holdover from earlier days when "synthetic" was an unpleasant word. They were quite charming botany drawings with the legend of each fabric inscribed below in quaint lettering: "COTTON (from Arabic *qutn*)—Seed Hair of the Shrub Gossypium"; "LINEN (*Linum usitatissimum*)—After Dewretting."

"HIGH-WET MODULUS RAYON WITH HOMOGENOUS FIBRILLAR STRUCTURE" marked a newer phase. The most interesting of all, from Chester's standpoint, was a meticulous line drawing of a synthetic process he himself had helped develop and patent, one that accounted for a good part of Pilgrim's—and his—prosperity: "CONVERSION OF SODIUM CELLUWORT TO XANTHANE." The spattered dark objects which from a distance resembled miniature dumbbells were actually, close to, identified as filaments on their way to an acid coagulate bath.

He walked past this four or five times without a glance. His mind couldn't even focus on whether he wanted a peanut factory. This wasn't due to Monday-morning muzziness, because today was Tuesday. He had taken Monday off to go over Festival details, the actual physical layout for music tent, exhibit stalls, illumination control board, parking areas. He had summoned, by helicopter, his best engineers and maintenance men. Trumbine had sent up three experts on open-air theater. All that was well in hand; the tangibles were being fitted into place. A rented Baldwin upright and a Wallenstein tape recorder had been installed in the guest house. Alicia Thorne too. But unlike the piano and tape recorder, her performance wasn't guaranteed for a year. And already he was tugged by occasional doubts.

His well-planed, medium-high forehead, under the wheaty blond hair, had a deep groove of worry line. Then the line eased and he grinned, remembering how Cassie Murdoch went about asking a favor. First she'd beat him two sets out of three on his tennis court, then flopped on the grass and borrowed his handkerchief. "When the sweat runs down into your eyes, doesn't it *sting?*" Then she'd asked about the guest house. He had made excuses, thinking if he kept the door shut, Alicia Thorne might still go away. He said, untruthfully, that Ross Trumbine (he started to add "My publicity man" but changed it to "My assistant") might have to stay there. Having to lie in a good cause made him sound very sincere and sorry.

Cassie's lovely blue eyes had looked even more darkly blue with concern. "Don't worry about it for a second. I'll ask her to stay with me."

He had felt a damp chill pervade his entrails. And it wasn't just from sitting on the early-morning grass.

"Oliver thinks it would be too hectic."

Chester did too, for different reasons. He was trying to think how to word his warning when Cassie went on, "Miss Thorne admires you so much. She told Prue you look well in armor. What do you suppose she meant?"

Chester shrugged and said he had no notion. But the phrase had a pleasing clang—of knights and jousting—that made him sit up straighter. He had won the first round with Alicia right after he met her. Jousting again, maybe every day till the Festival, would be quite a challenge.

"I'd thought she might be company for you," Cassie said.

Oddly enough, it had worked out that way the night before, not a joust, but companionship. Yates had been shut up in the guest house taping the opening number so that the choreographer in New York could get started on it. Alicia had strolled up to join Chester on his terrace, where he was smoking an after-dinner cigarette. Smoking outdoors seemed healthier somehow; and seeing the tip glow in the dark intensified the still-guilty pleasure. He was so preoccupied with this that he didn't even see his caller until she appeared right in front of him. She was wearing something long and palely wraithy, but there was nothing wraithy about her voice: "If I hear that beautiful damn song one more time, I'll scream. Like this." And she had let loose with a scream as forthright as Medea's when jilted. Chester was so startled he'd jumped a foot sitting down. Alicia giggled. "Could we go inside and shut all the doors to drown out that noise and have a brandy?"

When Chester poured Rémy Martin into small glasses, she said, "Thank God you don't go in for that ritual sniffing. Last night Pickett was clasping a brandy inhaler as if it were a globe of the world and he could mutter incantations and make it shrink."

Chester's ex-wife had taken all their brandy inhalers and he'd never got around to telling his secretary to buy new ones. Now he was glad. Alicia didn't smoke, so from then on he smoked for two. His lungs felt strong and refreshed; he no longer felt guilty in the least.

"You said Saturday your grandfather was a scutcher. It's a fascinating word—what does it mean?"

He was astonished and flattered that she'd remembered. "They beat the woody pulp out of the plant fiber—scutching."

"So that's where it comes from—'beat the pulp out of him.' Tell me some more."

Chester told her, at first rather shyly, some of the trade phrases he liked. "Everything's 'gray goods' until it goes to be dyed and finished." He enjoyed watching her react to new words, so vividly she seemed to be tasting them.

"So many people are gray goods as long as they exist—without color or design. How I despise the gray-goods sort. If I ever fade into that—but I'd kill myself first."

She said it with such passion—her voice actually trembled —that he was somewhat alarmed, but moved too.

"Tell me I won't be gray goods."

"You couldn't," he said. "You're like wild silk."

This felicitous comparison made her sparkle. "Describe me—my fabric."

"You're a natural—done by wild silkworms instead of cultivated. Beautiful, unusual texture. It has what we call 'a rich hand.'"

"A rich hand—oh, lovely." When he gave her more, she repeated in a kind of chant: "Linen has a cool hand—Dacron has a crisp hand—chiffon has a soft hand." She used her slender white hands charmingly, ticking off each fabric.

Over a second brandy, Chester warmed even more to his role as teacher of an obviously fascinating subject: "A polymer is a natural fiber. But nylon, for example, is the molecules of two substances that hook together alternately—that's called copolymerization."

"Molecules copulating alternately." She wrinkled her perfect nose at him mischievously: "But how do they know when it's whose turn?"

"A machine tells them." He lit a cigarette, then discovered he already had a lighted one in the ash tray.

"Imagine having a machine program your sex life. Thank God I'm wild silk. That's the prettiest compliment anyone ever gave me. No, not pretty—that's a flutter-butt word. Magnificent. Better than emeralds. I don't like jewels anyway. I've never been bought with anything but words and—" She broke off to listen; the music in the distance had stopped. "I really must go." She put down her brandy half finished.

It was so abrupt Chester was hurt and angry. He felt as if he'd been used to fill in time. He was polite, but cool, at the door.

When he switched on the overhead porch light, she moved, instinctively, out of the glare before she lifted her face. "You know, don't you, that your Festival is having an extraordinary effect on all of us? I haven't been so excited about anything in years."

He said, "I'm glad," in a courteous, unglad tone.

"I'd so much rather stay here with you. It's been the most

marvelous hour—I feel all recharged and wild-silken. But I have to go back to check the lyrics on the tape. Oliver's a talented boy, but he shouldn't fancy himself a writer. He tries to simplify words till they're simple-minded. And the way he bellows when he sings—he carries a tune like a football."

There is nothing pleasanter than having another, younger man run down by a beautiful woman. When she asked Chester to walk her back—"It's so black now I imagine wild beasts glaring"—he didn't point out that the path to the guest house was perfectly well lit. Or that the wildest beast around was a woodchuck.

Alicia took his arm as they started off; she didn't cling, she just curved close in a way he found very stimulating. And she was the only woman he could remember walking with who took long steps, not striding but flowing easily with his own. On the little patio in front of the guest house, she kissed him very swiftly, lightly, on the cheek. "Bless you for everything —good night."

She had said she was coming into town around noon the next day; she wanted to collect more books on early New England. He had offered to bring up a batch to Bevington: "I already have my staff working on Festival background stuff." But then it had occurred to him how much pleasanter to have her stop by his office, and he'd take her to lunch. It wasn't just that he wanted her to see him in his natural habitat; he wanted to show her off. He hadn't had a woman call on him in his office since his wife left. At least, no nonofficial women. Plenty of the home-furnishings sort. But nobody like Alicia Thorne.

Standing now before "Conversion of Sodium Celluwort to Xanthane," Chester looked at his watch, went back to his desk and buzzed for his secretary, who arrived in an unhurried way. Miss Barsted was a strongly boned woman of around thirty-five, probably five years younger than her employer. He knew she was married, but it was part of her efficiency image to go on being Miss Barsted. She was extremely capable and all-knowing. He so seldom caught her out that when he said, "Call the Bevington *Bugle* and have my subscription started at once," he couldn't resist adding, "Too bad you didn't attend to that sooner."

Miss Barsted's strong bones stiffened slightly, but she made no other acknowledgment of "*Touchée.*" Having scored his tiny jab, Chester said, "Matter of fact, I should have thought of it sooner myself."

Miss Barsted nodded, meaning, That's more like it. "I'd better get three subscriptions—one for Mr. Trumbine, one for the file here, and one delivered to you in the country."

He said "Right" as if that was what he'd meant all along. "Then switch the call to Miss Murdoch—she's the publisher's daughter. And tell her the choreographer already has the tapes."

"Oh, the choreographer asked to see you as soon as possible. I told him you had a very full morning. I knew you wanted to go over that précis and have the meeting on it. But he can't seem to understand. He's out in the reception room now. The switchboard girl says he gets up and twirls around on one foot." Her voice expressed what she thought of such goings on.

"I'll talk to him after the meeting."

"By then, he'll probably be taking his clothes off. I'll put him in a display room off to one side so people won't see him."

"Let them see him." He felt suddenly, jauntily lighthearted. "It's a teaser for the Festival."

Miss Barsted emanated disapproval of the Festival. She looked pointedly at the précis, recalling him to solider matters: "Do you want to dictate any additions to that list before the meeting?"

Chester said he didn't.

"About that paper towel plant, were you thinking of converting it to flowered paper sheets and pillow cases?"

Except for an involuntary grunt, Chester didn't betray surprise. "We're debating it." His interior debate had started that instant. Paper sheets had been tried in the past, and had never worked out. They'd looked like the paper towels in a men's room—muddy tan. But flowered! And with some of the newer processes . . . if they could get a smoother, firmer finish . . . but not too crisp or—

"If they were too crisp they'd crackle," Miss Barsted said. Mind-reading was one of her minor accomplishments. "I don't think people want to crackle in bed."

"That depends." His mind was already scouting the marketing possibilities: motels, hospitals, tired mothers, army, navy, moon settlers. . . . It could be bigger than paper napkins. "We'll discuss it at the meeting."

"Mr. Trumbine wants you to call him when you're finished. He said he's getting a good bag of politicians for an honorary committee."

Chester, thigh-deep in flowered paper sheets, extricated himself like a man caught in a bedroom farce. No point in sinking capital into experimenting with new products. The Festival was a big enough investment, more important to his future. He reminded himself again to tell Trumbine about Alicia working on the Festival. She'd be a good name for publicity.

"It's seven minutes of eleven," Miss Barsted said.

"If Miss Thorne comes, give me a buzz."

Miss Barsted disliked having a loose name floating around, unpigeonholed. "Is she a buyer from our mill?"

"From the mills of the gods." He was surprised but pleased to hear what he'd said. It had a literary flavor that was quite unlike his usual prose style.

"The Mills of the Gods?" Miss Barsted frowned and gnawed her upper lip, which was fringed with a light moustache. "Is that a new one?"

"Very old," Chester said solemnly. "Slow but dependable."

"If it's one of the companies you're taking over, I think you should change the name. It sounds too old-fashioned."

"So does Pilgrim. People want to get back to the simple virtues of the past." He gathered up some papers, whistling.

"If Miss Thorne comes while you're still in the meeting, shall I bring her in here to wait?"

"Bring her into the meeting."

"Into the *meeting?*"

"Just to say hello." Let the head of New Products Testing and the business manager and the Consultant on Subsidiary Acquisitions at Advantageous Tax Losses see the kind of women who called on him. "Then you can bring her in here afterward. And have the research girls line up some of those books for her."

On his way down the corridor, Chester passed a display room and stopped in mid-stride, mouth ajar. He had met the choreographer, Scollit, several times in the television studio, a man with springy calves who looked as if he could bend over backward and touch his head to the floor. Right now, Scollit was running amok in a draperies display that hung from ceiling to floor. As Chester watched, the choreographer wound one of the draperies around and around his torso, then unwound in a dizzying twirl and lunged out with a curtain rod. He was lunging at a mannequin posed by a bedspread who represented a contented housewife surveying her Pilgrim Mills matching décor. Using the rod, Scollit thrust, withdrew, and thrust again at the mannequin in what struck Chester as a rather peculiar spot.

"Oh, hi, Mr. Humboldt. I wanted to see you." Scollit talked like a flute with a lisp. He skipped across the room still brandishing the curtain rod. "I have most of the graphs worked out for the 'Grow a Liberty Pole' opening. I'm using the Laban system of notation—it's faster." He snatched a sheet of paper off the floor and waved it at his employer—some sort of diagram with tiny squares, little sticks and squiggles. To Chester, who had been in the Navy, it looked like a plan for battle stations. "We'll use the pole as a phallic symbol. The thrust—" He lunged again, demonstrating, but this time at Chester, who pulled back hurriedly to protect what his mother had called his private parts. "And we'll play up the phallic symbolism with strobe flashes and xenon—dark, light . . . in, out . . . down, up . . . But Clappworth said I should check with you first on the theme." (Clappworth was the program director, who would be in over-all charge of the Festival's songs and dances.) "He thought maybe you wanted more the old Plymouth Rock pageant stuff. But I'll tell you right now, Mr. Humboldt, it would lay the biggest turkey egg of the year."

Chester didn't want to lay a turkey egg, even a little one. On the other hand, he didn't want a show so phallic it would offend Bevington's old families. But what was offensive, these days? And if the show was a smash hit, wouldn't that win him enough kudos, even in Bevington, to offset the shaky old pillars like Miss Maulridge? Anyway, Miss Maulridge wouldn't know a phallic symbol from a hole in the ground. For that matter, some tombstones were sort of phallic. . . .

He told Scollit to go ahead. "But I'll rely on you and Clappworth to use your good taste. No burlesque striptease—nothing cheap."

The choreographer's mouth writhed with joy. "Believe me, it won't be cheap. We want to get Nikolais for lightning and Cassandra for costumes—she used to be with—"

Chester said he was due at a meeting.

Only Ross Trumbine was waiting in the office when Chester came back a half hour later.

"I played the tape for the Governor over our direct wire and he says it's the greatest affirmative tag since "America the Beautiful." Greater, because it has action, upbeat. . . ." Trumbine never let enthusiasm ruffle his hair or manner. In an underplayed, seemingly casual way, he was so well tailored and well ordered he might have been sprayed with a fixative. "I've already sent out the first releases: 'Bevington's Growing Liberty Pole Beats Jack's.'"

"Who's Jack?"

"Jack in the Beanstalk. We won't go into that much, but it makes a good hook for a headline. I have a lot more ideas we can noodle through if you're free for lunch."

Chester was about to say he had a date when Miss Barsted came in. "Miss Alicia Thorne called. She has to stay at Lincoln Center with Mr. Latham."

Trumbine made a small, choked sound. Chester was too busy digesting the disappointing news to notice.

"She said she wants to interest him in the Festival. And she'll report when she sees you at home."

As soon as Miss Barsted had gone, her backside as firm as her front, Chester said more casually than he felt, "We're O.K. for lunch, then. Good. Shall we go?"

But when he glanced at his public relations man, Trumbine didn't look in any condition to go any place: he was very pale, an almost greenish white; his eyes were sunken; even his hair gave off an aura of disarray.

"Alicia Thorne," Trumbine said in a mangled voice. "What has Alicia Thorne got to do with the Festival?"

"She's writing the lyrics with Yates."

"Oh, God," Trumbine said. A piteous sound. Not a curse, more a prayer. Perspiration stood out in droplets on his pale forehead.

"Are you sick?"

Trumbine shook his head. "Just mentally ill. We have to get rid of that dame."

"But you raved about her lyrics. And she's living in my guest house."

"Lady Macbeth," Trumbine muttered. "Queen Boadicea. She's a combination of Boadicea and that kid who opened the box—What's-her-name. . . ."

He wasn't making any sense whatsoever. Chester tried to calm him by asking simple, direct questions. "Where did you meet her?"

"I never met her," Trumbine said. "But she's my mother-in-law."

Chapter
Nine

"I ordered forty gross of the bosom bottles," Mrs. Tyndale said. "We worked out a shape in plastic—simulated bubble glass—it's so much lighter. They promised delivery the third week in June."

Mr. Loomite's eyes were so protruberant they too might have been simulated bubble glass. "But I particularly stressed authentic artifacts."

"Not for souvenir items, sweetie," Mrs. Tyndale said. "And I defy you to find an old bosom bottle. I phoned the New England Antique Dealers' Association—they don't have a single one listed. I suppose the original bosom bottles all got broken, one way or another. You can see how it would happen."

"But how will I ever face Alicia Thorne and tell her 'plastic'? She was so gracious about giving us permission to use her name."

"That was just party talk. Anyway, it's better advertising to call them the Bevington Bosom Bottle." In her own shop, Mrs. Tyndale had a considerably brisker twang. Tyndale Antique Bibelots and Unpainted Furniture was already the impromptu headquarters for volunteers mapping Arts, Crafts, Souvenirs, Baked Goods and Games for the Festival. The two ladies were sitting on a raw pine reproduction of a deacon's bench, with books, some molting, piled on a gate-legged table before them.

The store was in the middle of Bevington's main business block overlooking the leafy Village Green, which divided the main thoroughfare, Tranquillity Street, and served as a traffic island. Traffic, especially on weekends, had become so heavy that newcomers sometimes spent a half hour marooned on the island before they dared leap to make the crossing. On the other side of the Green, directly opposite, were Bilton's drug-store-newsstand, Farwell's Hardware and Garden Sundries, and the Bargain Boy chain grocery. All three had almost identical fronts: white-pillared, pseudo-Colonial doorway with an eagle squatting on top, head turned to give the somewhat coy effect of looking over its shoulder—*suivez moi*. The glass on both sides of each doorway was cut into leaded panes, but largish ones allowing a reasonably clear view of displays. Bargain Boy's was bannered: "SALE—Giant Family Size Frozen Spinach Soufflé, 2 for 69¢." Farwell's Hardware was featuring a bird repellent called Pigeon No Likee, four brands of insecticide sprays, and canvas deck chairs in a searing shade of orange.

Mrs. Tyndale's front was Colonial without the eagle, but to make up for this there were eagles all over the place, inside. On mirrors, as brass bookends nestled beside a wooden decoy duck, decorating tin trays, and even topping one lamp, gingerly, like a bird getting the hotfoot. Most of the other lamps were converted brass candlesticks.

An oval hooked rug covering half the back wall featured still another eagle, this one snuggled in flowers. Below this, leaning against the wall, was a bird's-eye cannonball four-poster bed, just the headboard and footboard. A beautiful, very old Lazy Susan dinner table sat in the center aisle. The raised section, almost five feet in diameter, held a display of salt-glaze mugs.

"This would be an amusing cross-stitch motto for our souvenir stall." Mrs. Tyndale read aloud from *History of Bevington*

County: " 'OBSERVING THE SABBATH—He killed his cat on Monday—For catching a mouse on Sunday.' "

Mrs. Loomite shuddered. She had a Siamese cat that slept with her, which was more than Bevington would say of her husband, or conjecture.

"There's Al now," Mrs. Tyndale said, "carrying a flagpole."

"We must learn to call them liberty poles. Did you know that one they raised near here before the Revolution was higher than a church steeple?"

"Don't tell Al that," Mrs. Tyndale said. "It would make him feel frustrated. He seems to be measuring it now against the front awning. I suppose they ought to reach about twenty feet up."

Mrs. Loomite glanced out the window, then leaned and craned to see farther down the street. "Oliver must be going in to pick up his tapes. He ordered more yesterday. Such a dear, talented boy."

"For some reason, he always makes me think of spaghetti without the sauce. So lank and white."

"I certainly prefer that to the red-faced supersalesman sort," Mrs. Loomite said, glancing meaningfully across the street at Al Farwell, who seemed to be trying to poke his pole up through the store awning.

"It takes all kinds," Mrs. Tyndale said. She had a shop-owner's supply of the small, pat phrases that forestall argument.

"There is such a searching for Truth and Beauty among some of the younger generation. Like Oliver. One can feel the dedication burning in him like a flame. That sensitive face. . . ."

"At least he doesn't wear whiskers."

Mrs. Hinck trotted in, sat down in an unpainted replica of a Brewster chair, put her feet together neatly on the floor, clicked open her purse, and pulled out the typed lists of a born organizer.

"Cassie Murdoch and I had an eight A.M. patrol together at the Hollow Bog bus stop and things were so quiet we made out a list of good cooks." Since neither Mrs. Loomite's or Mrs.

Tyndale's names appeared on the list, she added tactfully, "The ones who have time. I already phoned quite a few. Mrs. Mervin was at Dog Obedience class but I'm sure she'll say yes. She always does."

Mrs. Loomite said restively she didn't see why they bothered with baked goods. "That's so humdrum. We must get away from the stereotype image of county fairs and church bazaars."

"Homemade food always sells," Mrs. Hinck said. "It's such a treat. You can't even hire a cleaning woman around here—let alone a cook. Wait till you hear the dishes we're planning. Cassie found some of them when she and Oliver were rooting around at the County Historical Association."

Mrs. Loomite sniffed. "I really doubt if Oliver was looking for recipes."

"Cassie was. Among other things. Listen to this—'Spiced Punkin Bread.' You make it with mashed pumpkin. We'll have to use frozen now. But I'm going to try it again around Halloween. . . . 'Corn Ball Cakes'—they sound delicious—you drop the batter in bacon fat with. . ."

She went on with her list of eighteenth-century dishes. "'Fried White Man's Foot.'" Mrs. Loomite looked distressed. "It was an Indian dish—broad-leaved plantain. I think bananas would do just as well. With a good, rich sauce. And for another dessert—'Beggar's Pudding.'"

"What's in it?" Mrs. Tyndale asked, somewhat apprehensively.

"Mostly stale bread and chestnuts. The 'Currant Poundcake' will probably sell better. But you never can tell—'Beggar's Pudding' is a clever name. We could always use it for something else. Mrs. Mervin makes a lovely gingersnap pudding."

Mrs. Loomite held out for "the true, simple fare of our ancestors."

Miss Maulridge, who had dropped in on her way to the cemetery, said, "It's a pity we've given up the simple home remedies of our forefathers. My dear father knew quite a batch. I remember 'A leaf of fennel keeps you awake' was one.

He used to say the minister ought to pass out fennel before the sermon."

There was a decent titter of response.

Mrs. Tyndale waved to Charles Wood as he came out of the drugstore with a clutch of newspapers. He crossed against a red light by fast footwork, and came in to say a slightly alcoholic hello. Since his enforced retirement, he had tried to abide by the rule of "No drink till the sun is over the yard-arm." But there were days when the sun seemed to creep and he got tired of waiting.

Miss Maulridge was saying to Mrs. Hinck, "And the juice of the sassafras to cure toothache."

"That's fantastic," Wood said. "When I was in Taormina last winter I had a hell of an abcessed tooth, and all the dentist would tell me was 'Poultice with sassafras tea.' And it worked. Do you know any more?"

Miss Maulridge did, although on some she was rather muzzy. "Juice of an ash to cure earache. Or was it the juice of an oak?"

"Ash, probably," Wood said, quite seriously. "We can check it. Let's get up a pamphlet of those remedies, with old wood-cuts. I know a printer who'll do a fast job for us. And it will fit right in with the Festival."

Mrs. Loomite approved the idea, and expounded on what had become one of her favorite themes: "The life of the early settlers was so like the Buddhist concept. The same rapport with Nature . . . the rustic simplicity . . . the purifying of soul and body."

Wood said, "I'd say the settlers were a damn sight more like the early Romans. Rough and tough. And you know what happened to the Romans after they softened up on high living. Do as the Romans did—and brother, we've had it."

Mrs. Loomite didn't regard Wood as a true intellectual, because he had edited a mass-circulation magazine that made money. Resentment clotted her genteel voice as she began to take exception. Mrs. Tyndale pulled out another pacifier: "There's something to be said for both sides."

"Especially if you're a two-headed calf," Wood remarked.
"Hello, Gail, come on in."

Lo had told Gail to ride herd on La Loomite and the art
thing, but she didn't know how to begin. She had been
hesitating outside Tyndale Antiques until Wood, a kindly man
drunk or sober, took her by the arm and brought her in. "We
need your help."

Gail ducked her head and shifted from one foot to the
other, in a motion reminiscent of a bull pawing the floor in a
china shop. Mrs. Loomite explained the principle of home-
squeezed art: "They boiled their own berries and tree bark for
dyes. And I hope our local artists will follow the quaint old
ways for our show."

"Sounds like a crazy lot of trouble for nothing," Gail mumbled.

Mrs. Loomite had her finger in Edwin Tunis: *Colonial
Living*, which she'd marked with a slip. "Here it is. They
boiled the bark of hickory, walnut, sassafras—"

"Sassafras, again," Wood said. "Amazing. I wonder if it's
good fermented."

"And pokeberries," Mrs. Loomite went on.

"Pokeberries! They're poisonous!" Mrs. Hinck dropped the
typed list she was checking. "I always warn the children
against them."

"But this is not an exhibit of children's art. And people will
hardly lick the dyes off the paintings."

"But artists might lick their fingers."

"I'll do one with pokeberries." Gail sounded almost girlishly
eager. "Put a skull and crossbones on it—and print the antidote on the bottom. Use a purplish lighting in Plexiglass—or
maybe black glass pillars."

"It could be hung with widow's crepe," Wood suggested.
"Before the unveiling."

Gail, in the creative throes, didn't hear him. "Press a button
and moans come out, or maybe a death rattle."

"It will be the talk of the art show," Wood said. "Mrs.
Loomite, you're a genius to have thought of this. But of course

you have that rare sense of embracing the *avant-garde* and rear guard."

Mrs. Loomite, who had thought more of primitive paintings of fat-cheeked, short-legged children, said gamely, "I do think that understanding the two gives one more inner balance."

Cassie Murdoch came out of Bilton's drugstore carrying a container of coffee and a waxed-paper packet. Mrs. Hinck went to the door to hail her as Al Farwell popped out of his store to say hello. Cassie was a favorite of his although he'd only tried to pinch her behind once. She had burst out laughing. "I'd better bring you some of Davy's pornographic pictures."

They had been amiable friends ever since. He reported to her now on the liberty pole situation: "Tom Devin's lined up seventy takers so far. And I talked the wholesaler into another five percent discount."

Across the street, Mrs. Hinck waved her lists vigorously in summons. "I'd better go over and see what she wants."

Al escorted Cassie across the street, holding her respectfully by one elbow. They paused on the Village Green, that divided Tranquillity Street, partly to keep from being run down by a station wagon that appeared to be driven by a large dog. "It's Mrs. Mervin's golden retriever," Cassie said, waving. "He insists on sitting in her lap. I heard he broke up the Dog Obedience class this morning."

As they stepped off the curb, a Honda roared past, and they jumped back just in time. It was driven by a helmeted male or female; at any rate, something in pants, shaggy-haired, with a baby attached to the rear in a kind of strait jacket. "Crazy kid," Al muttered.

"Jilly's a *very* good mother. She works at the Stick Shift. Her husband went on acid or speed, so he's no use at all, and she brought the baby all the way home from San Francisco."

"On a motorcycle?"

"On a Greyhound. When it was teething."

Mrs. Hinck was waiting for them on the sidewalk. "We've been going over the Baked Goods. I tried to stop Mrs. Mervin when she drove past but she didn't see me. Mr. Wood was just telling us her Flopper broke up the Dog Obedience class this morning."

"I'll do a little story for the *Bugle*," Cassie said. "Has anybody seen Oliver? I promised him I'd run the tape recorder while he tapes the second number."

Mrs. Loomite gave the latest bulletin.

"Then I still have a few minutes. He has to collect his car at the garage." She settled on a high, three-legged stool, feet swinging, and took out a sandwich.

"I had another idea for Baked Goods," Mrs. Hinck said. "Cookies in the shape of a little red schoolhouse. Like the one on Downhill Lane that's been made into a Landmark. We could color the dough with old-fashioned vegetable and berry dyes."

"Not pokeberries," Gail said. "Unless you want to knock off enough kids to lower the school tax." As an exit line, it was thought-provoking.

"Bear grease," Miss Maulridge said suddenly. "It was supposed to be good for rheumatism."

Wood said bears were on the scarce side in Bevington County.

"And they used bear grease on their poles," Miss Maulridge went on. "For climbing. The contests at the old market fairs."

Cassie bolted a large bite. "Hey, let's have a greased liberty pole. And give a prize to the fastest climber."

Several of the ladies thought it sounded messy. But Al Farwell and Wood backed Cassie. "The kids would love it." Al said he'd get a half-dozen heavier poles for climbing.

Miss Maulridge had drifted into a kind of trance again, as if she were listening for messages from some forefather. She emerged with, "Pigeon hunts were very popular then too. The men went out with nets."

Al Farewell shouted, "They can hunt on my roof any time."

"Roast pigeon," Mrs. Hinck said tentatively. "For Baked Goods."

After spirited pros and cons it was agreed that pigeon hunts

117

—and therefore roast pigeon—were out. "They don't really fit."

Mrs. Loomite, still the main fount of printed lore, had her finger in *Colonial Living* again. "They always roasted half an ox, for fairs. Look at this charming drawing. See, a dog turning the spit." She read a caption. "They trained their dogs to wear a special harness and work a kind of crank that turned the spit."

Al Farwell said that was a new one on him. "We oughta get the Dog Obedience class onto that. It would make a great gimmick for cookouts. What time is it? I'd better get back so Sam can go to lunch."

As he crossed the street, the Honda roared past again.

"There goes that degenerate creature with her child," Miss Maulridge said. "The county should take the poor little thing away from her."

"Oh, no!" Cassie repeated her defense case for the mother. "Jilly would never give up that baby."

"Which is more than you can say for Alicia Thorne," Wood said idly. "She ran away with Harley Craig the day her baby was christened."

Cassie's foot stopped swinging.

"It made a dilly of a scandal. Alicia's family was so mortified Mrs. Thorne didn't use her box at Symphony Hall for a whole season. And Thorne left all his money to the grandchild. Funny thing—the kid's not a bad writer. We bought a little story of hers a couple years ago. I recognized the name because I knew Alicia's first husband. Knew Harley too, for that matter. He bit off more than he could swallow."

Cassie got down off the stool holding her half-eaten sandwich, wadding it absently in its paper wrapping. "I knew she'd eloped. But I didn't know she'd abandoned her baby."

"She didn't leave it on a doorstep," Wood said. "Both sets of grandparents were loaded."

"But to *leave* it."

"She couldn't very well elope with a diaper service."

"I don't see how Prue could have gone on being her friend.

118

She's always been wonderful with children. And Prue's so kind."

"What am I so kind about, darling?" Prue Washburn put down a bag of groceries to hug her godchild. "I had to park two blocks away and I saw you when I came out of Bargain Boy, so I just ran in to see how you're all making out."

"There's Oliver's car now," Mrs. Loomite said. "At the red light—Why don't you ask him to come in? We'd love to hear more about the music."

"He's picking me up at the *Bugle*." She put her arm through Prue's and edged her toward the door before she said softly, "We may get married even before the Festival, as soon as Mother and Daddy get back. I'm going to tell Oliver this noon." She turned to wave to the others. "Sorry we're in such a rush. I'll ask Oliver to stop in soon, Mrs. Loomite. Or even better, we'll play the tapes for you. 'Bye, everybody. I love what you're doing for the Festival."

Wood joined Prudence Washburn at the door, and they watched Cassie run to the corner. "Whenever I think there's no justice in the world," Wood said, "I remind myself Wes has that girl for a daughter."

As Prue turned, he was startled by the look on her face: yearningly tender, then fierce. "If anybody hurt that child, I'd kill them." She giggled. "Heavens, don't I sound bloodthirsty."

"I myself am just plain thirsty. Miss Maulridge, let's include a simple home remedy of the early settlers for hangover. After all, rum and hard cider for a steady diet—or unsteady diet. How did they get up at five A.M. to feed the pigs and yoke the oxen? They must have had something better than bromos."

Miss Maulridge said she'd look in her great-grandfather's diary. "If that's not too late a period, historically."

Wood said not at all. "Because these things are handed down in a family. Unfortunately, all I got from mine was 'a hair of the dog that bit you.'"

"Did you hear Mrs. Mervin's Flopper broke up the Dog Obedience class this morning?"

"Good," Prudence said. "Silly business. I hope when the

instructor said 'Heel," Flopper bit her in the heel like Achilles. That reminds me, during the Festival it might be nice to use the old names of things. The dogcatcher would be a hayward. I mean, a hayward collected stray animals like cows, so it's close enough. And for the house tour, use the old names on the programs—the keeping room, borning room and so on. And we might have men demonstrate some of the old ways of doing things. You know, when I was remodeling my house, we found so much hair mixed in the old plaster, to give it strength or something."

"Shades of Edgar Allan Poe," Wood said. "I hate to think who was walled up, or snatched bald. Ladies, I leave you to your ghoulish fancies. Miss Maulridge, may I call you this afternoon—say, around five?"

"That would be very nice." To have two men seeking her out, for her knowledge of the past's own treasures, brought out a long mislaid feminine graciousness. "I have to go to three cemeteries, but I'll be back before then."

"Three funerals in one day? Like a triple-header?"

"Just to read tombstones," Miss Maulridge said airily. "Mr. Bender and I have a thing going."

Lo came the long way around to the guest house, from the back road, so that he could see what the workmen were up to. It wasn't just his own bubbling curiosity that propelled him; he loved to collect news—any fresh developments, to pass on, generously stretched or even embroidered over in a whole, vivid new pattern. Toward the right, a few hundred yards away, he could see three tractors with sickle bars chuffing over what had once been the old Mortly pasture, clearing the space for the music tent.

He walked through a small woods carpeted in ground pine that bounced his footsteps along. A tiny garter snake, curled on a rock sunning, turned tail and wriggled under a fern. Lo picked up a stone to throw but was instantly deflected by the shape of this weapon, interestingly triangular. He examined this carefully, and put it in his jacket pocket.

Oliver and Cassie were having the kind of tight, controlled quarrel that's the worst kind for lovers. Things had gone wrong from the minute he parked in front of the *Bugle* to collect her. A toothy boy with a cracked voice had come out to say, "Cassie's stuck on the phone. She said to tell you to wait. She loaned her car to somebody, so she has to ride out with you."

Even under everyday circumstances, Oliver wasn't good at waiting. He was so congenitally, absent-mindedly tardy himself that he somehow took it for granted Cassie would be the one always there and joyously ready. She had called that morning and offered to come over during her lunch break. And he had said yes unenthusiastically. All his mind, his being, was geared to Alicia's return that evening. They had worked very late the night before; at least he thought virtuously of the hours they'd been together as a work session. Alicia had talked a good bit about herself too, and about him, but it all flowed together in his remembering. She affected him not so much physically as like a work of art, sweeping, exultant, tender, sorrowful, stormy. He wanted to set her to music. Her talk was already music—the words soared and sang in him. He had done parts of three more Festival songs after he left her. He was willing to have Cassie hear them, but already, getting Cassie's opinion seemed a minor wayside stop on the way to a special destination. And sitting in the car in front of the *Bugle*, with the late May sun stickily warm, he fumed. How dare she waste his time, when she was the one who had pushed him into the Festival in the first place?

It was six or seven minutes before she came out, on the run. "Sorry, old Mrs. Troxell called—she's at least eighty-seven. And when she found Daddy was away, she wouldn't talk to anybody but me. Some kids stole the fountain from her garden—I mean the statue of Eros or somebody. She and her husband bought it in Florence on their honeymoon sixty-six years ago, and she's all broken up. She said the police sound as if they don't care. So I promised her I'd do a story. I couldn't just brush her off."

"If you care more about the feelings of some senile old dame—"

"That's not fair. She's not senile. She's done a lot for this town. And it would have been cruel not to listen. She's so vulnerable now. Hey, I almost forgot. I heard something so awful about Alicia Thorne—*watch it!* You almost ran through that stop sign."

Cassie was a much better driver than Oliver, and this made him all the angrier. "If you'd shut up a minute, I might be able to see what I'm doing."

"O.K. But remind me to tell you later."

To forestall any such recital, in the guest house, he had gone right to the piano and put penciled fragments of scores on the rack, ready to play. Cassie, curled on a sofa, was craning her pretty neck to look around the room, which soared two stories high. "Wow, what a studio this would make. I remember now—it was a studio once. Old Mr. Mortly's grandson was a painter or he wanted to be, but he had to come home from Paris because they stopped his allowance. And then he just petered out and became a bond salesman or something. Wouldn't it make a wonderful studio for Gail? I wish—"

Oliver began playing loud and fast, to shut her up. "Start again," Cassie said gently. "You felt too rushed. That was my fault." She listened with the same pure attention as always.

She thought the weaving song, "Thump the Batten," was a good jazz number. "Wind the niddy-noddy—hackle the hetchel—it's fun. All the sounds beat together."

But "A Leathery Man" didn't charm her. It was a folk song about a young rustic who had lost his own true love and become a wanderer in tatters, patched together with bits of leather till he was all leather, even his heart.

"It's too wanh-wanh," Cassie said. "It's not the pioneer spirit."

"It happens to be based on an actual case," Oliver said.

"One freak. But think how many pioneers were different. No matter what hardships they had, or whatever hit them, they'd get right back up, as big as life, and keep going."

"I think Miss Thorne is really more of an authority on old New England than you are."

"She's certainly no authority on the simple virtues. She has none. I don't care if she is a great writer. She's certainly not a good person. Let me tell you what she did—she ran away and left her baby. . . ." When Cassie was aroused her body seemed to take on angles of refraction, throwing back what she couldn't approve of.

"The trouble with you is, you hold up a paper pattern to people and want them to fit it."

"I do not."

"You'd have called Dostoievski a dirty child-molester."

"Was he? Well, I'd have gotten him into a good mental hospital till he was cured."

"Cured of his genius?"

"I never knew any genuises."

This was a mistake. Oliver's eyebrows veered in toward his bony nose in instant, frowning reflex. "And if I ever did know any," Cassie went on, "I'd still say that being a genius doesn't excuse cruelty to a child."

"I suppose you'd rather Alicia had abandoned her writing to be a wet nurse."

"She could do both."

"You and your pat moral judgments."

"It's not a question of morals. It's a question of responsibility. People have to be responsible for other human beings."

"An artist is responsible to his work."

"That's not enough. Not any more. The way the world is now, if we don't feel concern for other people, we're finished."

"Let's skip it," Oliver said coldly. "Right now I'm concerned about the Festival. And if Alicia Thorne hadn't come along, we wouldn't stand a prayer."

"She's the one who needs prayers."

"Oh, for Christ's sakes, you sound like my grandmother."

Cassie, stung, waded in deeper. "You're always blaming your father for not giving you a better childhood, but he could have blamed his mother, and she could have blamed *her* mother—and I'll bet Alicia Thorne blames *her* mother."

There were times when Cassie's mindless clairvoyance made him speechless. It was all the more infuriating because Alicia had discussed her mother the night before. They had had a deeply satisfying exchange on parents' ambitious pressures and Philistine values. Alicia had said, "If mother hadn't pushed me, I would never have married Geoff."

At the time, he hadn't questioned the idea that anybody could push Alicia, and he didn't question it now. He was solidly aligned in his mind with her and her reaching for freedom: the two of them had their own liberty poles for an axis. . . .

"And I'm sorry I ever talked Chet Humboldt into letting her use this place. I'm going to tell him straight out she's not what I thought she was."

"See, the paper pattern again. If somebody doesn't fit your neat little do-gooder notions. . . ."

"I'm merely saying I don't want him to fall for her. He's too nice a man."

"Alicia wouldn't have him. She came back from there last night and imitated him yakking about polymers and copolymers. She said all he needed was a pointer and a chart to roll down when the polymers copol."

"If she accepts his hospitality, the least she can do is be loyal."

"Bull."

"And if she had a baby, the least she could do was to act like a mother."

He had never heard her so implacable before. Almost archaic. He crashed an atonal chord to express his irritation. "You don't even know the circumstances."

"I know she wasn't desperately poor or starving."

"There's more to it than that. She was in an atmosphere that made it impossible for her to write. She told me so. And I understand that, even if you don't. I have no intention of being surrounded with yammering brats."

"You picked a fine time to—"

The clanging on the door drowned her out. Lo burst in

while the knocker was still reverberating. "The workmen laying the cable have uncovered a nest of coral-colored snakes—a writhing mass, highly poisonous. And a cache of ancient Indian warheads. Look." He pulled the sample out of his pocket.

Even Cassie didn't bother humoring him. "It just looks like a stone to me."

Oliver wore his most sullen, put-upon look. "I'm trying to get a score done, if you don't mind."

"I didn't come to see you. Where's Alicia?"

"In purgatory. Or condemned to eternal hell-fire. Cassie decided just now, so of course that settles it."

Lo said, "But ducks, her kind doesn't have to be good. If Alicia were good, it would be simply too much. Was Cleopatra good?"

"That's different. Anyway, I've always sort of liked Cleopatra because she was short. She was at least two inches shorter than me."

Oliver's lips twitched in the beginning of a smile.

"And I wouldn't judge Cleopatra or anybody else on moral grounds. Any more than I'd want to be called immoral for sleeping with Oliver."

"If Cassie gets pregnant," Lo said, "I know where we can borrow a shotgun for the wedding—a musket in good working order."

Cassie said in an odd, small voice, "Drop it."

"I didn't bring up the subject. You got me off the track with your silly premarital squabbling. What I came to tell Alicia—I have the most fabulous costume worked out for one of the male lead singers—a jackanapes suit. Rhinegrave breeches looped all over with ribbons. It's the exact period. A British sea captain wore it in Boston."

"I hope they dumped him in the harbor," Oliver said. "Like a teabag."

"But the pioneers wouldn't wear things like that," Cassie said.

"You promised me some Tories. And for the settlers, I've

found something I'd even adore for myself—doublets fastened in front with tassels. And spatterdashes—you'll never guess what they are. Not spats."

"I needn't bother guessing," Oliver said. "Because you aren't doing the costumes for the show. They're all being designed in New York."

Lo's plump cheeks crumpled. "That's a lie."

"You're a great one to talk about liars. Ask Humboldt if you don't believe me."

"Cassie?" It was a half wail.

Cassie picked up the pieces rather tiredly. "Oliver had no right to say it that way."

"Why not?—since it happens to be true. I believe in putting things plainly. It's easier on everybody."

"I'll remember that," Cassie said. Oliver caught a note in her voice that made him look at her intently, for the first time that day. She avoided his glance. "Lo, Mr. Humboldt thought this would be easier because the singers will rehearse in New York, so they can be fitted there. But we're counting on you to do the other costumes. What the volunteers wear on the grounds will be much more noticed. Reporters won't describe what singers wore. Who cares?"

"I care," Lo said, with sorrow. "I've been up almost all night making notes."

"But you can use them where they'll be most effective. We're going to have men volunteers in charge of the games, and the tasseled doublets would be groovy for that. As soon as you finish one we'll dress up a model and take photographs ahead, and send them to AP and UP."

" 'Bender Puts Tassels on Men.' And spatterdashes." Lo's sun was emerging again. "They're leggings that come up to here." He slapped himself high on the thigh. "And I'll do face masks for the women. Ladies wore fancy masks outdoors to protect their complexions."

Oliver snorted. "They can wear these to hold up the Festival customers. I can see Mrs. Hinck in a mask, with her children carrying toy machine guns. As a matter of fact, it would make an amusing number. I'll tell Alicia. A founding fathers' and mothers' chorus—'It's always been American to give a child a gun.'"

"I will never allow a child of mine to have a gun," Cassie said.

"That's hardly relevant. Just because you have a mother fixation—"

"If you're starting on that again," Lo said, "I'm leaving. I've thought of a new twist for the women volunteers—we'll call the good-looking ones Liberty Maidens. And I'll give them wickedly low-cut bodices. Such a nice change from the apron and bonnet bit. Fiera Young would make a good Liberty Maiden. We could charge admission to her bosoms. And put a scarlet V in her cleavage. V for 'virgin.' She told me she would never 'surrender' her virginity before marriage. Cassie luv, I want you for head Liberty Maiden. Or Matron. Ta-ta, ducks."

As soon as the door slammed behind Lo, Oliver said, "I hope you're satisfied—we've wasted the whole hour. I can run the tape recorder myself. You'd better get back to the office."

Cassie stood up. For a small girl, she managed to look, if not tall, somehow in command of her space. "There's one thing I'd better say first. Since you believe in plain speaking. Something you won't want to hear."

Oliver said wearily, "Haven't we already had enough of that?"

"This isn't about Alicia Thorne. It's about me." She paused. "And you're concerned too."

Chapter
Ten

"I'm going to have another martini," Trumbine said. He had
slurped his first one like mother's milk. For a man who nor-
mally drank Scotch in reflective sips, this was an ominous
sign.

Chester signaled a waiter, and this too was out of keeping.
The three or four times they'd had lunch before, his public
relations man had always done the ordering. Not in any
aggressive way. Trumbine wasn't the sort to raise his voice or
snap fingers. And he wouldn't have chosen a restaurant where
that sort of thing was tolerated. The Gray Humor Pub on East
Forty-sixth Street wasn't a pub in any hearty, drop-in-for-a-
half-pint sense; it was more like a club with stiff dues. The bar
was crowded and all the tables were occupied, but the noise
was corked; only a steady hum, no more obtrusive than a
well-oiled motor.

Trumbine had his usual table, one of two red-leather-pad-
ded corner spots facing each other at the front end of the
long, narrow room. Not the most private, but the most
sought-after. Whenever a new restaurant was picked as It,
following that mysterious system which also sets the migration
of birds and gypsies, Trumbine always seemed to have known

the headwaiter from some earlier place, perhaps even from some previous reincarnation involving family retainers. They were friends; no tugging of forelock, no bribes. Rolfe, the headwaiter of the Gray Humor Pub, had taken their first drink order himself and had known instantly that something was wrong. When he came back to answer Chester's latest summons—"Another martini, nothing for me"—Rolfe had glanced at Trumbine, outwardly calm but somehow exuding anxiety neuroses, and had given Chester a conspiratorial flick of an eyelid. Chester felt quite set up; he had been accepted as a member of the inner, inner Ins. And to find that Trumbine was shakable, and a husband whose wife had left him, was gratifying to the son of a mill hand and a cuckolded ex-husband.

"We aren't doing anything about a divorce," Trumbine said. "She's gone to Mexico for a while—her current thing is primitive cultures. The poor kid wanted to be a writer, but she's not in a class with Mama. So now Allie's decided she'll be the greatest expert on pre-Hispanic civilization because that way she can outstrip Mama. It's the damnest love-hate syndrome."

Rolfe brought the second martini. Chester was hungry; his stomach rumbled a threat. Hot food or else. But it seemed crude to order lunch while Trumbine was suffering liquidly. He compromised by ordering a first course, the soup *du jour*, which turned out to be beef noodle, an awkward dish to eat in a listening attitude.

"Once Allie kept me awake till four A.M. telling me about the time her mother visited her at school. She told me, 'When Mother came in, she was so beautiful I could have just sat and looked at her forever. I know I shouldn't have tried to hug her —that was gauche.'" Trumbine fished the lemon peel out of his glass and wrung it fiercely, like a neck. "Mama really let her have it. 'Do you have to wear those hideous braces *all* the time—like a mouthful of Brancusi? Can't you *do* something about your skin?' The poor kid was already going to a dermatologist and not even eating desserts. Even now, if she gets upset, or eats the wrong things—Gods knows what that beans and chocolate molé bit is doing to her in Mexico. She wanted to write her mother when we were married, but she got so worked up over it I wouldn't let her."

"My wife hated flying because her mother hated flying," Chester said. "Whenever I had to fly to Europe on business, her mother would say, 'Why can't he go by ship and take you along?' "

Trumbine, usually so gifted a listener, simply seized on the words that fitted his single track. "Allie's crazy about flying. She soloed in a Cessna two-engine job, but I've made her promise not to take up a plane alone. Traffic's too heavy. Boats are bad enough. Her father used to take her sailing a lot before he married again, and she's a nut about that. Last summer in East Hampton, the small-craft warnings were up —big storm on the way—and Allie took the boat out and hit twenty-foot waves. The Coast Guard got her just in time. We had a helluva fight about it. . . ."

After several minutes more of this, a need to jar Trumbine into reciprocal listening made Chester say, "Mine had an affair with another man."

He might have dropped his little stick of dynamite into a bottomless pit. Trumbine said, "Allie doesn't play around. She has this fanatic thing about honesty—she says whatever she thinks is right. It was a bummer bit with my clients. She asked Senator Mallow one night straight out, 'When is the last time you confronted your conscience?' I'll say for Ed Mallow he didn't blow his hairpiece. He said, 'I have an annual confrontation with my conscience and my dentist.' Allie liked that. She can be pretty funny herself, when she's not on one of her crusades."

"She sounds like Cassie Murdoch," Chester said. "The little girl who dreamed up the Festival in the first place. She wants to take this country back to the simple virtues—honesty, hard work, love one another."

He had a sudden picture of Cassie on the tennis court, running toward him in sunlight; it was so bright, so charming he felt a warmth roll up his spine and down again. "When she gets a cause she wants to drive it over the net."

"I was going to tell Allie about the Festival the next time I wrote. I wanted her to come up for the opening—I thought it would be a good gimmick to get her back. But if she found out her mother's involved—I don't want to do anything to upset her—she's keyed up enough already. I'd better bow out —that's the safest."

They had been through this before; Chester said again he didn't want to do without Trumbine. It wasn't just the Festival, it was the undertones that would color his political future, the things only Trumbine could handle properly. "If it comes to a choice, I'd rather get rid of Alicia." He felt rather nervous at the notion, even a little regretful, but he had done other unpleasant things in his time to protect his career.

"We'd be cheating ourselves," Trumbine said. With the second martini, he had begun to sober and sound more like himself. "Thing is, literary types are big politically now. I can get across the idea you've got that charisma that draws Alicia Thorne, and we'll line up some more writers and actors. . . . Oh, another angle, I got the facts from Miss Barsted today about that integrated housing hassle in your Georgia plant. I'm sending out some stories that play up your championing the blacks—insisting they have equal housing and—"

"No," Chester said. "Lay off that. I'm damned if I want to be made out a bighearted benefactor for giving Negro workers what they always had a right to."

Trumbine looked shocked. "You've got a lot to learn, fella. If you're going to be in politics, you have to take credit for anything that sounds good. You have a solid reputation with the unions—"

"It's O.K. to say that," Chester said. "But don't single out anything I've done for Negroes. It sounds like the plantation owner treating his darkies mahty sweet."

"Allie would like that. She'd say you'll bring Honesty to government. But the point is, you can't get elected in the first place if you don't sail with the wind. That's what Allie could never get into her crazy red head. She thinks I'm too adjustable. Last fight we had, just before she left, she said, 'You take your principles out of the closet the way you choose what you'll wear—whatever is suitable for the occasion.' She's quite a girl. I wish you two could—" The sentence was snapped off as if he'd bitten it in two. He clutched his companion's arm. "I should never drink gin."

"You're doing fine," Chester said. "All you need is food. How about—" he consulted a menu—"scrambled eggs and sausage?"

"Sausage," Trumbine muttered vacantly. "Either I'm stoned or that woman coming in could be her sister. It's uncanny."

Chester's first thought, when he saw Alicia Thorne, was that she'd come to join him. He had left word with Miss Barsted, as always, where he'd be, and Alicia must have finished her business at Lincoln Center earlier and rushed to meet him. She was wearing a violet cape—the kind of cloak that in fairy tales may render its wearer invisible. In this case, it rendered Alicia distinctly more visible; her skin looked more translucent, her hair more burnished, her legs, under the swirling cape, were more enticing than ever.

As she approached the table, escorted by Rolfe, Chester leaped up, waving and grinning boyishly. "So you made it after all."

From her face, and the surprised jerking back, he knew instantly she hadn't expected to see him. And he felt like a fool. In the few seconds it took her to change her expression to How-lovely, he had switched to a prickling anger.

"Willy Latham insisted we'd talk better here. I was hideously disappointed." She was talking too fast. "Will you forgive me?" She glanced at Trumbine, who had risen automatically, and took him in: English hand-tailored, good bones, built-in breeding. She smiled even more enchantingly: "To think I might have had two such attractive men all to myself, for lunch. The sacrifices I make for your Festival!" She glowed at them, waiting to be introduced. Chester was stubbornly silent.

Trumbine said, "I went to school with Willy Latham's cousin." He seemed entirely at ease, as he and Alicia chatted about Lathams. Chester's anger sharpened. Their sort always recognized each other; no caste mark on the forehead, just

some casual, tossed-out phrase: "I knew". . . . "I went. . . ."
Without premeditation, he said bluntly, "This is Ross Trumbine. He's your son-in-law."

Just for a moment, Alicia looked almost ugly from shock; mouth pulled in, nostrils pinched, eye make-up suddenly garish. Chester was appalled at what he'd done, partly because of the Festival, but more because he wasn't used to stabbing women in the chest.

"We'd better all have a drink on that," Trumbine said. "We need it. Rolfe, will you tell Mr. Latham that Miss Thorne will be along in a minute?"

Alicia sat down slowly, shakily, but she rallied within seconds; it was as if she'd given herself a transfusion of pride and spirit. "Tell me, what did my ghost wear to the wedding? Beige lace over sackcloth?"

Trumbine laughed, genuinely, with admiration. "It was very Come-as-you-are. Allie wore a simple little suit—St. Laurent. I can see now where she got her clothes sense. She looks a lot like you."

Alicia frowned. Trumbine added quickly, "But she'll never be as beautiful."

Alicia looked ten years younger. She took a sip of her martini and held out her glass: "To the groom! I must say she picked well. I wouldn't have guessed, the last time I saw her. . . ."

"She's given up wearing braces. A great improvement. . . ."

Chester, listening to them chat and laugh, had a queasy feeling; they were too stinking civilized—all manners and brains and charm. . . .

But then Alicia said in a low voice, "I think of her in the night, even now. When I can't sleep, and I don't dare take any more Nembutal. She must hate me."

"Not altogether," Trumbine said. "Let's say, ambivalent feelings."

"And you—do you hate me?" She threw back her cloak; her golden eyes searched and yearned.

"I've been tapped by a wand," Trumbine said. "I grunt at your feet."

Chester thought that was laying it on with a trowel, but Alicia took it, with a half-sad smile, as her due. "Seriously," she said, "I've never cared a hoot what most people thought of me, but I feel that you and I are so—I'd like you to know my side. It was Geoff's parents—they wouldn't let me have custody. I spent every cent I earned, for years, fighting their lawyers."

Chester, watching her, was half convinced himself. So was Alicia. She was tearful, in a non-red-eye way, and her voice throbbed with emotion. "Maybe I deserved that. But I was so young—and Geoff was so wrong for me."

Trumbine said, with sympathy, "I can see now how he would have been. I find him a bit heavy going myself. So does Allie. The only thing they can talk about together now is sailing."

"Yar!" Alicia said. "Oh, the yars and yars I went through that. Hoist on the slice. . . . Do they still sail down at the Cape?"

Trumbine brought her up to date. "And now Allie's in Mexico, headed for the Aztec Fertility Rites Festival or some such." He and Alicia were amused and superior together.

They've forgotten I'm here, Chester thought. His beef noodle soup had gone cold; he was no longer hungry, just smarting and indigestive. He decided to leave—make some excuse —and had made the first wriggling motion of withdrawal when Alicia turned her gaze on him, full strength. "You'd have been bored to death by Geoff too. He'd tell you there are better ways to spend your money than putting on this magnificent Festival. And he'd quote *Barron's Weekly* on stocks— which one declared a double debenture. . . ."

"Pilgrim Mills stock tripled, so I can afford a small fling with a Festival or two." He knew it was childish, even low-class, bragging, but it made him feel much better. He even felt rather genial, softened up enough to enjoy Trumbine's describing him to Alicia: "Hum's the Don Quixote who'll lick the system."

"Hum, I forgot to tell you, I was talking to a man in the

State Department yesterday and they may be interested in sending the Festival singers abroad on tour."

Chester was tempted to say, "Do you still want to bow out because of your wife?" but he no longer felt like making mischief.

Trumbine told Alicia her lyrics were fabulous. "That opening number—as soon as you have more set. . . ."

"I can give you a few more right now. We worked out some ideas last night, and I worked on the train coming in." As she took a memo pad out of her black suede pouch, she was so businesslike she reminded Chester, ludicrously, of Miss Barsted about to brief him on messages.

"I finished 'Him's a Trimmer.'" When she explained to Trumbine about trimmers, Chester had the mildly catty notion Trumbine was avoiding his glance.

Alicia flicked through her pad. "'A Leathery Man'—oh, here's one you can do more with—'At the Tavern of the Headless Woman.'"

"We can sell an album on that title alone," Trumbine said. Now he was all business, like Alicia.

"It's going to be a narrative kind of thing."

"Head music," Trumbine muttered, "very hot now. Even on the jukes."

". . . when Sam Adams and John Hancock and some of the others are plotting the Revolution. Actually, they met at another tavern, but Oliver thought—er—I decided it would be more effective this way."

Chester noted with amusement that Oliver wasn't to get any credit. This was Alicia's show. As she mentioned more song titles, with concise summaries of what each was about, Chester had a new respect for her, perhaps the first real respect he'd felt yet. He was good enough at his own job to feel the flash of recognition.

Trumbine was so impressed he was, for him, almost humble. Once Alicia had their full appreciation, she was endearingly modest, anxious, even self-critical. She tossed out one song on the spot—"Come the Revolution"—with "How could

I have thought that was great? When I try to be cute, I'm terrible."

Rolfe came back to say tactfully Mr. Latham had a three-o'-clock rehearsal and was about to order.

"Poor Willy. I must go and coax him into a good humor so he'll help us."

She blew a kiss as she swirled off; and to Chester, for lagniappe, "See you at home tonight." He caught the two men at the next table staring enviously; under the circumstances, it was impossible to feel ill-used. He was, in fact, so cheerful he forgot to tell Rolfe to omit the sausage from his order; sausage was a goad to what the doctor called his incipient ulcers.

Trumbine ate scrambled eggs absently, and ate part of Chester's sausage too. "I was going to avoid her like the plague, but now I can see that would be ridiculous. Allie never told me her mother tried to get custody of her. I think she must have exaggerated that scene at the school. She was only fifteen and she probably got it all distorted in her mind. I can't imagine Alicia being so crude, can you?"

"She's not crude," Chester said cautiously. Things were going along too well to upset the cart again.

"And less than two hours ago I was telling you to throw her out. Incredible. It would have been the worst possible thing to do. Allie needn't know a thing about this till later."

He chewed and swallowed reflectively. "You know, Alicia's really unbelievable. I had to keep telling myself, 'Remember, she's your mother-in-law.' "

Chapter
Eleven

"Then the only thing left is for us to get married." Oliver had intended it as a somber statement, to fall like a stone, but somehow it came out at the end on a rising note, more a question.

Ever since he'd known Cassie she had always had the right answers, the answers that comforted and buoyed him. And he still couldn't quite believe she would let him down now. He hadn't formulated the exact words she would say, but something along the line of, I want to do whatever's best for your work. Instead, she said, "We were going to get married anyway. It's just a matter of doing it sooner."

If she'd sounded humble, apologetic, he wouldn't have resented it as much. But she sounded so calm, so taking-for-granted that it struck his quivering nerves like, You'd already stepped into the trap, so I can spring it sooner.

"Why the hell couldn't you have been more careful?"

Cassie went to the door without another word. He ran after her and grabbed her arm. "Wait, I'm sorry. I didn't mean that. It isn't your fault."

Cassie looked at him steadily. "I'd never thought of having a child as a fault."

"I know you didn't do it on purpose—not consciously. But you were hipped on having a child."

"With you as the father—yes. It's your child too."

Something stirred in him then—tenderness, pride, some feeling as old as caves and "begat." He was leaning down to kiss her gently on the forehead—little mother-to-be—when she said, "And you always knew how I felt—that people like us are responsible for their actions."

The flat-footed phrase "responsible for their actions," reviving the argument over Alicia, made him furious. "And you knew how I felt—I'm responsible to my work." It seemed to him that Alicia had opened the door—to fame, fulfillment as a composer, and Cassie had waylaid him on the threshold of greatness acknowledged. A phrase he'd read somewhere about a frustrated life came into his head: "He died with all his music locked in him." He had thought when he read it that it was poignantly sad. Now it fitted like a shroud, and he could have wept for his early demise. "You're sure you can't get something done?" "Abortion" was too harsh, too abrasive for his tongue; Cassie should have spared him this blunt-axe discussion.

"I'm sure I won't." Her chin was so firmly set it reminded him of a bulldog. And her neck's too short, he thought meanly.

It was a pretty, rounded neck that sat well on her shoulders, but right then everything about Cassie seemed implacably thick. Even her high young breasts. He had often laid his head there; the idea of a shiny-bald, congested-red baby sucking there, dribbling rancid milk, was offensive.

"You told me your roommate's sister and another girl had it done in Sweden."

"That was different. They were just practicing sleeping around. Why did you ask me to marry you if you didn't want—?" Her voice broke. She rubbed her hands across her eyes like a child.

This was so unusual, for her, Oliver felt rather ashamed. He wanted to say something loving, but the sense of being victimized was still too strong. He muttered, "I didn't think it was any immediate problem." I thought the Pill was safe. And if you'd taken it regularly the way you were supposed to. . . .

"I have to get back to the office. Why don't I take your car so you won't have to drive me? Then you can get on with your work."

Again he felt ashamed, because she wasn't being sarcastic, just thoughtful. She said she'd send the office boy back with the car. "He can bring his scooter so he'll have a ride home." This was so like her, to have practical solutions for everything, Oliver was vaguely reassured. "I have to write a half stick on Mrs. Troxell's lost statue of Eros." She said it matter-of-factly, but Oliver thought he heard a tinge of irony beneath. It may just have been the mention of Eros.

He had parked his car behind the guest house instead of on the driveway because he was ashamed of its shabbiness. When he and Cassie went out he looked at the rust holes in the hood, the cracked back window, and his resentment swelled and burst: "For one thing, I need a new car. I thought as soon as I got some money ahead. . . ."

"Give me the key," Cassie said.

"I'd take you in if I weren't so swamped with all this Festival stuff." Even to his own ears, his voice sounded tinny, whiny. He said quickly, "I took your suggestion about the lyrics of 'Him's a Trimmer.' I pared them down. Alicia's going to be sore. But I thought you were right."

"I often am. This windshield is filthy."

Oliver took out his handkerchief in a burst of atonement.

"Don't use that—you'll ruin it. I have a Kleenex."

Again this was so soothingly like the old Cassie he watched her quite fondly as she rubbed the glass above the driver's seat, and he offered to do the outside himself.

He was proceeding with ostentatious efficiency when a scream rang from the wooded area behind them. Lo came running toward them, not jogging, but bouncing along like an unleashed yo-yo. He was waving something that looked like a stick. "Arrow!" he panted. "Nearly pierced me through the heart. I pulled it out of the tree and brought it to show you as proof. You wouldn't believe that stone was an Indian warlock. Look at this—steel-tipped."

Oliver took the arrow and examined it. "Made in Japan. Probably some kids playing in the woods."

Cassie leaned out. "Lo, how awful for you. And it's not even hunting season."

"Yoo-hoo, Mr. Bender, did you take my arrow?" Humboldt's housekeeper, Mrs. Gifford, came bounding out of a thicket carrying a large bow and a quiver of arrows slung over her shoulder like a golf bag. She was wearing leather-thronged sandals and what appeared to be a sawed-off toga.

"I take your arrow!" Lo's round face bulged with fury. "You aimed it right at me."

"But I wasn't aiming at anything. That's the whole theory of Herrigel's Zen Buddhist archery—the only target is yourself —the freeing of buried hostility. You just let fly without looking and—" She raised her bow to demonstrate.

"Don't do it again," Lo shrieked. "I'll have you arrested."

Mrs. Gifford's buried hostility surfaced and hissed. "This property happens to be posted. No trespassers allowed. If you'd had legitimate business here—I was very careful to stay away from the area the workmen are clearing."

"Because workmen belong to a union," Lo howled. "And no union would let you get away with this. They'd put an apple on your head and fire back."

"They'd put an apple in your mouth, you—you pig."

Cassie had got out of the car; she and Oliver exchanged amused glances, and suddenly he felt a peaceful, even happy sense of closeness. "Let's bust this up," he murmured. "Before they take aim at twenty paces. Ask Lo if you can give him a lift to wherever he left his car."

Lo accepted, pettishly. "Although an armored truck would be safer, with this crazy Zen Cupid on the rampage."

"You have no right to say that. You have no right on this property."

"He's working on costumes for the Festival, Mrs. Gifford. And I do want to tell my brother Davy about the Herrigel theory. He's just taken up Zen Buddhism and he'd be so interested."

"If you know what's good for you," Lo said, "you'll tell Davy to stick to something harmless, like overthrowing the government."

Cassie managed to coax him into the car. Oliver, in a rush of affection, called to her, "See you tonight, dear," and formed his lips in a kiss. Cassie's tactful expression of mediator changed to a radiant smile. "Fine. I'll pick up a steak."

Mrs. Gifford said, "Oh, Mr. Yates, I nearly forgot to give you the message. From Miss Thorne. We had such a delightful little chat when I saw her this morning—on Kuan Yin— the Goddess of Mercy, you know."

It sounded to Oliver like a code of some sort. "Did Miss Thorne want me to do something about the Goddess of Mercy?"

"We must all hold her in our hearts," Mrs. Gifford said. "And think ill of no one."

"You make it damn hard," Lo said.

"The message," Oliver reminded her.

"Oh, yes, the message. About tonight. Miss Thorne is expecting you for dinner at seven. In the guest house. She arranged with me before she left."

"Miss Thorne should have arranged with Oliver," Cassie said. "She's taking a lot for granted. I'm expecting him for dinner too."

"It's a work session," Oliver said hastily. "Have to put the Festival first. We'll work right through dinner. You know how it is."

"*I* know," Cassie said. "But does Miss Thorne? Maybe she's just hard up for dinner dates. She's getting on—her daughter must be as old as I am. Maybe that's one reason Miss Thorne never wanted a child around." She started the car so abruptly Oliver had to jump back.

As they went down the driveway, Lo said, "Are you still on that moral kick, luv? Because I'll give you a teensy hint—it's getting boring. And it makes Oliver seethe."

"Let him seethe. Do him good to hear a few things about that woman."

"Not from you, ducks. He wouldn't believe a word of it. But he didn't even want to meet her, at Humboldt's party. I had to drag him over. Honestly. All he wanted to do was go look for you. He was clawing at my arm yelling, 'Where's Cassie? Was she shot? Are you sure she's all right?' I had to calm him down."

"Oh." She drove on, silently. "This car still hiccups," she said finally. "They didn't fix the choke right."

"Do you think we could have horse-drawn buggies at the Festival? It would be amusing to crack a whip. You know, I've never cracked a whip."

"I cracked one today," Cassie said, more to herself. "And the animal bolted." She reached over and patted Lo's hand. "You've said what I needed to hear. You're really a very perceptive man."

"Yes, I am," Lo said, complacently. "I'm an eighteenth-century product in the age of the giant computer. Ducks, I found the most fabulous drawings of gentlemen's wigs in seventeen fifty." He gestured with both hands: "Shoulder-length on one side, and on the other, halfway down the chest."

"Sounds like the kids' hair now. You ought to put on a teen-agers' fashion show at the Festival."

Lo thought the idea utterly divine. "The hair *and* the clothes." He chattered on happily ". . . leather pants fringed, midi-length . . . gorgets and steenkirks—so much more chic than turtlenecks . . . Come back to the school with me and I'll show you my sketches."

Cassie said she had to get back to the office; she told Lo about old Mrs. Troxell's statue. "Lo, would you have time to go and talk to her? Tell her I sent you. She's so lonely. And she's had two eye operations—she's nearly blind."

"I could pose in her fountain like Eros."

Cassie said it would be more helpful if he'd talk to Mrs. Troxell about art and costume ideas. "She'd enjoy that. She's traveled all over, and it's awful for her to be old and shut off from everything."

"She might adopt me. I'm a bit overage for adoption but I could bring joy and colorful confusion to her last years. The patter of little tongues." He waited expectantly. "Why don't you laugh? I thought that was quite a good line—'the patter of little tongues.'"

"Isn't that your car up the lane? I'll drop you here so I won't have to turn around."

As Lo wriggled out, he said, "You weren't meant to be bitchy, luv. Your claws are too stubby. And your heart is too cup-overfloweth. I can be bitchy. Alicia can be bitchy. But you can only be nice. It's like being born with six toes."

Cassie laughed. "I'm glad Mrs. Gifford's arrow hit a tree. I'd hate to lose you."

"Longfellow!" Lo said. "I just realized—that's who Herrigel stole his Zen Buddhist nonsense from: 'I shot an arrow in the air—it fell to earth and hit God knows where.'"

"I may take up archery," Cassie said. "I need to release hostile feelings."

"Voodoo is safer, ducks. Just a bit of modeling clay, a packet of pins, and a hair tweaked from the head of your enemy. If you want any more advice, I'll be at the Stick Shift tonight."

Soon after five, Oliver drove into Bevington to mail the tapes of the second number. At the post-office counter, he said, "First class—certified," and was slightly appalled when the clerk said, "That will be four seventy-two." He was so conditioned to cutting corners, paring any outlay of actual cash, that he hesitated. If somebody was going into New York in the morning . . . but Humboldt might not come up again until the weekend. Then he remembered: he was on expense account, for the first time in his life. Humboldt had made that clear Sunday. With a wonderful sense of release—lavish, high-riding release—Oliver said, "O.K. Make it special delivery too." He made a notation of the exact amount on the back of an envelope, then put down another three dollars for gas and oil. There was something about an expense account that invited overstuffing, like a goose. Humboldt could damn well afford it.

The idea of Humboldt's having a Bechstein piano annoyed him. A man with no talent—probably inherited a few million and spent most of his time playing squash. And getting a massage afterward. Oliver had never seen a squash game, but it had the squishy sound of soft living. He had never had a massage, either, but he hankered after one. Especially today. He'd had almost no sleep the night before—he had worked till dawn doing the piano arrangement—and had a class in Solfeggio at nine. Bunch of stupid brats. Even Phillipson, the best music student of the lot, had been acting half-witted, tittering. . . . I should have canceled the class and slept through. The back of his neck, in fact his whole body, felt like a wire pretzel; walking back to his little second-hand car, he thought, when I've got it made, I'll have a masseuse—no, a masseur—come in twice a week. Five times a week.

In the meantime, he had to get a haircut; Alicia said he looked shaggy. And go back to his room to take a shower. He would have liked to take a shower in the guest house, but he hadn't dared. The night before when he was working there and had asked euphemistically to wash his hands, Alicia had startled him by refusing: "I can't bear having anybody else use my bathroom. There's a maid's lavatory in the basement." In a way, this fastidiousness had pleased him. Made her even more glamorous. But it also made things a bit awkward. He had risked using the toilet in her bathroom today in her absence, but he had felt furtive about it. And if he went to his room now and took a shower, Lo would hear him and start banging on the door. No chance for a nap; Lo would yak about costumes, nag him about Cassie. . . . He felt pushed from all sides. If Cassie cared anything about his work, she'd have agreed to—his mind still shied away from "abortion." Just a minor, hygienic removal of an unwanted growth. . . . Maybe someday when he had a duplex apartment with a soundproof workroom. . . . And have the nursery soundproof. Or have a nurse and the baby live in a separate apartment and just come in for a half hour mornings and evenings. He could play lullabies every evening . . . put a lullaby in the show? . . . young mother singing over one of those old wooden cradles: *My wish for thee . . . to grow up free . . . in a land all green and peaceful.* . . . The tune unwound in his head as clear as a road he must follow. It was so simple and right and lovely he wanted to cry. He'd play it for Cassie tonight—no, he was supposed to see Alicia tonight. Something told him Alicia wouldn't like a lullaby. Might not even want it in the show. Well, he'd do it anyway. He could write the lyrics himself. And she needn't start ranting. He knew a damn sight more about song-writing than she did. He must clip that tendency she had to overwrite. He'd certainly improved "Him's a Trimmer." He sang the revised lyrics to himself:

> *"It's always fair weather*
> *When you and him's together*
> *Because if trouble blows a gale*
> *That trimmer turns his tail. . . ."*

Do more choruses . . . barber-shop quartet . . . have each man sing a chorus about the other, pointing, accusing, then close harmony again on "Him's a Trimmer." He'd make notes for the director. Better go into New York and see him. Alicia needn't be involved. She always wanted her own way . . . highhanded. And the way she'd arranged with the house-keeper about dinner without even asking him ahead. . . . It reminded him of a movie he and Cassie had seen, about a young man engulfed by an older woman, a friend of his parents, who arranged all the assignations. . . . He, Oliver, would watch his step. He wasn't going to be sucked into anything.

He was a half hour late for dinner, partly out of a show of independence. He banged the brass knocker on the front door of the guest house and stood there with the tense, tight-nos-triled look of a man who intends to watch his step. The door remained blankly shut. He banged again, harder. Still no Alicia. And no sound from inside. He pounded the door with his fists, and felt a small-boy desolation. She had stayed in New York; she was abandoning the Festival and him. Or had

Cassie made Humboldt get rid of Alicia? But even in his frantic state he rejected that; Cassie didn't play tricks. And she wouldn't do anything to hurt the Festival. It was Alicia who'd gotten bored. No, Latham; Latham at Lincoln Center. He would have advised her to get out, not to squander her talents on anything so provincial and thrown together. . . .

"You're here!" Alicia came around the side of the house and he was shaken by a fresh astonishment at her beauty, and by a relief that made him feel limp. "The gardener was showing me through his greenhouse and I forgot to watch the time. I'm not even changed. Oh, good, you aren't either."

Oliver had put on his one summer suit, the tan-striped seersucker, but he was conscious now that the sleeves had shrunk. Or his wrists had stretched. He felt adolescently awkward, ready to scrunch. Alicia was wearing a simple beige knit dress, and her bronze hair seemed woven with light. "I have so many exciting things to tell you. And I worked on the train. If you don't like these new lyrics, I'll throw myself off a mountain." The chimera of a conniving older woman evaporated like smoke. When she reached out both hands in welcome, he clutched at them. "I—I thought you'd had to stay in town."

"Willy wanted me to. There's a do at Lincoln Center tonight. And a party for some singer afterward—Mila somebody —you probably know her."

Mila Calacci was one of the most famous contraltos in the world. Oliver swallowed, and said he knew her records.

"Oh, you might have liked to come in and go with me. But it's a bore to have to lug in dinner clothes."

For Oliver, it wouldn't have been a bore—it would have been a wizard trick. He had never even rented a dinner jacket.

"Anyway, I wanted to get back here so we could do a lot of work. I needed to work and work and work. Don't you find it's the one cure when you feel beleaguered? If I couldn't work I'd go mad. Wouldn't you?"

Oliver agreed fervently. How she understood!

"Fix us a drink, will you? What extraordinary hands you

have—the long, supple, strongly boned fingers, as if they had a separate life of their own." She put out her own slim left hand, adorned with only a plain square-cut emerald, no wedding ring, and touched his wrist lightly. "So beautifully articulated. Sanetti would like to sculpt them. He often asks me to help him name his pieces for an exhibit. If he does your hands, we'll call it *Concerto*."

Oliver was a little nervous over this style of conversation, which seemed larger than life. Not name-dropping, but more like gods and goddesses dropping in for a drink; there was the danger Alicia would walk too serenely tall, accustomed to celestial domes, and would bang her head on the low ceiling, the obscurity of Oliver Yates.

"I'll just take a glance around the kitchen and see if that so-called housekeeper, the Zen Buddhist warbler, left some things in the oven." She called from the kitchen, "Don't you detest fanatics and crusaders? My ears were rubbery with listening. . . . Willy's coming to the Festival. But I won't tell you the real news till we're settled."

When she sat down beside him a few minutes later, and raised her glass, turning to face him, he noticed for the first time that her full upper lip was deeply indented in the middle; not a Cupid's bow—more delicately carved and vulnerable.

"Here's to our opera," she said. "Willy's commissioning it. I gave him the idea today and he's mad for it."

"Your story—the one I'd been working on—" He was so overcome he could hardly talk.

"Not that. It would bore me to work on something I'd already done in another form. This new idea is much more powerful—you'll adore it. And incredibly timely. We're to start work the minute we finish here. Willy's lending me his house in East Hampton—he'll be in Europe all summer—and you can come down and stay."

Oliver stammered something about not being sure he could leave.

"But I thought you'd be so excited," Alicia wailed. "I could hardly wait to tell you."

Oliver said hoarsely he was excited. "But if you stay on here we could still work together."

"Impossible. I'd be depressed in this atmosphere. I had a horrible experience today. I ran into Humboldt and his assistant or something when I went to meet Willy for lunch. And the other man knew my—my first husband, and he blamed me —I know he blamed me. And I could feel Humboldt giving off righteous rays. But when I married I was so young—so incredibly naïve. I was such a little fool, I even got pregnant on my honeymoon. It nearly wrecked my life."

Oliver's insides constricted.

"How beautifully you've managed to stay on course and not let yourself be parceled out in pieces. Since I've been working with you, I feel such a marvelous new sense of direction. I'd gone stale—I'd dreaded holing up for the summer and flogging myself to write. And now!" She flung out her arms, embracing new continents. "Willy's house is ideal. Nobody there but a couple to do for us. We can each have a floor to ourselves."

Oliver blurted out, "I'll talk to Cassie tonight."

"The little girl who helped you on research? Who was it described an ingenue's face as looking like pink and brown china doused in hot soapy water? And that delicious story of Flaubert's—the simple-minded young girl who was 'tender as new baked bread.' So fresh—and so doughy inside."

If the implication drifted past that Cassie had a shiny, perspiring face and doughy insides, and was simple-minded to boot, it was all done so fast Oliver had nothing to hold onto. He wanted to give a fairer picture of Cassie, and he groped through his mind in confusion, not knowing what words to pick up. He was as baffled as if he'd had to describe air or nourishment or sunlight. "She's an awfully nice girl."

"Of course she is. She has it written all over her—in capital letters. But don't tell me you'd let that child decide what you'll do or not do."

"We decide things together." But even as he said it, he was

bitterly resentful all over again at Cassie's stubbornness. If she doesn't have an abortion—in his resentment he seized on the word without flinching—I'll be finished. I'll never be able to write with a brat screaming night and day. . . .

"Of course I can always get another composer."

Not just the words, but the way she said them—coolly, like a stranger—"I can always catch another cab"—frightened him so much he felt sick. Suddenly she seemed as implacable as marble. "To be frank, Willy would prefer someone better known. But he was so enthralled by my idea for the opera he humored me when I insisted on you. Obviously I made a stupid mistake. You're not interested. You don't like working with me. I'll bow out of the Festival too. I'll leave tonight."

"No! Please! Please stay."

It was so desperately unhappy a cry Alicia's face softened. "You must admit you haven't been very encouraging. You haven't even asked me what my idea is."

He had to beg her for several minutes to tell him. But once she relented, she was so vivid as she talked that he basked in the look and sound of her, and caught only snatches of words ". . . Tavern of the Headless Woman, where the rebels met. Benedict Arnold was one of them. Benedict Arnold—that's it!" She stopped and looked at him eagerly. He tried to think what he'd missed. What had Benedict Arnold to do with it?

"He's the opera—his life—don't you see? He was one of the original Revolutionaries. But then he was lamed early in the war—a leg wound—and he was embittered because they hadn't given him enough men—and he fell in love with an eighteen-year-old belle of Philadelphia—her father was a Tory—she was half Arnold's age, so he wanted money and power all the more. . . ."

Oliver was listening more closely, but uneasily, now. To trade the witches—Alicia's witch story—for Benedict Arnold —seemed a dubious switch. Benedict Arnold didn't arouse any music in him; witches did. And at the back of his mind there was a nagging thought that Cassie wouldn't like him to write about a traitor.

". . . came from a fine old New England family that went downhill, and his father became the town drunk. As a boy, Benedict Arnold resented his father horribly—he felt he'd been cheated, betrayed. . . ."

Oliver began to feel warmer toward Benedict Arnold.

". . . then when he feels betrayed by his country, he's justified in selling it out and he's in a key spot because Washington trusts him more than any other general. I think Benedict Arnold is so much more fascinating than Washington. He had dash and fire—he was complex, deviled—and he must have begun to see that democracy wouldn't work for long anyway. It hasn't worked. Look at this country now—mob rule by an ugly minority. Students look like apes—soon they'll have to mate with real apes—it's the only way the next generation will survive in this jungle."

She was so wrought up she trembled. Oliver got her back onto the story line of the opera mainly to calm her down. And once back on, she was beautifully concise—clear about where they were going: "The young bride would work on Arnold, threaten to leave him if he didn't give in. She was a spoiled beauty—mad about clothes . . . Major André had been a beau of hers, and that's how they got their first message through to the British. . . . When André was captured with the blueprints of the West Point fort, Arnold and his wife escaped to the British frigate, and the Americans offered to swap André for Arnold. It must have been a hideous decision for the British. André was so adored—like a son to his commanding officer—in fact, I'd suspect a homosexual tinge. We can hint at that. And of course the British despised Arnold as a traitor—'Not cricket, y'know.' But they had to keep him, and let André be hanged as a spy. I think end it there—with Arnold going into exile—in England—condemned to a living purgatory. Willy says we'll sell it to the movies too, but with a different ending. Washington and Arnold will meet in the hereafter and decide America wasn't worth all the fuss." She drained her glass. "We'll make scads of money every which way. Doesn't it have everything?"

Oliver said it did. He didn't have the nerve to say, But I'd still rather work on your witch story. And there was no question that an opera on Benedict Arnold would be more popular. And profitable. A movie sale. He could tell Cassie, In a year or two years at the most, I could afford a real household. . . . He fixed fresh drinks and clicked glasses with rising elation.

"You'll laugh at me," Alicia said, "But right after I left Willy I went to Bendel and ordered a dress for our Lincoln Center opening—white velvet, with a border of mink. . . . We might open next winter, if we hurry."

Cassie always claimed she cared about his music. Now was the time for her to prove it. Abortions weren't dangerous these days—get the best doctor. . . .

Alicia went out to the kitchen again, and he roamed around the room with a head full of things he'd say to Cassie. They sounded strongly convincing; clearly his was the only sensible solution.

When he saw Cassie's car go by the guest house and park a hundred yards up the driveway, he thought she'd come to make a scene, and he rushed out to keep her at a safe distance. In his childhood he'd been so torn by almost daily scenes between his mother and grandmother that the idea of two women fighting terrified him all the more. Cassie greeted him so gaily he was taken aback. "Hi, I'm on my way to have dinner with Chet."

At first he couldn't even think who Chet was, because he was so full of his own news: "Latham of Lincoln Center wants me to. . . ." He spilled it all out, not the logical, persuasive sequence he'd arranged in his head; it was as if he'd packed a bag neatly and then it burst open and dumped the contents, even the soiled underwear underneath: "You have to give me this chance. It's the only possible way."

"But if we got married now, I could stay here and work while you were in East Hampton. And I'd just come down weekends."

Oliver said sullenly, "If you insist on being stubborn. But it will ruin everything. I won't be able to concentrate. I'll feel as if a sword's hanging over my head."

"I see," Cassie said, too brightly. "Then let's forget the marriage bit."

"I didn't say forget it. All I said is, postpone it till I get things all set. I'll pay for everything—I can get an advance from Latham—get the best doctor—"

"Don't bother," Cassie said.

"Then we'll have to get married right away," he said angrily.

"No. I'm a free agent. If you're a free agent, so am I."

"Don't be insane. *I'm* not having a baby."

"No, you aren't, are you?"

"I didn't mean I'd leave you in a jam."

"And what if I told you I'm not in a jam," she said in a strained high voice. "That everything's fine now, as of this afternoon? That I just counted wrong and panicked?"

He was so wildly, wishfully relieved it came out as scolding: "And you waited till now to tell me? You nearly drove me crazy."

"You thought you were being blackmailed into it?"

"You know very well I didn't mean—"

"I doubt if I know what you mean about anything, any more."

"Look, why don't you stop by here and honk, when you leave Humboldt's? And we'll go to the Stick Shift to celebrate."

"With Miss Thorne as chaperone? You mustn't take any chances. Besides, I don't feel like celebrating."

It wasn't the most perfect moment for Alicia to stroll out. Although she couldn't have been more cordial: "You *will* loan him to me long enough to work on the opera?" she said charmingly.

"He's not mine to loan."

"Oh, but he thinks so. We'll put a sign on him—'Property of Miss Cassie Murdoch.' Wouldn't that make you feel safer?"

"I wouldn't dream of worrying about him when he's with you," Cassie said, in a dreadfully sweet voice. "Because you're such an old, old friend of Daddy's."

Chapter
Twelve

Driving up to Bevington in end-of-day traffic, with the Festival blueprints in a briefcase beside him, Chester felt extraordinarily untired. His stomach, usually mean at that hour, was being so quiescent he might not have had a stomach at all.

Sometime earlier that year, he'd gone to a trade dinner—manufacturers, textile designers, buyers—and one bouncy little man he knew only slightly had roared out, "How many you guys got a pain in your guts right now?" Chester for one, had; judging by the grimaces around the table, he was in the majority. The little man had slapped his own middle exuberantly: "I had my stomach taken out last year and boy, is that a relief! You guys oughta try it." The recital hadn't helped the digestions of his ulcered listeners, but it had given Chester an offbeat kind of pleasure. There was something almost jolly about a man with no stomach rejoicing in his state of Nirvana.

The smooth onrush of cars on the throughway, miraculously as uncongested this dusk as Chester's stomach, was part of his over-all sense of well-being. Not static well-being, or torpid contentment, but a feeling of going exactly where he wanted to go—home to dinner. It had been a long time since he'd looked forward to that homely ritual. Ever since he'd talked to Cassie Murdoch on the phone that afternoon, he had been in fine humor. He had made decisions—good, clear decisions—ping, ping, ping: buy the TV station and the Swedish textile firm; no peanut factory, no paper towel plant, no to five other possibles. He hadn't even considered asking Alicia Thorne to have dinner. He had recovered from the humiliating letdown over lunch, but he'd felt an instinctive need to be laved in genuine appreciation, as a dog knows when it needs to eat grass. And Cassie's natural, direct "I would love it" had begun the laving of minor wounds. The major wound, the cuckolding and divorce, was so much a part of him now it had become a livable pain, to be overlooked except in the murkiest hours of sleeplessness, when memory clawed him open.

"Let's make it around eight," Cassie had said, against the metallic jabber of typewriters in the background. "Then we won't feel pushed."

So he had that glimmering ahead of him. And he was supported by the all-too-human superiority he'd felt after Trumbine's revelations at lunch. Helluva sick situation, that marriage. And the way Trumbine had flip-flopped to side with his mother-in-law. Or pretended to. No, not pretend. Nobody could pretend much with Alicia. Being with her was like—Chester searched for a suitable simile and almost got hold of one but lost it in a sudden clogging of cars where the new underpass was going in. He was stuck in line twenty-five minutes. Oddly, he didn't fume about whether Cassie would wait.

But when he went racing up his driveway soon after eight, and saw her standing with Oliver and Alicia in front of the guest house, he felt short-circuited. He had imagined her sitting curled up on a chair in his living room, looking cozy and welcoming. But he did notice she was wearing a much more becoming dress. None of that bunchy look. She really had a nice little figure. And he was gratified by the enthusiasm of her greeting: she almost jumped in front of his car, waving. All the more because in contrast she was cool with Oliver, a tossed-off "See you" as she got into the front seat with Chester. Alicia was looking pinch-mouthed about something, but while they exchanged the usual token chitter-chatter about traffic and weather, she linked her arm through Oliver's, like a hostess closing in with her mate—solidarity, gracious couple—to speed the guests along.

Chester felt a sporting amusement in Oliver's expression: pleased but uneasy. He had been there once or twice himself, with Alicia.

"I can hardly wait to see our blueprints," Cassie said, just a shade too clearly. Either out of a sense of wanting to help her or to jolt Alicia, or both, Chester called, "I got a boot out of you and Trumbine. Talk about crazy coincidence. Hoist on the slice." He didn't need to look in the rear-view mirror to know Alicia was reacting unfavorably as he drove off. Let her explain that to Yates.

In the meantime, he threw it like a juicy bone to his passenger.

It had been his experience that women were always avid to gnaw on details of other women's mistakes in marriage. But Cassie wasn't avid. She said, "I knew she'd left her child," but she said it tiredly, almost absently. "Sometimes people are pushed into doing a thing they hate." She sounded as depressed as he suddenly felt. The evening seemed bogged at the start. Even the Festival was pointless; the idea of starting a new career made him skittish now. Why jump into the brambles?

While they were having drinks, he spread out the blueprints on the big, square coffee table, but more to give them something to talk about, some raft they could cling to briefly: ". . . Music tent here, electric illumination board right behind . . . eight hundred amperes so we can light up even these fields we'll use for parking lots. . . ." He thought, I'm sounding like a guided tour of Radio City Music Hall. Cassie was making enthusiastic noises, but with no feeling behind them. "Three smaller tents—I thought one for Arts and Crafts." Cassie revived enough to object. "If we don't separate the painters like Gail from the craftsy set, it will be murder. Let's put Crafts in with Antiques." Her voice lost that deadness as she told him what Prue Washburn was rounding up. ". . . Old Mrs. Troxell has a peacock quilt that's been in her family forever. And a quilt of Presidents' heads, a kind of linked medallion pattern, as if they're in oval frames."

The peacocks and Presidents' heads intrigued Chester. Great idea for bedspreads. Although the peacocks were safer politically than the Presidents' heads. But stop at, say, Teddy Roosevelt. Anyway, definitely before Harding and Coolidge and. . . . "Do you think Mrs. Troxell would let me copy the designs and pay her a royalty?"

"She'd grab at the chance. That big old house is the only thing she has left, and the school taxes alone have doubled in the last four years. She said why should she pay huge taxes so the schools can turn out more vandals and hairy hermaphrodites?"

This twanged a responsive chord in Chester. He sounded off on what he thought of the younger generation trying to tear up the world.

Cassie said she thought it was more like finding a wall with the paint peeling off. "You want to peel the whole thing and repaint."

"But not knock it down." Neither of them wanted the walls knocked down willy-nilly, but they disagreed on who was to blame for the current urge to bash. Cassie said, "With so much of the world in misery, and then most of the others just sitting fat-cat, not caring, the kids feel desperate. They have to do something. Like the Peace Corps. Or students giving up their Sundays to help at a playground in Harlem."

Even Chester approved of this form of revolt.

"But sometimes they feel so hideously frustrated because there's so much more needed. I know one Peace Corps man who nearly cracked up because of that. He said he felt as if he were teaching kids to brush their teeth on a diet of bread and water."

Chester listened restively to the recital of villagers' poverty. "They ought to do more with their own textile resources," he said. "For instance, in the Far east, urena. It's a bast fibre—a stem fibre—it could be manufactured cheap. And sunn's another."

"Manufacture sun?"

He spelled it out. "It's good and strong for sacks, fish nets—doesn't mildew, or rot in salt water. Help them start one industry like that and it could lift a whole district. I grant you they can't do it with a water buffalo."

Cassie vibrated with interest. "If you'd go down to Washington and talk to people there—"

"I might even run for Congress." The idea had taken fresh hold on his mind, with new, more positive tentacles.

"What a terrific idea! Did you just think of it this minute?"

She was so admiring, so trusting, Chester squirmed. "Look, I may as well tell you straight out—I got into this Festival to have a gimmick, a launching pad." This was harsher truth than he'd meant to offer.

Cassie looked stunned. She stared down at her drink.

"I know I must seem like a heel. But I couldn't let you think I was the great crusader. I want to do something to help. And I was hooked as soon as you got up in that meeting and talked about it. But I had my own selfish reasons too."

Cassie said slowly, "Maybe we all did. I suppose I wanted Oliver to have a launching pad." Her voice dropped until he could barely hear: "And now he's launched in another direction—away from me."

Chester had so strong a sense of her depression he said quickly, "Alicia bowled me over too. She bowls over every man in her path. For her, it's as natural as breathing. She needs it to keep her going the way a hurricane needs wind. But Oliver—" The idea of Oliver facing even a small hurricane struck him as so shaky he switched metaphors in midstream: "For Oliver it's like going to a play to see a famous star and she asks him backstage. He's dazzled—he's flattered, but he won't want to see the play every night for the rest of his life."

"He picked a stinking time to go to a play," Cassie said. But she did look and sound livelier.

Fiera Young came in to announce, "Dinner will be served in ten minutes if you desire to freshen up before." She was in her low-cut, brief-skirted serving costume again, but this time with a large black velvet bow in her hair instead of a flower; it looked like a nesting crow. "I saw the menu," she said conspiratorially. "First, you're having vicious saws."

Her listeners were understandably puzzled. "Baked in a cake?" Chester asked.

"It's not a dessert—it's a cold potato soup," Fiera said. "Personally, I think soups should be hot."

"I love vicious saws," Cassie said solemnly. "I make it with a dash of curry powder."

"Makes it more vicious," Chester murmured.

"And for the entry, Beef Burgoyne in red wine sauce."

"That sounds very suitable," Chester said. He had always liked history. "Very colorful. Thank you, Fiera. Tell Mrs. Gifford we'll be ready in ten minutes."

He found to his surprise that he was hungry. Part of it was the contagion of Cassie's appetite. But partly it was due to a kind of blessing she'd given before the meal: "I think you'd be absolutely great in Congress. And if the Festival helps, I say fine."

Mrs. Gifford had retained enough backsliding bourgeois instincts in the midst of Buddhist meditation to do her employer and his dinner guest proud. Fiera, in attendance, provided a more informal note: pouring a splash of wine into Chester's glass, she said, "Mrs. Gifford says, 'Let him taste it before you keep going.' Okay?"

Chester, who had learned the ritual gestures the hard way, suddenly saw the whole thing as ludicrous. He said to Cassie, "What am I supposed to do if I don't like the wine? Spit it out like strained spinach?"

Cassie giggled. Fiera said, "That's a good one. I gotta tell that to Mrs. Giffrod. She's been tellin' me about the Buddhist bit. Far as I can make out, you ask a lot of dumb riddles and you get dumb answers: 'Master, where is God?' . . . 'God is in a stick of dry dung.' What kind of disgusting talk is that?"

"This vichy—uh—vicious saws is much better than mine," Cassie said. "Tell Mrs. Gifford I'd love to have the recipe."

Chester liked the tactful way she got rid of Fiera. By candlelight, she looked more grown-up, more romantic, until she said, "Hey, you haven't tasted your soup."

He picked up his soup spoon. "I got used to stalling way back, so I could see which silver the others used and grab the same thing. The first time I took out a patent I was invited to dinner on Park Avenue—man who heads one of the biggest synthetic combines. And there was a footman behind my chair. I felt as if he were a monitor watching to make sure I didn't cheat on exams. The big thing is not being born with a silver spoon in your mouth, but knowing which spoon to put in. I'd bought an etiquette book and it said you start at the outside and work in. But you have two sides, and sometimes you aren't sure whether you ought to use a fork or a spoon. I wasn't scared on the business end—I knew what I was doing —but I was scared stiff of that line-up of silverware."

"It's hard to imagine you being scared," Cassie said. "You always seem so in balance. Maybe partly because I'm used to being with kids who are always ranting about something or dropping a tab."

Chester said he'd heard of picking up a tab, but not dropping it.

"Drugs," she said. "Some of Davy's friends drop three or four tabs a week. They try to escape from thinking about war and nuclear bombs. They figure if they're going to be destroyed, they want to do it their own way."

She shivered. Chester wanted to say what he thought of the tab-droppers, but he also wanted to cheer her up again and that impulse was stronger. He said he'd had some crazy kinds of escapism of his own: "I'd dream about going on safari. Once I went into Abercrombie and priced an elephant gun. When I moved into this house I actually thought of buying an elephant gun and having it lie casually on the piano."

Dragging the piano in was a mistake, because Oliver came with it, or his unwelcome ghost. "Oliver's terrified of any kind of sport, even tennis. If anybody handed him a gun, I think he'd faint." Then as if she'd heard what she was saying and couldn't let it rest there, belittling, she said, "But he has a lot of courage in other things. He won't write electronic music because he thinks it's all negative—all nonmusic. If he'd gone *avant-garde,* he could have had a lot more grants and fellowships."

Chester said, "When I read about some of these fancy grants for far-out writers, it burns me up to see money wasted like that when people are starving. And I don't approve of one person getting so many grants. It's like living on somebody else's credit cards. When the credit's cut off, they scream they've been robbed."

"But they need a hand up. You have no idea how tough it is to be a young composer. You have to pay at least eight hundred to have the vocal scores copied, then a thousand or more for the instrumental parts, and changes come to several hundred more. Then you only get about fifty dollars a performance. And you may not get more than four performances altogether. So grants are just about the only hope. Oliver says if creative people can't do the work they want to do, then the world's not worth saving."

"If the others can't get enough food or decent housing— can't get jobs—then there won't be any world anyway. Even in the South, the worm's turning. . . ."

He had turned off Oliver. Cassie wanted to hear more. Fiera Young brought coffee into the living room: "Mrs. Gifford's going to show me some yoga exercises. You stand on your head and it clears your brain." Chester had an irresistible picture of Fiera standing on her head, complete with nesting crow, while bits of string and fluff drifted out of her brain.

And in the foreground he had Cassie sitting behind a Georgian silver coffeepot handling the hostess chores with unself-conscious grace. He was feeling so contented that when she said, "You were going to tell me about conditions in the South," he was mildly jarred. He even felt a counterstreak of appreciation for Alicia; there was a lot to be said for women who were so charmingly distracting you forgot about the mess the country was in. But once he'd started talking about the problems, he was soon galloping through statistics: "Twenty years ago, only eight percent of the cotton in this country was harvested by machine. Now it's ten times that— around eighty percent. And that's fine, in some ways. But we're just beginning to realize you can't let the men sit and rot away. Or push them into the cities on welfare. We've got to figure out ways to involve them—build 'em up—the way we do our businesses. New methods—new training—new products. For example, alginates—they've never been developed much here commercially. . . ."

Cassie was listening so nicely he went rather overboard on algae: ". . . spin on a viscose system . . . use a cationic agent . . . so far, it hasn't been profitable for mass production, but if they come up with a new process—and there's no reason they can't—"

It seemed to him suddenly that the "they" should be "we." Get a bunch of chemists, oceanographers, manufacturers together. . . . He entangled his guest even deeper in undersea growth. "Alginates are impervious to infrared—they've been used to make military targets invisible to the enemy. Must be some element there that could be used in lighting effects. . . . Maybe that's why we don't see more mermaids. They wear seaweed to make themselves invisible." He had broken his own spell. He laughed sheepishly. "I've probably bored you stiff."

But Cassie was as bright-eyed as a child who's heard a fairy tale at bedtime: "It does me good to hear somebody talk hopefully, for a change."

"The whole southern coastline ought to be a gold mine for alginates. If we could set up plants in the poorer states. . . . I'll talk to some of the men about experimental stations when I'm in Georgia next week."

"You're going away? Just when we're getting the Festival set?" She sounded so wistful Chester felt quite indispensable. He said he'd try to cut down on the business trips. "But we've had a hassle over integration at one of the Georgia plants. We promoted a Negro to foreman because he was the best man for the job. . . ." (Actually, the hassle had been settled weeks before; the foreman was doing fine, and Chester was going down to check on a new dye process. But he wasn't above using a Cause to gain Cassie's approval.)

"That's *really* important," she said. "Of course you have to go, and you must stay just as long as you need to. The least I can do is keep an eye on things for you here. I got you into this Festival and I want to make sure it doesn't go haywire on exhibits and things while you're gone. Let's go over the blueprints again. Why don't I make us more coffee?"

Chester's stomach flinched; it reacted sourly to caffein after ten P.M., but he felt it would be unmanly to say so. And he enjoyed watching Cassie in the kitchen. She didn't bustle; she had that same quick sense she'd shown about finding vases for lilacs, knowing exactly which cupboards to open, which dial to turn. "What a fabulous stove, with its own Roto-broil, and that plate-warmer shelf above. . . . How about some cheese and crackers? . . . Crèma Danica, mmmmm . . . I love coffee strong and black, don't you?"

Chester said he did. He was holding an interior dialogue: *You'll have heartburn all night.* . . . Your stomach would kick up anyway, so enjoy yourself while you can. . . . *You're old enough to be her father.* . . . Not unless I'd married at fifteen. She's more like a kid sister.

He liked that idea; he had a boyish urge to tousle her hair.

Chapter
Thirteen

Alicia said, "Europe knows how to honor its composers. How you'll love it. Italy most of all, I think. Sometime you'll have a villa at Spezia and work there with the Mediterranean lying at your feet."

They were sitting in front of the fire Oliver had just lit. Small curling drifts of smoke came out into the room and floated toward the ceiling. He knew he ought to get up and kick the front log—it was too far out—but he was caught in the exalted lassitude often found in opium dens or at old-fashioned pot parties, when the dream is action enough. Anyway, he'd worked like a dog all evening. He had set two new lyrics Alicia had written on the train. One had been fun: "Me and Thee Here in the Stocks—And Baby, Is It Worth It!" The second had been more like running the gauntlet, with Alicia jabbing. She had called her version: "A Neighborly Stone Bee." "All the men would help a new settler build his house, heaving stones into place from dawn on, and then their women brought food and cider. . . ." Oliver had shied off "neighborly"; He said it sounded like imitation Rogers and Hammerstein. He had argued for "Throwin' a Stone Bee."

Alicia's dilating nostrils showed what she thought of *that*. "You say my idea's derivative. You practically accused me of plagiarism. And then you come up with something that's a direct steal from that gruesome story by Shirley Jackson—all the villagers throwing rocks to stone a woman to death."

When Alicia was on one of her irrational streaks, grappling with her was like tangling with ectoplasm laced with barbed wire. Oliver protested he'd never even read the story.

"Of course you read it. Everybody read it when it first came out." She stopped, perhaps remembering Oliver might have been in kindergarten then. "There was an even more frightful one by somebody this month. Every New Year's a huge savage dog would lope out of the forest and come to some house in the village, and that was the signal for the family to put out a tender young child as sacrifice. The dog ate the child right there, crunch, crunch—in full, loathsome detail, and left a bloody pile of bones. That's what literature's come to—this senseless sadistic rending of flesh into nothingness. Can you wonder I despair? If the dog had carried the child away and eaten it off-stage—" Alicia was beginning to be amused at herself—"that wouldn't disgust me. But to eat it right on the front lawn—revolting."

In the end, Oliver had got his way: "Throwin' a Stone Bee." Somehow Alicia wasn't being as difficult tonight. And she had poured out other ideas till Oliver felt like somebody who races along after a pinwheel and tries to catch all the golden shower of sparks. And now that they'd finished work, what she was saying about his future was so shining golden with promise he still wanted to catch every word. The smoke from the forward log was beginning to sting his eyes, but he sat in thrall listening: ". . . must visit the Provençal cliffs where the troubadours sang and the love courts were held . . . Fado in Portugal, a bitter chocolate, dark melancholy—like no other kind of singing. . . ." Vaguely he sensed a shift as she went on talking. "At the Music Festival in Glyndebourne when performances start in the sweet, wholesome English afternoon, the audience turns out in full evening regalia. By the way, if you want to order a new dinner jacket, I'll ask Willy the name of his tailor. He uses the same tailor as my ex-husband, but

I'm avoiding my ex-husband because I refuse to be coaxed back into that box. I'd rather confide our problems to Willy. He's one of those safe, charming men one pats on the cheek in passing."

Even in Oliver's lightheaded state, this posed a two-pronged question. Did she expect him to wear a dinner jacket to the Liberty Pole Festival? (He had a sudden picture of them together, suavely dressed, taking curtain calls on opening night as the audience shouted "Bravo.") Unconsciously he pulled in his bony wrists. It was time he had a suit made to order. Two suits. But how could he pay for them? Charge it. So that answered one question. But Alicia's description of Willy Latham—"Charming man one pats on the cheek in passing." Did she mean that he, Oliver, was another?

". . . such a stiff little bookworm," she was saying. He must have missed something. Was her ex-husband a stiff little bookworm? ". . . until I was thirteen and began to wriggle out of the cocoon. One afternoon I went into my father's library and pawed through *The Golden Bough* looking for juicy parts about sex. I knew I was safe because my mother never went into the library. She disliked books, although I will say for her she liked elegant bindings. But my father happened to come home early and he caught me on that Golden Bough. I said I was checking on a sociological reference, and he thought that was funny. He told my mother later as a joke, and she began to watch me like a Puritan witch. The best witches were Puritans. Still are. Boston has more than its quota per district."

Oliver's mind drifted back to Alicia's Salem witch story. That aria he'd written before he met her—do it instead as a witches' quartet—handled like "Him's a Trimmer" but slyer, sinister—key of F minor? . . . Smoke getting too thick. . . .

"It might be instructive sometime to do a study of love-making by cities," Alicia said. "In Chicago, I'm sure they do it with all the windows open—breezily."

Oliver caught up with the conversation at the tag end: "I'll open a window."

She burst out laughing. "I didn't mean we had to demonstrate each city's methods of making love. Although it's an amusing notion."

Oliver blushed, an adolescent, true-hued blush. "It's smoky in here."

"Poor Oliver Twist," she said teasingly. "Am I too much of a change of diet from gruel? Remember what your little girl said. She wouldn't dream of worrying about you when you're with me. What a smuggie she is. The small-town mentality—you get born at one end of Main Street and die at the other, with a stop at the church in between. And nothing else is important."

Oliver roused on that one. "Cassie isn't like that. She cares about what's happening in the world. She's been thinking about joining the Peace Corps."

"She's been thinking about getting married," Alicia said. "She's the sort who'll have triplets out of sheer verve in motherhood." She mistook the spasm of distaste on Oliver's face. "I know—I'm being utterly horrid. Sometimes I remind myself of that murderer who scrawled with lipstick on a mirror, 'Stop me before I kill again.' I can't stop myself when I get this way." She looked distraught and beautiful. "Forgive me. But it's just that the domestic prison with diapers and bottle-warmer nearly snared me so young. And when I see somebody with your talent, I get frantic for fear you'll make the same mistake."

Oliver said hoarsely, "I know."

"We're alike, you and I. Amazingly so. We can't stand being lassoed and branded as belonging. We have the flexible hollowness. We have to be free and open to every sort of experience, especially when we're young."

What she was saying was so much what he needed to hear that it was like a powerful local anesthetic quieting any guilt over Cassie and releasing his tongue to babble. Without meaning to, he told Alicia most of the confrontation that day. ". . . And then when Cassie found out she wasn't pregnant after all, I felt as if I'd been hauled up and rescued from drowning."

166

Alicia was marvelously understanding. And movingly anguished for him, for the ordeal he'd been through. A belated, watered-down instinct of fairness made Oliver say it must have been hard on Cassie too.

"But she was using it to get what she wanted. She wants to 'drive life into a corner' and tame it. To be brutally frank, dear Oliver—and I realize this will be painful for you—I'm afraid she made the whole thing up to force your hand. It's really too melodramatic to ring true, in this day and age. When she found you wouldn't knuckle under—oh, how I admire you for that!—she had to change her story."

Oliver said Cassie would never lie to get her way. But even as he said it, he was beginning to doubt what he said. After all, there was something fishy about Cassie suddenly finding she wasn't, when she'd sounded so positive before. . . .

He replayed that scene in the driveway in his head, and this time he saw that Cassie's behavior was definitely suspicious. She'd even withheld the good news as long as she possibly could.

"To do the little thing justice," Alicia said, "she was probably driven by jealousy. Which is pathetic, and ridiculous. Just because you and I have an extraordinary rapport in our work doesn't mean that I'll reach out rapaciously. I am not a spider weaving gray webs." She patted his cheek, lightly, fleetingly, not at all like a spider. "You're safe."

His cheek tingled from her touch. And his pride, his maleness crackled against the word *safe*.

By midnight, Cassie had made three pages of notes on the Festival while she and Chester talked: "For the Town Crier, to keep him from being just quaint, let's have him announce some things—I mean local crises—that are happening right now," she said. "And have him call concerned citizens to action. In the old days, people didn't wait around for the government to do everything. They acted on their own."

"Well, they didn't have a federal government," Chester said reasonably. "And now we have too much. When it gets too swollen, it can't see down past its belly to tie its shoes and move fast. But everything's tending that way now. In five years, there'll be only three or four textile companies—billion-a-year giants sprawled all over the world, and swallowing all kinds of businesses. We're diversifying more at Pilgrim Mills all the time." With Cassie, it didn't seem like bragging. Or if it did, it was a natural kind, not to get his own back, but to report on everyday happenings: "Just today, we bought a TV station and a Swedish textile firm. That reminds me, I may have to go to Sweden soon."

"Sweden!" Her whole manner changed. Instead of being curled up comfortably, she was coiled like a spring. "I may have to go to Sweden this summer."

Chester was puzzled. She didn't seem like the kind of girl who would deliberately go to Sweden; it was a country too prosperous, too well run, to need a Peace Corps. Unless . . . "You mean on your honeymoon?"

She looked as if he'd hit her.

"I'm sorry. It's none of my business." He blundered on. "But you'd told me you were getting married—"

"We are," she said carefully. "Except that we can't do it just yet. Oliver doesn't want to until he makes some money. But it just happens I got pregnant." As if to keep him from saying anything—he was too flabbergasted anyway—she rushed on: "Several girls I know have gone to Sweden for abortions because you don't have to run a risk there. And nothing's furtive. You're in a good hospital with a good doctor. So it's really very aboveboard. It happens all the time now." When she tried to manage a smile, Chester was ripped by pity. "It's not as if I'm a wronged woman. I knew exactly what I was doing." For the first time, her voice trembled: "I thought I did. I thought as long as I didn't do anything to hurt other people —people I loved—then I had a right to live the way I wanted to. But you can't tell ahead what will hurt people. Oliver, Mother and Daddy, even Davy. I felt tonight as if I'd had to stand on my head and look at my life upside down. Because

I'd always planned to have children. And then to have it come at the wrong time. . . ."

"You can still get married right away," Chester said. The words hurt his throat but they pushed up anyway. "Money's no problem at all. I'll give Oliver a salary, or a lump sum for the whole job. There's no reason he should volunteer his time and talent. I should have realized sooner."

Cassie smiled rather sadly. "It was more my fault. We always expect people like Oliver to donate their services to a good cause. And of course the Festival will help his reputation. I'm sure he'll get offers."

"He can be paid for his work too. I ought to be kicked for not thinking." Yates was the one who ought to be kicked, always wanting women to do his dirty work. "I'll mail him a check tonight."

Just for a second, Cassie looked eager and happy. Then she shook her head. "He's afraid to have children right now. He thinks my having a baby would ruin his concentration."

"That's nonsense. He'll think differently when he has money in the bank."

"He'd still feel trapped."

You're the one who's trapped, Chester thought. "I'll mail him a check anyway. And I think we need a drink."

He was so upset for her that when he poured out brandies, he had to restrain himself from gulping down a slug.

"I know Oliver loves me," Cassie said. "And if he knew I was really pregnant—"

"He doesn't know! My God, girl, all you have to do is tell him."

"I did, I tried to. But he got so frantic—he's under a strain right now." She gave Chester an abbreviated and charitable account of the scene with Oliver that evening in the driveway. "I was damned if I'd plead and beg. I'm not used to—to being a victim. He'd have married me if I'd insisted, but I had to be independent. I had to for my own sake, and for both our sakes, so he'd think of me that way again. Can't you understand that? If you were pregnant and somebody acted like that, wouldn't you do the same thing, and say you weren't?"

Chester, although biologically handicapped on putting himself in her shoes, tried honestly to consider. "In those circumstances—maybe yes. But don't forget what I said—he'll get over this infatuation in no time."

"Oh, I don't mean he'd *sleep* with her," Cassie said. "She's too old. But right now she's all tied up with his work. The opera is what he's always prayed for. Not just to be commissioned, but to have Lincoln Center behind it. That's the top of the world for him."

"It may fall through. Alicia's not anybody to count on."

"She needs Oliver too." Cassie sipped her brandy reflectively. "At first I thought she was being so kind and generous. But that's not it. She's slipping. She's not as famous now. And Oliver is young and terrifically talented. He's probably more talented than she is. And I have to admit they're good collaborators. I can't be a drag on him now."

"Cut out the wee martyr bit," Chester said angrily. "You could never be a drag and you know it."

Cassie grinned. "I was sounding entirely too noble. I'm really very good for him. But he does need a big success to make him feel sure of himself. Then he'll stop being so afraid of things. He'll be grown-up enough to want children."

Chester lit one cigarette from another. Of all the crazy over—simplification. . . . "Some men never want children."

"Is that how you felt?"

It touched him that in the midst of her tangle, she could still reach out and be interested.

"It turned out that my wife couldn't have any. And we talked about adopting a child, but then she backed away from the idea and I didn't want to push her."

"It doesn't work anyway," Cassie said. "I tried to push Oliver around like a—like a baby carriage. So I have to take the consequences. Oh, I forgot—nobody knows about this but you."

He felt such tenderness he couldn't say anything; he took her hand and held it tightly.

"I hadn't meant to tell anybody till after it's over—not even Mother and Daddy. I have five thousand dollars my grandmother Murdoch left me in trust. I get it when I'm twenty-five. But I could borrow on that at the bank, don't you think?"

Chester said he was sure she could. He knew the odd sort of independence she'd worked out for herself was too important, and too precarious, to interfere with.

"I'll just say I'm going on a trip. I mean I'll say I want to see Europe before I settle down. If you say you're going on a trip, it sounds so ominous now. When you mentioned Sweden, it had been so much on my mind I just blurted everything out. Do you think you might possibly be over there then? Say, right after the Festival?"

Chester pressed her hand more tightly. "I'll be there."

"I wouldn't want you to make a special trip. But I don't know anybody in Sweden. And it would be so reassuring to have a friend around."

"Nothing could keep me away." He had an aftertaste of the line. Like dialogue from a bad movie. But it didn't worry him.

"Of course things can change overnight," Cassie said cheerfully. "Oliver might decide he needs me around when he's working on the opera in East Hampton, and he'd say we ought to get married right away. In that case I'd tell him I'm pregnant, but he'd know it's his own free choice."

Her on-again, off-again attitude, her torturously illogical logic, rather shook him. Even shocked him.

It was almost one o'clock. Cassie insisted she ought to tidy the kitchen but Chester overruled her.

He walked her down to her car, and noticed that the guest house was dark. "I'm sure Oliver's back working at the Talladay studio," Cassie said. "You have no idea how he drives himself."

Chester watched her taillights winking down the driveway and turn off onto the main road. He was still so wound up, so caffeined and confused, that he dreaded lying down in that lone prairie bed. Lilacs scented the night with a kind of sadness. He had no reason to connect his ex-wife with lilacs —she had preferred considerably more sophisticated flowers and scents—but he thought of her anyway. He remembered how anxious he'd been to make excuses for her. How much he'd wanted her back.

He remembered when it was she who'd done the pleading: "But it's our anniversary. And we've had tickets for this show for so long. Can't you postpone the meeting?" He tried to remember what meeting—there must have been some crisis—but he couldn't think what it had been. And he had been too busy to realize for six months that he'd lost his wife.

Now he walked, without noticing, until he found himself in one of the fields cleared that day. Good thing he'd bought more land than he needed. When the deed to the old Mortly place was being searched, his lawyer had told him about a deed from 1770, setting the western boundary: "Said land to begin at a rock near the corner of the field where Jonas sowed wheat." Chester sighed for the simplicity of it.

Pale moonlight washed the leveled hummocks; the woods behind were dark, unfriendly territory. Someday he'd explore all his property, in daylight. He ought to get a dog. But striding around, country squire with dog bounding, no longer seemed so attractive. Cassie had said in the kitchen, "When we were little, Davy and I used to come over here and go back in the woods to the stream. We'd make a dam and catch pollywogs and have a picnic lunch. . . ." Might ask her to walk some weekend. Was it all right for her to walk now? Yes, walking was safe right up to the end. Somebody ought to tell Yates the truth. Was there any way he could act as mediator? But she'd trusted him. He couldn't betray her. All he could do was try to persuade her to tell Yates. Even if she didn't stay married, at least she'd have her child. He'd send Yates a check in the morning. That might help push the guy in the right direction.

Having decided that, Chester felt drained—sad and empty

but strangely at peace. He was so tired now he took the shortest way home, cutting around in back, past the darkened guest house. There was a car parked behind, almost hidden in the bushes. He was mildly surprised at its shabbiness. Didn't seem like Alicia—to have such a junk-heap. Then he saw the glint of another car beyond, moonlight reflected in the glossy dark surface. A Chrysler convertible. The junk-heap wasn't Alicia's.

Chapter
Fourteen

"It's like being shut up in a boiler factory with a cage of canaries," Alicia said. "That ramshackle hall. And the same bloody tweet-tweet, toot-toot, squeak-squawk, crash-bang, over and over and over."

She had said it to Oliver at the second or third rehearsal with the orchestra in New York. Not the first day, when the singers had gathered around her paying court, and Oliver had felt left out. He'd brooded about it; from the way they acted you'd think she wrote the music too. If they knew how much I had to do on her lyrics. . . . But when they'd got down to business, it was Alicia who was left out.

He was rather bewildered that she didn't share his excitement, hearing, feeling the texture of the music gathering strength and richness and shimmer, as the instruments wove in the harmonies. For somebody who loved music so passionately—by her own admission—this seemed to Oliver incredible. But in another way, he was relieved when she stopped going to rehearsals. There had been one day when they'd listened to the new soprano, not a Pilgrim Mills television regular, but a girl hired just for the Festival. The fact that the girl was good-looking simply melded in Oliver's mind with her singing voice. When he murmured after her first solo,

"Beautiful, beautiful," he was innocent of lust, or at least of anything but aesthetic composer lust for a perfect purveyor of his art. But Alicia had turned on him in one of her cockatoo rages: "You think she's more beautiful than I am. You deliberately want to hurt me. . . ."

They had made up over lunch, a long, tender lunch in a little Armenian restaurant near the rehearsal hall on Second Avenue. Alicia was touching in her contriteness, and lavish in her praise of the singer's voice, the way it had warmed their love song. "But we must be sure she's well padded with falsies. Otherwise she'll look like an ironing board." Alicia had glinted at him then, and laughed deliciously. "If you call a spade a diamond, you can say much blacker things about it." After lunch, she had taken him to Willy Latham's tailor to be measured, and Oliver had missed half the afternoon rehearsal.

Even after Alicia stopped going to rehearsals, she insisted on going into New York the days he had to go in. "I refuse to stay here and be nagged by Prue. Much as I love her, I simply will not listen to any more of her lectures. I make up my life as I go along. We're free—free—free—you and I."

Oliver didn't feel all that free. He discovered Alicia had told several people in Bevington that she loathed rehearsals and couldn't be dragged to another. Oliver had said uneasily, "But they'll wonder why you always drive me in. It's better if they think you have to be at rehearsals too."

"Better for who?"

Oliver was silent; he had learned not to invite one of her tempers.

"Better for Cassie—I know. Prue already scolded me about that. I told her to make up any excuse she likes—say I'm a compulsive shopper, or that I have to see my publisher—anything."

One late afternoon when she picked Oliver up after rehearsal, she told him, "I bought you a present this afternoon. Two, really."

One present was at his place at dinner in the guest house, a little square Tiffany box: gold cuff links in the shape of music clefs, snuggled in chaste black velvet. He had never owned anything from Tiffany's before, and somehow that excited him more than the cuff links themselves. He never used cuff links anyway, so they didn't seem awfully practical. And in his sartorial ignorance, he hadn't realized he'd need them with his dinner-jacket-to-be until Alicia mentioned it. She was like a child when she gave a present, glowing, greedy for more and more praise of the object, pointing out any feature he might have missed.

The second present, which he saw late that evening, was even more of an eye-opener because Alicia was wearing it: a pleated chiffon negligee slit up the sides, definitely not opaque. A ripe golden color that was marvelous with her eyes. Although at the moment he wasn't concentrating on her eyes. . . .

If only she didn't have this thing about leaping out of bed right after they made love: "I can't bear to lie there like a roast braised in its own juices. I have to get up and shower and feel my bones clean and upright. . . . You *can't* be sleepy. I'm so wide awake my mind's blazing. You have to stay and talk to me for hours. . . ."

Mostly, she did the talking: "I wish I'd been born in the era of garden parasols, and hats laden with Renoir fruits and flowers. Trailing gowns and glories. . . . I'd meet you under a yew tree and we'd drink wine from silver goblets. . . . Yew trees and nightingales, and that heavenly scent of an English summer night. The first time I went down to the country there for a weekend, the host gave a vast dinner party and dance for me. Most of the girls looked so perspiringly shiny and toothy—I was the belle of the ball. Some man walked me out on the terrace between dances and said, 'Do you smell the wallflowers?' And I thought, What a *peculiar* remark. Till he pointed to the blossoms clinging to the stones. It was one of those enchanting bursts of revelation one has—'But of *course*, that's how. . . !'"

She had gone to England, she said, "because Harley's wife was being beastly. She wouldn't give him a divorce. And a

London paper took him on as critic. Even my father was beastly about it. I would have expected that of my mother. She was only upset because of what people would say. But my father never gave a damn about gossip—and yet he cut me off."

Alicia was sitting up very straight, as if she were on trial in a courtroom, giving testimony to prove her innocence, to establish that she was the victim of persecution. "My father wrote me through his lawyer that I had behaved in a totally irresponsible manner by eloping. But I was behaving responsibly to myself—to every instinct in my heart and mind. Father said I should have waited till things could be properly worked out. But it's wicked to wait. Time congeals the impulse. A life can't be measured in length—it's the heights and depths that count—not the dull, endless plateau. How could he judge me for *being?*"

Oliver said his mother had been rigid in a different way: "Nothing mattered but work. She even set up the models for me to copy." He told Alicia about the sepia-tinted photograph of Verdi hanging over his bed, and how mother and son had read *Lives of Great Composers* together. "Not that I always reacted the way she planned. When Verdi was writing *Rigoletto,* he wanted to have the Duke's and Gilda's great love duet come right after the Duke had seduced Gilda. But in those days it was considered sinful to be exuberant and lyrical after the act. Lovers had to be remorseful. So Verdi gave up the idea. He told a friend, 'Think of what the parsons would say.' My mother approved of that."

Alicia could be so responsive she flowed into his mind like quicksilver. "We must use that in our opera! Right after Benedict Arnold decides to sell out his country, he must sing in glorious defiance—he'll be rich, famous—he'll cover his beautiful wife with jewels—the war will be over—the aristocrats will triumph. . . ."

She scribbled words excitedly on the amber bond paper she always used. "It's so magnificently right!"

Her tantrums could flare up as sharply and suddenly as her

raptures. When Oliver tried to doctor one of her wordy verses: "How dare you tell me lyrics aren't meant to be read—they're meant to be sung? My words have always sung —every line I wrote. Every critic has mentioned my poetic cadence. I won't change a syllable."

But five minutes later she would be sobbing in his arms, begging him to forgive her, saying she hated domineering women, that she wanted to be "feminine."

With her, Oliver felt a queer mixture of elation and sinking. Or not so much a mixture as one following upon the other, often lickety-split. The lucid lightheadedness of fever, floating, soaring, seeing new marvels in the landscape of her mind and body. And then, unaccountably, the anxiety—at its worst moments almost like the sensation of falling one gets in a nightmare.

Part of it could have been lack of sleep. There were times when he moved through the days so exhausted he felt sandbagged. He had told Cassie he always went back to the Talladay studio to work late on piano arrangements, after he finished work with Alicia. But the truth was he was so tired by then all he could do, usually, was fall on the couch and sleep. A sleep filled with such violent dreams he woke up tireder than ever. But turning out music faster than he'd ever done in his life.

This was the big thing he stressed whenever he talked to Cassie. He phoned her every day, mostly to tell her how frantically busy he was. And he'd left a duplicate tape of the last songs at the *Bugle*. She had praised several of the songs, although not the way they deserved. But obviously, she was biased about anything he did with Alicia. At least she never nagged him. And she was very matter-of-fact, even cheerful, about Alicia's driving him into New York so often. "Prue told me why she goes in." Whatever excuse Prue had made, it seemed to be remarkably effective. And Cassie was jammed with work herself, checking on a hundred Festival details, acting as peacemaker between splinters of committees, doing her regular stint at the paper. The last three issues of the *Bugle* had given a generous amount of space to features on the Festival—stories about Oliver, about Alicia, Lo's costumes for the local Liberty Maidens. And a story about Humboldt.

Personally, Oliver thought the *Bugle* had been unnecessarily generous to Humboldt; all the guy had donated was money.

Cassie had asked him only one awkward question. Right after Humboldt went away, she had said, "Did you get the check from him?" Oliver had said, truthfully, no. But the check had arrived in the next mail, and Oliver had avoided saying so. No business of hers what he did with his money.

In the almost a month he'd known Alicia, his views on money had changed so much he was like a country that suffers a sharp devaluation of its currency. The more money he and Alicia figured gleefully they might make soon—recordings of Festival songs, royalties, their opera, a movie sale—the more things Oliver realized he needed. Alicia wasn't in the least greedy about money; she simply looked on it as a divine right. There would always be more coming.

Once, driving back to Bevington, she had started a minor tirade about her hairdresser in New York. She had had her hair done that day while Oliver was at the arranger's, and the man had been "incredibly stupid. It was as if he'd never seen my hair before. . . ." Oliver's mind often wandered when she was talking what he thought of as female floop. But when she said, "After all, I pay forty or so dollars each time," it yanked him back to attention. Forty or so bucks! He'd paid less than that for his seersucker suit . . . Cassie washed her own hair, in the shower. He remembered watching her emerge rosy and naked and laughing. . . .

"I know I look horrible," Alicia said. She clenched the wheel and looked straight ahead at the road, in brooding concentration. Usually her haphazard method of driving, talking and gesturing all at once, made Oliver nervous. She was a much surer driver than he was, in her own reckless way, but so much more erratic than Cassie that Oliver couldn't quite get used to being her passenger. But her focused silence now, vibrating in the car like the hum of discontented bees, made him nervous in another way. And yet resentful too. Sometimes he begrudged paying these constant high tolls to ensure smooth passage. "Your hair looks O.K. to me," he said, rather offhandedly. More silence. Head high, proud reserve. In profile this way, she was, if anything, even more beautiful. His resentment evaporated; he moved closer and slipped his arm through hers: "Silly girl, you couldn't look horrible." But even as he said it, and she responded with a quick turn of her head, vivid smile, he had an echo of his voice saying "Silly girl," and he was somehow embarrassed for himself and her too. And once when she glanced in the rear-view mirror, the thought popped into his mind that she watched people around her—men, even women—through a kind of interior mirror, all in relation to herself. Making sure they were following. Making sure nobody passed her.

"Will you brush my hair for me tonight?" She sounded so wistful, so childlike, he was touched all over again. How dependent she was, really.

It was only a few days later that she announced she was going to try a local hairdresser. And it was typical of Alicia that as soon as she'd made the appointment, she was exuberantly expectant: "They say this girl is fabulous. And I'll save a fortune. That cretin homo in New York knows I can't stand hair spray, but he sprayed me with something that made me stiff as horse's hair. . . ." Oliver's mind took an intermission, but the buzzer rang early; Alicia never let anybody's attention wander from her for long: "I forgot to tell you. I had an idea for a square-dance number. The fiddlers used to string their bows with a hair from a horse's tail. Let's bring a horse right on stage and have the fiddler circle around him trying to get close enough." She circled Oliver in droll mimicry: "Just one hair, horsey, horsey." She stroked his head; he leaned back against her unsuspectingly, then screamed *"Ouch!"* Alicia crooned, "You can spare one hair, out of that thatch." She nibbled his ear. The nibbling became rather heated. . . .

When Alicia went off for her hair appointment the next afternoon, Oliver was trying to do the last sixteen bars of

"Fiddle with a Horse's Tail." He had arrived after his two-o'-clock class, just as she was leaving. And he hoped to finish the song before she came back because she hated what she called "the dum-dum-dumdums." But the tune wasn't coming right; it trailed off toward the end. He kept lighting and stubbing out cigarettes; his chest felt pinched in, as if he were getting bronchitis. He scratched out some notes on the music paper, then threw down his pencil and rubbed his face wearily. Get some air—have to get some air. Maybe walk over and take a look at the music tent. Might try to test the acoustics.

The tent was enormous, bright yellow, so festive that, tired as he was, he felt a surge of excitement: My tent—my music —my show. Several workmen were laying cables near the entrance. "Watch it, buddy. Nobody allowed in here now."

Oliver was childishly annoyed. He said stiffly, "I'm the composer."

One of the men stuck his head inside the tent and yelled, "Miss Murdoch, some kid here claims he's the composer." He winked at a fellow workman. "Don't look so composed to me."

"Hi," Cassie said. "I see you're still using that same old smudgy pencil. You've got it all over your face."

"These Paul Revere lanterns look awfully tinny." Mrs. Tyndale was unpacking a carton of Festival souvenirs. "Like Mexican tourist junk."

She trotted to the back of the store and called down the basement stairs: "Al! Come up here a minute. I need your advice."

Al Farwell appeared, red, beaming, with bits of excelsior stuck here and there like confetti. "Your basement's gettin' worse'n mine. I got so many liberty poles stacked up I hardly got room for merchandise."

"Don't unpack any more of the Festival stuff," Mrs. Tyndale said. "I just wanted you to spot-check for damage. Al, do you think I should send back these Paul Revere lanterns? They look so much flimsier than the sample I ordered from. I'm sure it's a different model."

"No time to get a new batch. We only got ten days to go, and by the time you allow for a computer muckin' up the order, and maybe another truck strike. . . . Why d'ja order so many gravy boats? I been unpackin' gravy boats till they're comin' out my navel."

"They're not gravy boats. They're witch lamps—exact replicas."

"No kiddin'!" A worried haze overcast his beamishness. "You think that's gonna be a popular item?"

"It was a delightful old superstition." Mrs. Loomite, deprived of wandering geese, snatched at this newest cause: "If you lit the lamp at dusk and let it burn till daylight, you were safe from witches."

Charles Wood muttered, "I can think of at least three customers." He was sitting at a drop-leaf table correcting proofs on *Homely Herbal Remedies.*

"I'm not sure it's a good idea to have all those witch lamps and spitboxes and things in the same tent as the homemade food," Mrs. Hinck said. "Some of the ladies are very upset."

"Cassie'll talk 'em out of it."

"She is doing entirely too much. She looks peaked."

"Why wouldn't she?" Mrs. Tyndale said darkly. "Oliver's with that Thorne woman every minute."

Mrs. Loomite's eyes bulged with indignation. "Theirs is a purely working relationship."

"With that dame, I'd work at it too." Al Farwell guffawed.

"Prue Washburn told us herself that Cassie and Oliver planned to be married this summer."

"That was weeks ago. I don't notice she's talking that way now."

"Cassie would be the first to resent these innuendoes," Mrs. Loomite said. "Oliver has done thirteen songs in a month—a truly inspiring score. And a perfect mating of talents. I had the privilege of hearing one they taped last week. 'Will I Trade My Lover for a Bag of Salt?'"

Wood said, "My God! Does that come under the heading of stoned-soul music?"

Mrs. Loomite said it was a deeply moving war ballad. "It seems that if a man enlisted in the Revolutionary army, the state of Connecticut gave his family a bag of salt, and the song develops that theme so beautifully. Miss Thorne was gracious enough to allow me to copy the lyrics." Mrs. Loomite wailed:

> *"But if I lose my love . . .*
> *Do me no favor . . .*
> *My tears will be salty . . .*
> *And life will have no savor."*

Her listeners looked slightly dazed, but the ladies murmured politely. They were glad to have old Miss Maulridge appear as diversion.

"I'm on my way to see Cassie now." She perched girlishly on the edge of a Windsor chair. "Lo is at the Women's State Reformatory—they're sewing the Liberty Maiden costumes for him. And I found the most delightful new epitaph just now. So I thought I'd take it right over to Cassie to give to Oliver." The ladies exchanged significant glances; obviously Miss Maulridge wasn't up on the current gossip. She was fishing in her reticuleish bag for a tiny blue-leather notebook. In a quavery voice, she recited:

> *"Here lies John Konkepot.*
> *God be as good to him*
> *As he would be to you*
> *If you were he*
> *And he were John Konkepot."*

Wood said, "I'd cut the last two lines."

Miss Maulridge's turkey wattles tensed. "I feel the last two lines are intrinsic to the meaning. Without them, the humor is lost. I'm sure Lo Bender would agree with me. After all, it is Our Song."

Mrs. Hinck's finger moved hurriedly down her list of old games and jabbed at random: "Huzzlecap? Anybody know how to play Huzzlecap? Oh, I forgot. Pickett already tracked that down. It's pitching pennies."

Miss Maulridge was flouncy in disapproval. "I do not feel that this Festival should promote gambling."

"If the Catholics can have bingo, we can have Huzzlecap."

"This Festival is for all faiths, creeds and colors. As Cassie mentioned in her story in this week's *Bugle*. And we have quite a few Negro volunteers."

"The blacks were hardly responsible for settling this country." Miss Maulridge snapped her bag shut. "That is a distortion of history. All they have done is make trouble since they were given their freedom."

"You read the wrong history books," Wood said, rather grimly, for him. "You and Tom Devin. If you merged the D.A.R. and the John Birch Society, you could call it Daughters of White Birch."

Mrs. Hinck jumped into the breach on all fours. "What I was leding up to—about the all faiths and creeds—is that the Dog Obedience teacher wants us to have an interdenominational Blessing of the Animals."

"What animals?"

"People bring their pets to the Festival to be blessed."

Mrs. Loomite clasped her hands together, expressing pleasure for herself and presumably her Siamese cat. "What a charming notion."

"It's an old Scottish rite some of the settlers brought over. We'd have ministers and a priest and a rabbi—"

"And a guru, I trust," Wood was sounding more cheerful again.

". . . to the accompaniment of Scottish bagpipes."

"The Lions Club has a buncha fellas that's taken up playin' bagpipes. They gotta practice in the club basement because their wives won't allow it at home."

Miss Maulridge prepared to take her leave in the midst of considerable caterwauling over bagpipes. "Oliver may be working on the tombstone song right now. I really must take this to Cassie."

Mrs. Tyndale brushed herself absently with a feather duster.

184

"Are you sure Oliver's not in New York with Miss Thorne today?"

Al snickered. "Layin' on sumpin' softer than a tombstone."

"If you are casting aspersions on Miss Thorne's character," Miss Maulridge said, "You are being unjust as well as ungentlemanly. Prue Washburn told me why Miss Thorne has to make those frequent trips to New York—she is being fitted for dentures. I believe it's now called a reconstruction of the jaw. But she's still very sensitive about it, Prue says, so Prue has hardly told a soul."

"The piano was promised for this morning and it hasn't come yet," Cassie said. "But we can test the acoustics anyway. I'll go down on the stage and project, and you sit near the back."

Oliver clambered thankfully to one of the upper tiers of seats. He felt more comfortable at a distance from Cassie these days.

Sitting there, he felt as if he were under a giant yellow umbrella. Spokes radiated out from the center pole like ribs. But no gusts would blow this one inside out. The massive main pole was already hung with lighting rigs. Eight or nine aisles tapered down to the stage, which was set at the bottom —oval, bowl-shaped. From where Oliver sat, Cassie looked rather like a midget. She was standing just behind the footlights. "Can you hear me?" she said, in her clear young voice. "Do I reach you?"

Oliver cupped his hands: "O.K. Now move to the back and talk some more."

A workman came on stage wheeling what looked like a mover's dolly. He wanted to talk to Cassie about something. Oliver heard, "When the piano. . . ."

He began thinking uneasily about the piano parts. He had been too busy, what with one thing and another, to do the harmonies himself after the first two or three songs. Pilgrim Mills' musical director was taking care of that, but not well enough. The arrangement for "Will I Trade My Lover" (Alicia's favorite) was too thin—sounded whiny. If I shifted to B flat, Oliver thought now, and used more bass instead of that damn plinking dulcimer . . . talk to the arranger about it tomorrow . . . no, tomorrow he and Alicia were to have lunch at her sculptor friend's studio. Maybe he could skip that and spend all day with the orchestra. . . . But Alicia wanted the sculptor to do Oliver's hands. If he broke the date she'd get sore. And in the afternoon he was supposed to have a fitting at the tailor's. . . .

He sat back wearily in the comfortable seat—surprisingly comfortable for a music tent—and scowled down at the stage. Cassie was still yakking with the workman, probably asking about the man's wife and kids. Ignoring the fact that Oliver didn't have a minute to waste. Forgetting he was nearly killing himself for her Festival. Good thing classes were over next week. Funny that Phillipson hadn't turned in his last harmony exercise. The kid had been such an eager beaver—only talented one of the lot. No discipline, though. Spoiled bunch of brats. To hell with all of them. He'd be able to get more sleep after next week. Maybe he could sneak in a nap today before Alicia got back from the hairdresser. Have to go to his own room, though . . . Alicia wouldn't like walking in and finding him asleep. When he slept on his back he snored. . . . The idea of a nap was so hypnotically restful. . . . Oliver's heavy eyelids, heavier than ever these days, pulled down, down, down. . . .

Sound jarred him awake; he stared foggily. Where, what—? Oh, yes, Cassie, testing. But there was definitely something wrong with the acoustics. It sounded as if she were saying, "How are Alicia's teeth?"

It so happened that Oliver bore the marks of Alicia's teeth on his right shoulder.

"Hey, how are Alicia's teeth?"

Cassie couldn't be saying what he was hearing. There was no possible way she could know anything. He used his hands as a megaphone: "Say something else."

"I have," Cassie yelled. "I've been talking till I'm blue in the face. So finally I tried Alicia's teeth."

"Wh-what about teeth?"

"Her new FALSE TEETH. Do you mean she hasn't told you? Upper and lower plate. Prue said she's very sensitive about it—probably doesn't want you to know."

Oliver had a sudden picture of his grandmother's teeth leering at him from a glass of water beside her bed. As a small boy, it had frightened him into hysterics.

"Can you hear me? Do you want me to try from stage center? There may be a blind spot here."

Oliver said no.

"What?"

"NO," he shouted. "The sound's O.K." Whether it was or wasn't, he wanted to cut this short. Instead of waiting for Cassie to join him, he loped down an aisle and ducked out the nearest exit. A freshly dug hole—actually a long trench—stopped him abruptly. By the time he'd detoured around it, Cassie appeared. He was afraid she'd offer to drop him off at the guest house, but she didn't.

"Chet will be back this weekend. I didn't like to ask him on the phone about the check—I'm sure it just slipped his mind because he's been so busy. But I can remind him this weekend."

Oliver stammered, "I—I finally got it. But it was only fifteen hundred."

"Only!" Cassie looked at him oddly. "That's almost four times what you make in a month at the school."

"It won't begin to pay for a new car," Oliver said. "But at least I can make a down payment—I have one on order now." He didn't want Cassie to ask what kind, because it wasn't exactly an economy model; he hurried on: "And I'm having a couple suits made. Willy Latham's tailor." He had never met Latham, but saying "Willy" made him feel more secure, more justified in extravagance.

"I see," Cassie said, still in that odd voice.

"I certainly couldn't go to the Festival in this." He gestured distastefully at what had been, a few weeks ago, his best light suit. "Alicia will be dressed to the teeth."

It was an unfortunate choice of words. Cassie smiled wryly. "I gather you're taking her to the opening."

"I guess I'm stuck with it," Oliver said. "Being collaborators and all. But I know Lo would be glad to take you. I'll ask him. And we could all get together at intermission and—"

"I'll make my own dates. And they won't include Alicia, with or without her teeth."

He came near blurting out, "That false teeth thing is just a joke." What stopped him wasn't caution, but an uneasy sense of doubt. Why would Prudence Washburn say a thing like that if . . . ? The horrid thought wriggled back into his mind like a garter snake.

Two workmen were now heaving dirt a few feet away, extending the trench for a cable line. The stout one pulled out a gray-looking handkerchief and wiped his face. "I could go for a beer."

Oliver thought suddenly, nostalgically, of cold beer. Once he'd asked Alicia if she had any beer on ice, and she'd looked quite pinch-nostriled. Cassie loved beer; he remembered a night in bed with her when they'd sprinkled each other with the stuff, and licked. . . . He began to feel an upsurge of the old affection, warmed by looking at her there, so guilelessly young in the bright sunlight. But then he was chilled by a counterwave. How could she even have thought she was pregnant? And if she'd only claimed she was—inventing the fact to fit the need—and switching her story so abruptly. . . . He said, "I'd better get back to work."

"Have you finished the epitaphs number?" Cassie said. "Because Miss Maulridge just gave me a new one. And I meant to tell you earlier that in the North Fork cemetery there's one for a young soldier who died in the Revolution. It's—"

"If I keep on working this hard, I'll be laid out there myself." He wanted to divert her from a subject he had good reason to avoid: "And I still don't have a closing number. We may just do a reprise of 'Grow a Liberty Pole.'"

"I wish there could be one somewhere that gives the spirit of the settlers themselves—the way they faced up to things and. . . ."

Oliver cut in restively: "How did you like 'Will I Trade My Lover for a Bag of Salt?'" He agreed with Alicia that the song would become a folk classic. And he wanted to nudge Cassie into admitting how great it was.

"To be quite honest," Cassie said, "I think it's a phony tearjerker. And the music is thin—it isn't up to your standards. But it may sound better on a jukebox."

Oliver's pride was so raw that he forgot to be discreet: "Which is more than you can say for an epitaphs number. That's out." Alicia had turned against the idea of a cemetery scene; she said it was ghoulish. "We aren't going to touch it."

Cassie's dark blue eyes were enormous in dismay. "But that's the one number Lo was to do the costumes for. And the idea's so fresh and—and true."

"Not that fresh," Oliver said. "It's been done before. In *Our Town*. The cemetery scene with umbrellas—a schmaltzy family wake."

"I cried when I saw it. Even in a high-school production. But of course you don't approve of that kind of feeling—families loving each other. You were probably glad when your father died."

This bit too close to the bone. Oliver said harshly, "You think everybody has to love their mothers and fathers and forefathers and all members of minority groups."

"I'll tell you one thing," Cassie said. "I'm glad you weren't one of the early settlers—we'd never have made it."

"You and the early settlers can go to hell." As Oliver stalked off, one of the workmen said, "What is he—some kind of Communist?"

"Prue! Prue-blue! Where are you?" Alicia went straight to the foggy antique mirror above the mantel and gazed at herself, patting and poking.

"I'm up here in the attic."

189

"Come see my new hairdo." Alicia strolled to the stairs and peered up. "Hurry. I can only stay ten minutes."

Prue's voice now came through muffled, like somebody shut in a trunk. "Cassie wants to bring Lo Bender up here and . . . I'll be there as soon as. . . ."

Alicia picked up the phone by the stairs and dialed the guest house. She listened, frowning, for eight or nine rings. "Prue!" she yelled. "I can't wait forever."

Prue's squat little body appeared, looking more bean-pottish than ever at the top of the narrow stairs. The risers were so far apart her short legs had to grope their way step by step down the two flights. Toward the bottom, she steadied herself by putting her hands flat against the wall.

"Pet, I'm sorry about last night—canceling our date so last-secondish. But we're working at such a pace. Do you like it?" She lifted her lovely throat and turned her head.

"Your pace? No."

"My hair! I had it done fuller at the sides. Don't you remember? This is the way I used to wear it in school."

"Was it?" Prue said. "That was so long ago." She took a long-handled brush out of the fireplace rack and went at the hearth vigorously, as if that were the only reason she'd come down.

Alicia's mouth quivered. "I was so happy, and now you've ruined it. You want to make me feel old and ugly." Her voice wailed up: "Don't you like it at all?"

"I don't like what you're doing. You dreamed up that opera just to take Oliver away from here. He and Cassie were going to be married this summer, and you had to make mischief just to be sure you still could. The way you had to make Wes Murdoch sit up on his hind legs and beg—not because you wanted him, but because I did."

"Prue! I swear I didn't know! I never thought of you as the kind who—"

"Who would get a man? Because I never had any looks to lose?"

"Oh, Prue! You know I say things I don't mean. I was so

190

bitterly sorry afterward. But you have to believe me about Wes. You have to."

Prue sat down heavily on the sofa. Alicia knelt beside her and looked up at her imploringly. "Say you believe me. You must—you must." She took Prue's freckled hand and laid it against her cheek.

"All right," Prue said. "Maybe you didn't realize. And maybe there wasn't much to realize anyway. But you can't claim that about Cassie—you knew just what you were doing. And you don't care a fig more for Oliver than you did for Wes."

"That's not true. I've changed. He's changed me. I'm new. I know now I was never young before. He's given me my youth."

"I've heard it too many times. Each time, you say you've never felt like this before."

"But this time I never had. Do you realize that of all the men I've been with, the others were just conveyors—appreciators?—and then they'd turn jealous of my talents because they weren't in my league. They were never creative. But Oliver is. It's so glorious. Our minds rush together as lovers. I've never been so alive."

"And how do you think Cassie feels?"

"She'll still have him for forty years. Don't begrudge me this lovely snatch of joy."

Prue pushed back her grizzled gray hair, half despairing, half resigned. "Whether I begrudge it or not, I know you well enough to know I can't stop you. The one good thing is that it won't last long."

Alicia smiled rather sadly. "This may be the last time around."

"Well, the sooner it burns out the better. And it's a good thing Cassie has her hands full with the Festival. I don't think she has any real notion of—"

"Those Festival volunteers are really the weirdest lot."

Prue frowned.

"Really, pet, I'm not exaggerating. I went by that shop

where they hang out, and they all behaved so peculiarly. They kept sneaking looks at my mouth, as if I were a ventriloquist or something." Prue's own mouth twitched up at the corners. "Then the old biddy who haunts cemeteries said I must have patience and not be discouraged. Oh, yes, and she said I should stick to soft foods for a while. Why on earth should I stick to soft foods?"

Prue said blandly, "I can't imagine. Miss Maulridge gets muddled sometimes. She may have confused you with the head of the Historical Association—the one who had her gall bladder out."

Alicia shuddered fastidiously. "Ugh. Lamb, I must dash." She jumped up lithely and went back to the mirror. "It really does make me look younger. Don't you honestly think so?"

Chapter
Fifteen

Chester Humboldt, seeing Bevington for the first time in a month, felt slightly stunned, as if he'd been hit over the head by Beauty. Liberty poles stretched like a double rainbow along both sides of the main street, with a third brilliant line of poles down the center on the Village Green. Some were swirlingly striped, or festooned with bright streamers that floated airily high. Some bloomed with fresh flowers in pots bracketed here and there, the height of a child or a man. And some wore silvered harrow discs like shields, glinting in the sunlight. He couldn't slow down to gape for long because of the heavy traffic. It was a Saturday six days before the Festival.

As he drove out of town toward his own place, the brightness still beckoned him on. Almost every house along the road had a liberty pole in front. A few of the home-grown decorations—papier-mâché Puritans, a neon sign blinking HOME OF THE FREE—made him wince. He had sent up some of his best designers and display people, and he had counted on them to veto. But as Cassie had said on the phone, "It wouldn't seem right to keep saying no, no to people with bad taste when this is a Festival celebrating freedom. After all, it's their yard."

Chester had called her long-distance the first time to tell her he might be delayed a few days getting back. That had been toward the end of the first week. But the problems at the mills had multiplied like rabbits, and it soon seemed natural, in fact, essential, to call Cassie every night, usually around eleven when he finally got back to his motel. Their conversations had taken on a comforting domestic flavor. "How did it go today?" she'd say. And it made him feel better to tell her. If he'd exaggerated to her originally, about having to settle another racial upset at one of the mills, the truth had overtaken him with a vengeance.

But at least there was one cheerful piece of news to tell Cassie. His plans for an experimental station to develop new products had gone ahead faster than he'd expected. "The algae conversion isn't practical yet—two varieties are toxic—but somebody here came up with another idea using peanut husks." Chester had bought the peanut factory after all, and he tried giving Cassie the fascinating technical rundown on experiments, but she wasn't scientific-minded; she simply leaped over peanut husks to grasp the results—the maybe-results. Good things always seemed within reach when he talked to her. And she kept assuring him she was fine, that everything was all right there and he mustn't worry about not getting back. Sometimes he thought that meant she had made up with Yates. Maybe the check had had something to do with Yates's coming to his senses—if he had come to his senses. Chester felt shy about asking Cassie straight out. For one thing, he wasn't sure how much she knew about Alicia. She only mentioned Oliver in the context of the Festival. And if they spent ten or fifteen minutes on the phone every night discussing Chester's problems—the mill's new integrated housing development or whatever—they often spent twice that talking about Festival preparations. Chester had expected Trumbine to go up to Bevington and be in over-all charge. But Trumbine's agency had hauled him away precipitately to handle a senator's hot potato that might explode any minute without professional cooling. So Cassie had had to take on considerably more superintending than Humboldt had planned. She said, "Your idea of using only local electricians sounded fine." (It had been Trumbine's idea, originally, to "yoke the locals and make them feel involved.") "But the only trouble with that," Cassie said, "is they're all too busy wiring the new schools."

Chester's men had helped her round up a crew, and he gathered that Cassie and the Pilgrim Mills employees on loan had established a matey relationship. She gave him bulletins: a display man's roommate had left him for, of all things, a woman. "I hope it's the start of a trend." The head engineer had bursitis: "He's getting treatments from some machine that shoots out rays like science fiction. . . ."

She said she often took her lunch sandwich over to eat with the workmen, and Chester could picture her casually sprawled on the grass—no lipstick, vivid little face shiny—as she'd been that day beside his tennis court. "They want to put plastic grass around the exhibit tents because the ground was so dug up. It costs a dollar and a half a square foot! But Al Farwell can get us a good discount. Is that O.K.?" This too had a cozy domestic flavor, as if they were building a new house together in a slap-up hurry, and must confer on everything from grass to the shade of orange for the seats.

Because of these day-by-day bulletins, even more than the blueprints and color sketches air-mailed to him, Chester had expected not to be surprised by the finished result. But as he drove in the entrance to the Festival grounds, his first feeling was astonishment. He was wearing dark glasses against the late afternoon sun he'd driven toward, but they couldn't dim the impact of this bright new world that had sprung up on nine of his acres.

The last weeks had been so grimly serious, with the black-lash, white-lash crises, that the Festival had often seemed to him like some absurd make-believe. Except when he was talking to Cassie on the phone, none of it had much substance. Yet the reality of it was so gay and natural that, as he got out of his car, he grinned like a boy at his first carnival.

Not that this looked like a carnival, even with the tents.

There was no midway. The main part had been laid out in the shape of a wide-pointed star with an open plaza in the center and Liberty Poles circling a fountain. Grassy walks led down each of the five points toward a tent. Only one of these walks had outdoor stalls along it, of yellow and white striped canvas, shaped squarely, rather like the tents at knights' tournaments in movies. All of them had their rain flaps cautiously lowered. Cassie had said, "We have to get most of it ready a week ahead so the *Look* photographer can shoot, but we're sending up anti-rain prayers." One of the stalls was bannered in Old English lettering: THE TOTAL ABSTINENCE LEAGUE. Chester recognized this from phone bulletins as the soft-drink stand, but he was a bit startled at the bannered exhortation over the stall directly opposite: TAKE A TRIP ON SNUFF! Cassie had neglected to brief him on that one. Had she deliberately not told him because she thought he was too middle-aged? Not that forty-one was middle-aged; he made a mental note to tell Cassie he thought this stall was fun. Did her generation still say something was *fun?* The word sounded curiously old-fashioned.

Most of the workmen had gone for the day—it was after five—but there were a few teen-agers putting up more signs on stalls. One, which said tersely in flame-colored letters How THEY CAUGHT FIRE, struck Chester as somewhat ominous. His faith in teen-agers' "terrific ideas" was not as shining as Cassie's. Five or six long-haired youths in identical costumes—pants sawed off and fringed at the shinbone, tasseled jerkins—were in a huddle in front of the stall when Chester went over to investigate. It was some sort of demonstration by a blond boy with longish curls. "See, man, you put the shreds of cloth in this tinderbox." The boy held up a small metal box. "Then you hold the flint in your palm and knock it with this piece of steel. And when a spark drops on the cloth you fan it like this, till you get a real fire." His companions watched as if mesmerized. One of them said, dreamily, "You know what, man? I'm going to get one of these gimmicks and carry it around for a cigarette lighter."

Chester was relieved and somehow touched; he wanted to

find Cassie and tell her. He had expected her to be here to welcome him. The night before on the phone she had said, "Oh, I'm so glad you're coming home."

He had thought about this on the way back till his imagination was so inflamed that when his plane had to circle two hours over La Guardia, he pictured Cassie as frantic, standing under a liberty pole waiting and worrying. When his mind did a replay now of the words, the tone, they seemed less ardent, reduced almost to social chatter. But he went on looking for her anyway. He couldn't see her Volks in the impromptu parking lot on the left, an ex-pastureland where cars were scattered higgledy-piggledy. Have to work out a system before opening night, he thought; ropes and illuminated markers, and maybe use teen-agers to park the cars. He remembered from the blueprint that there must be another parking lot at the far right. On his way over there, he decided to glance into the music tent, and bedlam assaulted him. Scollit, the choreographer, was down on the stage with a dozen or so leaping figures carrying what looked to be spears. Scollit was screaming, "*Tour en l'air!* Higher! Higher! Thrust! Withdraw! Thrust lower!" It didn't look awfully phallic to Chester, but the lights were changing so erratically he couldn't really judge. An electrician squatting in the stage apron was shouting to an accomplice up in the booth perched like a bird's nest: "Give it a cool. . . . Flesh tone's too lavender. . . . Try the follow spot. . . . Mushrooms, more mushrooms. . . . We're missing a male connector."

The choreographer turned to scream at the on-stage electrician, and Chester ducked out before Scollit could recognize him. Between this tent and the next (Food, Souvenirs) there was a large grassy space bannered "GAMES PEOPLE USED TO PLAY. Woo the Widow! Shinny Up the Greased Pole!"

Whether wooing the widow entailed shinnying up a greased pole was not altogether clear. A man, or an apparition, got up from a bench and came weaving toward Chester. He, or it, wore a stovepipe hat tilting perilously, a long frock coat, and spats. "Welcome back, Humboldt."

Chester squinted with that baffled Should-I-know-you? expression. He hadn't acquired the politician's fixed beam. "Charles Wood," the man said. "Currently editor of *Homely Herbal Remedies*. The *Look* crew were here today and I've been cavorting as a barker. We damn near didn't get the exhibit stalls ready in time. The carpenters wanted to knock off and Cassie stayed here till four A.M. feeding them coffee laced with brandy." Chester asked where Cassie was now. "Didn't I give you her message? She had to file a wire story but she'll still meet you for dinner—Bevington Inn at seven."

After hearing this, Chester was more inclined to be chatty. He said everything looked great. Wood's stovepipe nodded congenially. "It's wonderful what you can do with a little imagination and a lot of money."

The two men talked for a few minutes until Wood muttered, "Don't look now, but the ladies from the Food Follies have spotted you. They're converging like hens after grain."

Chester sprinted for his car. To hell with courting votes right now.

His housekeeper had already left for the day. The house seemed so large and lonely, with that impersonal neatness of a department-store display, that he wished again he'd bought a dog. Cassie liked dogs. He wasn't sure how he knew this, but the impression was so strong in his mind it almost barked at him. He could ask her at dinner about a good kennel around here. Maybe get two dogs—one big and one little. Although this disparate pairing had no conscious connection with Cassie, it somehow propelled him to hurry unpacking and changing his clothes. He had planned to call Trumbine in Washington, but he decided there wasn't time now; he got to the Bevington Inn twenty-two minutes early for his date.

He waited in the taproom, which was artfully littered with warming pans and old pewter. A blown-up map of Connecticut *circa* 1775, on the wall beside his corner table, showed historic spots and legends encircled in purplish red: "GENERAL ISRAEL (DON'T FIRE UNTIL YOU SEE THE WHITES OF THEIR EYES) PUTNAM took this route to the Battle of. . . ."

Chester thought that as military strategy "Don't Fire until You See the Whites of Their Eyes" was full of holes. He was trying to remember how General Putnam had made out in battle, or more important, how his men had made out, when Cassie appeared. Partly because of the lighting in the taproom —simulated early Revolutionary—he almost didn't recognize her when she came in. She looked smaller—not shorter, but thinner. It reminded him, inversely, that she was pregnant, and this made him feel oddly bashful. And he'd forgotten how pretty she was. But he thought she was being entirely too businesslike. She had brought along a wad of clippings to show him, most of them mentioning Chester, and for some reason this rather hurt his feelings. Did she think all he was interested in was publicity? They—or their disembodied voices—had been so close on the phone all those nights that their materializing together as people—fleshly sitting side by side—took some getting used to. From what Charles Wood had said, he knew Oliver was still in thrall; he sensed Cassie didn't want to discuss it, and this made an awkward hump in their path when they talked about the Festival. She asked him about the trouble at the mills, but he was suddenly sick to death of the whole subject of racial tension. He did think of telling her one thing the Negro foreman had said just before Chester left: "It's not so much black against white any more —it's decent people in the middle against the hate-hollerers on both sides." At the time it had struck him as a remarkable truth, but in the dusky, padded comfort of their surroundings, it seemed too irrelevant to mention. Instead he told her about being stacked up over La Guardia.

When they were finishing their drinks, Cassie suggested they have dinner in the almost empty taproom. "I'm not very hungry." She ordered blinis, which seemed unsubstantial considering the condition she was presumably in. Halfway through the meal, she said suddenly, "I thought that doing a thing on the early settlers would somehow make us more like them. But I'm beginning to think a lot of them were just plain mean and ignorant. Did you know anybody could go and take a child out of an orphanage and use it for child labor? They didn't even have to sign!" She sounded so horrified that Chester had to work up instant appropriate emotions, or sound as if he had. "And even real servants had no rights at all. They weren't supposed to have *sex*. One poor man got so frantic—I read this myself in the early records—it said, 'He buggered a cow.'"

Chester choked on a piece of steak.

"And you wouldn't believe what the town authorities did. They hanged him—and the cow too."

If it wasn't quite table talk *à deux* as he'd been conditioned to it, at least it was lively. And he liked hearing Cassie's voice take on feeling—sorrow, indignation, even a childish hurt over the past's not living up to its reputation. "It made me realize we aren't as bad now as most people think. If I'd been a woman then, in my middle-class income bracket, I probably wouldn't have been able to read or write. Imagine! Just carrying water and hoeing potatoes and baking in an oven that took three hours to heat."

Chester tried to picture Cassie as a middle-class illiterate carrying water—on her head?—and the idea was so ludicrous he burst out laughing. Cassie giggled, then collapsed with laughter. Both of them were hilarious out of all proportion. Whenever it died down, one or the other fed it with silly trifles that struck them as wildly funny.

"What a jolly little party."

Chester, looking at Alicia, felt a healthy male response in his nether region. She was wearing a clinging dress in a cool underwater color that set off her extraordinary skin and bronze hair. He noticed instantly that she had a new hairdo. And he sensed, just as instantly, that she wasn't pleased to have found him enjoying Cassie so uproariously.

She sat down and took a sip of Chester's wine, lifting it in salute, smiling at him full strength. She was on her way through to the dining room to join—she said—"friends from town." Chester understood this could only mean New York. Somehow Alicia could make even New York sound tucked in her pocket. "It's good of you to give this child a night out. She's been running her legs off. And Oliver's felt so guilty about neglecting her. He's at one of those screamie-meemie rehearsals, so I'm having a night off myself—till eleven. He always comes by afterwards to unwind."

Cassie smiled steadily, but Chester was as aware of her tensing as if he held her in his arms: "I've been trying to persuade Cassie to go off on a holiday right after the Festival and meet me in Europe. I have to go over on business." Even he was startled to hear what he'd said. Alicia was so taken aback she couldn't reload at once.

Cassie's hand under the table slid into Chester's, not squeezing amorously, just establishing contact with the rescue party. "I'm tempted," she said demurely. "If Daddy gets back by then, I ought to be able to leave."

"You look so tired," Alicia said. "Doesn't she, Chet? Do see that she gets some rest. And you must come have dinner with me one night this week."

This last was directed too pointedly to Chester. He said he had to catch up on a lot of work at the office and wouldn't have time. But when Alicia looked hurt, he felt caddish. Wood had said, "The funny thing is, nobody can really stay mad at her. Because she can't stand having somebody not adore her—she suffers the tortures of the damned, literally. An ego like the biggest aspidistra, and one rough word can wilt it. So you end up wanting to comfort her no matter what she's done."

Chester felt this strange reversal now. Groping about for the equivalent of a Band-Aid, he said, "Trumbine is still raving about your lyrics."

He had honestly forgotten for the moment she was Trumbine's mother-in-law.

Alicia hadn't; she looked downright sour. "It's a wonder I've been able to do any songs at all. The workmen swarm all over the place from dawn on, pounding and screeching. I'll be so relieved when this hoopla is over. Glorifying the settlers as if they'd been a new breed of gods." Cassie, who a half hour before had been expounding to Chester on the warts, was bristling as Alicia went on: "They were really quite a crude lot—except of course for aristocrats."

"What a snobby Victorian word," Cassie said. "It's so dated."

Alicia was just getting up; unexpectedly, she laughed. "You must take up knitting—when I go to the guillotine."

As soon as she'd gone, Cassie said, "I got so mad I came near asking her, 'How are your new teeth biting?'"

Chester was interested to hear about the new teeth. But he couldn't help wondering, silently. From what he'd seen of Alicia, she was still capable of devouring raw meat. Had he jumped to the wrong conclusion the night he saw the second car behind Alicia's? Maybe a workman had left it there. . . .

". . . so that's what he had to use your check for," Cassie was saying.

Chester, returning to the conversation, was adrift. Oliver had used the check to buy Alicia new *teeth?*

"Because he couldn't go to see her in old clothes and a rusty old jalopy."

Chester couldn't say what he was thinking, so he didn't say anything.

"It's childish and stupid, but that's the phase he's going through. I wish I could figure why I still love him. You know what I wish sometimes now?—that you could yank love out like a tooth."

When Chester went to bed that night, the rehearsal in the music tent was still going on. Even a quarter of a mile away, the noise kept him awake and made him even madder at Yates. His incipient ulcers weren't sleep-inducing anyway. Emotional frustration always played hob with them.

When he went down for breakfast, Mrs. Gifford told him she'd had a fascinating dream: "I dreamed I was freshly made coffee, and when I was poured I could feel myself curving to fit the cup. Such an amazing experience—the pure feeling of matter forming the simple rightness of thought."

This was such a far stretch from his own tangled dreams Chester almost envied her.

He had a tennis date with Cassie at eleven, and he half

thought of calling it off. She'd talk about Yates again. He felt sullen and middle-aged.

Cassie arrived in shorts, looking freshly laundered and glowing. And with a large basket. For one wild moment, he thought she'd brought him a puppy.

"You talked about going on a picnic sometime," she said. "And it's such a heavenly day I made us a little cold lunch."

In a burst of elation, Chester beat her two sets. And Cassie said his backhand had improved fabulously. He hadn't played for over a month, so he was surprised but gratified to hear this.

They went down to the brook for their picnic. When Chester saw the width of his stream—at least nine feet across and beautifully clear and flowing—he felt rather like Balboa. Cassie took off her sneakers to wade. "Come on—try it. The water's delicious between your toes."

Chester, with some trepidation, rolled up his pants and plunged in to his ankles. The water *was* delicious between the toes. Oddly, it seemed to quiet his stomach too. He ate two hefty roast beef sandwiches and two helpings of potato salad. There were a few ants; Cassie disposed of hers by knocking them off her plate and giving them a toss. Chester stepped on his, but not meanly.

Even the ghost of Yates didn't intrude. Chester thought once, Yates is the kind of guy who can't stand ants. After that, he didn't even mind an occasional ant crawling up inside his pants. He just squashed it against his leg without fuss.

Cassie said they could go over later and inspect the Festival grounds. "You didn't really see the exhibits yesterday."

Chester said if it was all right with her, he'd rather stay here. He yawned, not from boredom, but from sheer animal contentment.

"Take a nap," Cassie said. "I will too. I didn't sleep much last night."

Chester had never napped with a woman unless he'd made love to her first. He rolled over on his side a bit self-consciously, but even the ants didn't keep him awake for long.

Cassie was still sleeping when he woke up. She was curled in a ball, with her knees tucked up, and each time she let out a breath, quietly, sweetly, Chester felt his own lungs constrict with tenderness. Or at least something in the region of the lungs.

Chapter
Sixteen

On Monday, the thermometer outside the drug store was glued at 98°, and the overworked air conditioner in Mrs. Tyndale's shop thrashed and groaned like an animal in pain. Tempers were snappish. Mrs. Tyndale's veneer of shopkeeper tact was peeling off fast. The job of rounding up "genuine craftsmen" to demonstrate their trade was, she announced to a half-dozen listeners, driving her up the wall: "The only real cabinetmaker in fifty miles smashed his thumb yesterday in a car door. And the blacksmith has a full-time job as a welder and he says if it stays this hot, forget it. I could kill Prue Washburn for dreaming this up in the first place."

Mrs. Loomite was wearing the bouffant wig she'd bought especially for opening night; she was trying it out on the ladies, and Mrs. Tyndale rallied enough to say, "It does something for you," without saying what. Lo Bender rent even this temporary harmony when he gave his opinion: "You look as if you'd got your head stuck in a tea cozy."

Mrs. Loomite was so upset she retired to the lavatory to stare at herself and sniffle.

Lo was being attacked in turn. Miss Maulridge said his costumes for the Liberty Maidens were indecent. Either the cleavage would be filled in with ruffles (Miss Maulridge didn't actually say "cleavage"—she said "exposed chest section") or she would resign. Nobody could quite remember what her title was, or what committee she'd resign from, but most of the ladies managed an "Oh, no, you mustn't. . . . We couldn't do without you."

Lo snapped, "Better her than me. Just brand the Liberty Maidens H for 'whore.' "

"Apart from your spelling," Charles Wood said, "let's not go to extremes."

Lo tossed his head. "Where else is there to go? If there's anything I loathe, it's moderation."

Miss Maulridge said that was the trouble with young people today.

"The trouble with your generation," Lo said, "Is that the only four-letter word you know is 'funk.' "

Having shared a brief and happy bond in epitaph-hunting, once the cemetery number was dropped from the Festival he and Miss Maulridge had reverted to being natural enemies. Wood, as a kindly gesture to ease Miss Maulridge's disappointment, had arranged with a manufacturer to turn out plastic epitaphs of a size and shape suitable for bookmarks, to be sold as souvenirs. Lo had just heard about it that afternoon, and it infuriated him even more than having the number dropped.

As he pointed out to Cassie a half hour later, at Prue Washburn's, the tombstone idea was all his. "Oliver deliberately cut out that number because it was my idea, my costumes. He has to run the whole show. He's power-mad. Just because he's sleeping with Alicia doesn't mean—" Lo broke off and put his hand to his mouth like a child.

Cassie laughed. "Oh, you and your fairy tales."

"I didn't expect you to believe me anyway," Lo said, too quickly.

"I didn't. When Daddy got his new teeth, he was so miserable he slept in the guest room for weeks."

Prue came in through the side door waving a trowel. "I didn't hear you come in. I was out in the garden exhorting the iris to hold on for another ten days. The attic's a mess. Alicia came when I was going through the trunks, and I meant to go back up this morning, but it's too hot."

"You go on up," Cassie said to Lo. "I'll join you in a minute. I want to read Prue some bits from Daddy's letter."

Lo was sunny again with expectancy, and inclined to be helpful. He stopped by a pile of quilts stacked in plastic bags at the foot of the stairs. "Would you like me to take these up?" Prue said Lord, no, they were going over to the Crafts tent for exhibit.

Having offered his good deed for the day, or the week, Lo bounded up the two steep flights, and the musty heat struck him full force at the top. It didn't faze him; half-crouched under the slanting eaves, he crooned to himself, or to the invisible audience that always attended his adventures, "My very first attic." He knelt by a trunk with a rounded top and rusty brass hinges: "Ball gowns of twittering silk," he murmured, already preparing his account. "Dueling pistols. And a diary that should be preserved under glass."

He lifted the creaky lid and explored a first layer: old gas and electric bills, a moth-eaten mauve wool sweater, a high-school senior classbook. . . . . Below, ski pants, blankets, elbow-length white kid gloves . . . It wasn't until the bottom layer that he came on something more worthy of his imagination, a wooden inlaid box with a key conveniently in the lock. Inside was a packet of letters tied with a brown shoelace. To Lo, it seemed the most natural thing in the world to settle back on his haunches and have a good read. . . .

"I bought a smashing dress this noon," Cassie said. She and Prue were having iced tea. "Chet wants me to be his hostess at the dinner he's giving at the Inn before the opening." Prue leaned forward eagerly. "Don't get that matchmaker glint in your eye. He's still crazy about his ex-wife, so we console each other. Oh, I forgot to tell you Lo's latest. He says Oliver and Alicia are having a passionate affair."

"He had no business to tell you that." Prue's tone was so

fierce Cassie's eyes widened. Prue tried to cover her blunder, too late. "I mean it's just so ridiculous."

Cassie said in a low voice, "Yes. But it's true, isn't it?"

Prue was unhappily silent.

"Don't take it so hard. Being unfaithful doesn't matter that much any more. We don't really give it a thought."

"Don't you? Then I'm sorry for you. If you can't feel something that basic, you're not much of a woman."

Cassie managed a half grin. "All right, so it hurts like hell. And the thing that hurts most is that he didn't tell me himself."

"That doesn't help much," Prue murmured, more to herself.

"Maybe I knew it underneath, but I didn't want to. I grabbed at that false-teeth story of yours. You ought to be ashamed of yourself."

"I'm not. It was the most convincing lie I could think of in a hurry. And I wanted to spare you. Because I know what it's like. It happened to me when I was your age, and I wanted to die. My closest friend—"

"God knows Alicia isn't my closest friend. And I have no intention of dying. But it's settled one thing in my mind. I don't want Oliver's—" She stopped and looked startled. "Alicia was your closest friend. She did that to *you*?" Prue made a sad little face. "Did she marry the man?"

"She wouldn't have him. He went away for a while and met somebody else." Prue raised her head suddenly like an animal sniffing danger. "Did I leave the key in that box of—I'll just run up and make sure Lo found the right trunks."

"You sit right here. I'll go. I should have gone up with him in the first place. He's been ominously quiet. But maybe he just has heat prostration."

"I hope so," Prue said, rather grimly.

Trumbine arrived in Chester's office looking his usual imperturbably cool self. He had just flown in from Washington, and he said the heat was worse there. "It's not the humidity—it's what's cooking. They cook up a new batch of rumors every five minutes, and everybody runs around tasting and dishing out samples." He had got his erring senator-client off the hook, partly by cooking up counterrumors: "Where there's fire, there's smoke. And if you get enough smoke, you confuse the issue till people forget it."

He apologized for having to delegate so much of the Festival publicity to underlings. "But I kept my finger on the whole ball of wax. We planted some good stories. Did you notice we never tag you as a philanthropist? That's dead as a stuffed moose now. Our releases always plug you as a civic-minded young millionaire industrialist."

Chester was more pleased by the "young" than he'd have admitted.

Although Trumbine looked cool enough, he couldn't seem to sit still for long. He got up and paced around the office while he talked. Once he paused before the line drawing of "CONVERSION OF SODIUM CELLUWORT" and studied the inscription. " '—on Its Way to an Acid Coagulate Bath,' " he read aloud. "I know how it feels." He said he'd had to tell Allie about her mother being involved in the Festival. "She knew I was hiding something. She gave me a bad time at first, but she's calming down. She has some new project going and it seems to have done her good. She even offered to come back for the opening, but I'm trying to talk her out of it. She's not *that* calm. I'll go down there right afterward but I won't stay —I'll try to bring her back with me—because we're lining up a series of speeches for you starting in July."

Chester said he was tied up in July. "I have to be in Sweden." He gave the newly acquired textile firm as a rather lame excuse.

Trumbine pulled up a chair on the opposite side of the desk and protested at length. "What's one piddling plant compared to your political future? You've moved enough vertically, businesswise. Now we have to move you horizontally." (He marched his fingers across the desk to dramatize this.) "We'll broaden your base so you're known all over the country. You'd better hold off on Sweden."

Chester said that was impossible. Trumbine said surely Sweden needn't take more than a day or two. Chester was vague. He said he couldn't really tell yet. How long did it take to recover from an abortion? He remembered hearing about a girl who'd gone swimming the next day. But emotionally . . . if anything could throw Cassie off balance, this was it. She ought to stay over there a while. He could rent a car and drive her around. She'd be interested in the cooperatives in Sweden. He'd like to have a look at the workers' housing himself. Then go over to Greece—Cassie'd get steamed up over the poverty there. Do her good to get furious about military dictators. . . .

". . . want a picture of you with the Illegitimate Mamas," Trumbine was saying. The peculiar *sequitur* startled Chester so much his eyes nearly crossed. He had completely forgotten about the folk-singer group. Would Cassie be sensitive about the name?

Trumbine was talking about press coverage for the opening, but Chester went on worrying about Cassie. When she'd said she wanted to stay in the taproom to eat, instead of eating in the main dining room, was that because she wanted to avoid seeing people? In a town like Bevington, the gossip must have hopped like fleas. Cassie had never mentioned it to him. She'd cheered him up every night, on the phone, and kept her own troubles to herself. He should have realized that being pregnant made her more vulnerable.

He cut into Trumbine's recital: "I have to make a call." He buzzed the intercom and told his secretary, "Will you get me Miss Murdoch at the *Bugle*?" He wouldn't be able to say much in front of Trumbine, but he had to hear her voice.

Trumbine said, "She's the one who got us to switch the dinner from the country club. She said they accept Jewish members 'if they don't look Jewish.' We don't want to get caught on that, not when you're going into politics."

"I wouldn't want it anyway." Tom Devin had offered to put him up for membership at the club and he'd accepted without thinking. "I'll resign."

"I already resigned for you," Trumbine said. "I got two feature stories out of it: sponsor of Liberty Pole Festival fights discrimination as anti-liberty. It will help with the Jewish vote. But once you're elected, you'll have to soft-pedal the pro-Jewish, pro-Israel bit, and bow to the East at sunset. And not kick over any pork barrels. Or tell any Southern Mister Bigot what's wrong with his domain. A Freshman congressman has to go slow for the first few years or he gets slapped down. They can keep you off every committee that counts."

"There's no time to go slow. I'm damned if I want to go down there and sit on my ass making discreet noises when the country's in trouble. If that's the way they play, I can do more where I am." Would Cassie be disappointed if he didn't run for Congress?

"After what I've been through this month," Trumbine said moodily, "I am not one to tout our noble lawmakers. But it's more prestige. And the Festival gives you an edge. 'Patriotic citizen'—being a millionaire doesn't hurt either—'backing the solid pioneer virtues.' "

"They weren't all that solid," Chester sounded rather indignant. "They raided the orphanages for child labor and treated the kids like slaves."

"Better not go into that," Trumbine said. "The pioneer spirit is sacrosanct. Wait! It might be a fresh twist at that. Idea of, 'Don't tell *me* this country is going to hell. Consider our children—the way we treated our children then and now.' No —that could turn into a stink bomb. The rightists would yell 'Look at our kids now. Bunch of anarchists and criminals.' "

The intercom buzzed; Miss Barsted reported that Miss Murdoch was not at the *Bugle*. "They said she's at a Miss Prudence Washburn's. Would you like me to try her there?"

Chester said yes.

Lo was so engrossed in his letter-reading he didn't hear Cassie until she was halfway across the attic room. "Wait till you see these! You won't believe it! Alicia nearly wrecked his life and Prue shouldn't forgive him after the way he hurt her, but he can't do without her friendship—he values it more than anything in the world."

Cassie stood there frozen, staring at the familiar scrawl on an envelope, handwriting as familiar as the letter in her purse. Lo babbled on: "The earliest ones are the best. I've put those on one side."

Cassie said in a queer, throttled voice, "You can't—you had no right. Put those back."

"But you said I could read any love letters I found in Prue's attic." He sat back, pouting, jiggling on his buttocks.

"I didn't mean it."

"You promised. I know—because you didn't think Prue had any love letters. Duckie, were you ever wrong. The first ones are hot. Some guy who signs himself W something—his handwriting is terrible."

"Give me those."

Lo pushed the letters behind him. "I won't. I'm only half finished. It's the only fun I've had."

When Cassie went around to grab from the other side, Lo defended his find simply by sitting on the lot. "I won't tell anybody, honestly, ducks. Just let me read the last ones. I want to find out how it ends."

Cassie put a hand in his thick hair and yanked. Lo howled. "If you don't give me those, I'll snatch you bald."

The intercom rasped again: "Miss Washburn is on Three."

Trumbine said, "See you later," and went, with gratifying speed.

Chester pushed Button Three and picked up the phone. "Hello, Miss Washburn. . . . What's she doing in the attic on a day like this? . . . I hope the weather is better to us Friday. . . . Yes, I'll hold on. Thanks."

Prue Washburn's voice plinked on pleasantly; Chester was only half listening. Suddenly she let out a high scream: "No! Cassie!"

Chester could hear the receiver crash. And that was all.

He hung on, shouting into the phone, willing someone to come and tell him what had happened.

Chapter
Seventeen

That afternoon's rehearsal in the music tent had been going on for five steamy hours. Oliver could feel the dampness seeping under his armpits, staining his shirt. Smelly. It was one of the small worries flickering at intervals. Alicia was another. He had told her he'd be there by six thirty; now it was almost eight and he still had two vocals and a dance number to go.

The music director was shouting something: "Have to add six bars here to get them off-stage." Oliver held up a hand limply to show he'd heard. His skull was already pounding from the barrage of demands: "Cut twelve bars" . . . "add six" . . . "take out a harp" . . . "put in a flute" . . . "the last note's too high" . . . "too low." . . . The lead soprano said there had to be more rubato in the fifth and sixth bars of "Will I Trade My Lover." Too many words—she needed a pause there to breathe. Oliver knew she was right because he'd already argued that point with Alicia.

He should have fought it out with Alicia till he got his way. Often, when he was away from her, he told her off in long one-sided conversations when all she did was listen: When I'm trying to get a song done, don't make everything so personal and emotional. I can't think about you and Hummel's theory of the dominant chord at the same time."

Usually when he worked, he could close out all extraneous matter such as people. Most of his life, in fact, he had heard music far more clearly than he heard what people said. Cassie had understood that. Alicia understood it for herself; once when he'd dropped in she'd been working on a story, and she'd glanced up from the typewriter with a cold annoyance, a look of Who-are-you? He recognized the state she was in because he had spent a good part of his life there. But he resented being the victim. Perhaps, however unconsciously, he resented seeing his own self-centeredness reflected so ruthlessly in Alicia. She demanded total attention and got it. Her brilliance and beauty had dazzled him so much in the first weeks he couldn't have looked away. But now there were times when it affected him like a too-bright light. He wanted to turn it off, to shut his eyes and be in that hazy grayness of withdrawal which, perversely, nourishes creativeness. But Alicia wasn't turn-offable. The only one who could withdraw was herself. If he did it, she accused him of all sorts of slights and thoughtlessness. It was as if she wanted her own life and his too. She wanted him to like whatever she liked, loathe whatever she loathed—people, books, music. She seemed to take it as a personal insult if he didn't.

Oliver had had no sustained periods to brood on all this, but it was there, like the knowledge of a bill collector lurking. And in a sharper, more focused, immediate way, the thought of her anger if he didn't turn up for dinner. Although he couldn't even count on her anger. The week before, he'd had to arrive late and he'd found her in her sheer negligee reading Santayana. She had made him a drink, waited on him with a charming half mockery—"My lord and master"—and read him bits of Santayana: "'It would be so awkward in heaven, after all one had discovered, to have to put on a perfect innocence. . . .'" And she'd laughed and said, "That's one problem I'll never have." At times like that, her unpredictability was enchanting.

The director was shouting at Oliver again: "If we reprise 'Liberty Pole' for the closing, we'll need a new twist on the final chorus."

Oliver gestured O.K. Maybe a few crash chords—to give a feeling of friction, war threatening. Then build the harmonies to come out strong in the last bars. Spirit of the settlers—the do-or-die bit. . . . He seethed with new anger, remembering Cassie's parting shot: "I'm glad you weren't one of the early settlers. We'd never have made it." Typical of that cooky-cutter Girl Guide mentality. She'd never really appreciated his talent. Discouraging him from doing an opera . . . trying to whack him down to her size. . . . The Festival often seemed to him now like a smalltime finger exercise, with Lincoln Center towering ahead. Why should he sweat it out here all night? The changes weren't that important. If the music director thought he knew so damn much, let him do the rewrite himself.

But the thought of anybody else tampering with his, Oliver's, melody, made him as edgy as Cézanne would have felt if some butterfingers had tried to touch up an apple in a still life. It wouldn't take more than a half hour to write the new ending; he could stop by Alicia's to explain, then go to the studio. He should have done an entirely new song for the closing. But Alicia hadn't come up with anything after he'd shelved her "Crazy Sue Denham" lyrics. Some homespun New England Cassandra—went around prophesying wars and draft riots and racial violence, and her neighbors said, "Poor crazy Sue." Alicia had insisted they ought to end on that note of irony. And Oliver had half agreed, more to keep peace, but somehow he'd never been able to do the music for "Crazy Sue." He had been nagged by the thought that Cassie would hate that kind of ending.

Prudence Washburn, standing at the foot of the stairs holding the phone, saw Cassie start down, and then the fall that seemed to happen in a dreadful stopped moment of time. As Prue screamed, she flung herself over, pushing at the pile of quilts.

Cassie landed on them with a soft thud, and lay frighteningly still. Lo rushed down howling, "I killed her. It's my fault she's dead. I wouldn't give her the—"

"Shut up." Prue was taking Cassie's pulse. "She's just stunned. But she fell on her arm and it looks twisted. Tell Chet and then call the doctor."

Lo picked up the phone: "Cassie just fell downstairs. You'd better call back later." He banged the receiver down.

Oliver was so groggy by the time he reached the guest house, around nine, that when Fiera Young came to the door in her Liberty Maiden regalia—laced bodice, bursting-out bosoms, and a Medusa mess of curls—he reared back in fright. "Hi, Ollie, you sure are late. Dinner's already over, but I can make you a sandwutch. I wore my costume over to show Miss Thorne. She's in the bedroom."

As soon as Alicia came out, he knew she was tearing mad. "Prue's gone crazy."

He was relieved if that was all.

"She said you're to go right over. She kept saying, 'He's to come the second he gets there—on the double.' God knows what's on her mind. She wouldn't say. She was incredibly snappish with me. Probably a new lecture on morals."

Oliver collapsed into a chair. "She can go to hell."

Alicia looked him over distastefully. "And I suppose I can too. You arrive hours late—unwashed, unshaved, no tie, not even a jacket."

Oliver mumbled the first thing that came into his head: "You sound like my grandmother."

Alicia's mouth pulled in so tight she even looked like his grandmother—caved in, without her teeth. He hadn't the strength, or the nerve, for open combat. "I just meant she had a thing about neatness."

"A pity you didn't inherit it."

Fiera appeared in the kitchen doorway with a plate clutched against what Miss Maulridge would have called 'the exposed chest section.'

"Mr. Yates won't be dining here, Fiera. You may go."

"But it's only a sandwutch. It's already made." With a defiance befitting a Liberty Maiden, she marched over and put the plate on the end table beside Oliver. "You look beat. How about some beer? Wouldn't that go good with your sandwutch?"

Oliver nodded gratefully.

Alicia put on her Ugh-how-vulgar look and said there was no beer in the house.

"I brought some over from Mr. Chet's. I remember Ollie and Cassie they always liked beer."

"*I* do not." The queen being unamused.

But Fiera was already putting bottle and glass at Oliver's elbow. Then, bravery evaporating before Alicia's glare, she scuttled off. The back door slammed as one last gesture.

Oliver longed to get at the snack, but felt he ought to observe the amenities first: "The reason I was so late, we were having trouble with 'Will I Trade My Lover.' We finally got it set." Tiredness and hunger made him careless. "I had to pare down the lyrics some. The singer couldn't cram all those words into the space."

"And of course you put her feelings above mine."

"It's not a question of feelings." His irritation was getting too scratchy to contain. "It's a question of what's best for the song."

"It's never the music at fault—it's always the lyrics." When Alicia shrilled up like that, the sheer sound of it offended his ear, which was sensitive anyway. He shut his eyes, to express aesthetic pain, reached out blindly for the bottle of beer, and knocked it onto the floor. Beer cascaded over the rug while he fumbled, trying to find where the bottle had rolled to.

"For God's sake, do something. The whole place will reek like a brewery."

Oliver fetched a dish towel and got down on his hands and knees to mop. The towel was soaked long before he'd finished the cleanup operation. "Get me some paper towels," he said absently, still on all fours.

"I will not. I am sick and tired of your ordering me around, telling me how to write, changing my words without so much as a by-your-leave."

"I told you," Oliver shouted, or tried to shout. A man on his hands and knees is at a certain disadvantage in arguing. "The singer has to breathe."

"Why?" Alicia said coldly. "She gargles through her nose anyway."

Oliver scrambled to his feet and almost flung the sopping towel on the table in front of her like a gauntlet, but didn't quite. A few drops of residue beer spattered on Alicia's dress, a pale yellow silk print. "Look what you did, you clumsy idiot." She was so angry the cords in her neck stuck out. "You've ruined my Pucci."

Oliver strode into her bathroom—forbidden territory—and shut the door. When he came out a few minutes later, washed, combed, calmer, even ready to apologize, Alicia was sitting stiff-backed on the sofa, her skirt spread out as if posing for a commercial on stain danger. "It shouldn't leave a mark," he said cheerfully. He took the long-delayed bite of sandwich. "If you put on a spot-remover powder and let it stay on over-night." The last came out thickly, through ham and mustard.

Alicia's nostrils dilated. "I'll never wear it again."

Oliver swallowed a mouthful hurriedly and tried a new tack: "Did your dress for the opening come?"

"It really needn't concern you." She gazed into space. In a remote sort of way, he took in the whittled perfection of her profile. "Because I'm not going with you."

He was so tired that the meaning took a while to reach him, traveling in slow-motion spirals that finally hit him like a blow. He gaped at her stupidly. "But—but it's our show. You were the one who said we ought to be there together."

"That was before I realized you've always favored the music over the lyrics."

"That's not true. You know it. You said the music sparked you. You said that's why you wanted us to work on the opera."

"I've had second thoughts." Alicia poured herself a demi-tasse from a starkly straight-up-and-down Danish pot and dropped in a saccharine crystal. "So has Willy. He's decided Benedict Arnold isn't right for opera. He thinks it will be stronger as a play."

Oliver was too stunned to speak. The towers of Lincoln Center toppled and shattered around him.

"I met the playwright Willy wants me to work with—Malcolm Pugh—he's had several things on Broadway."

"I've heard of him," Oliver said mechanically.

"He's terribly excited by my idea of how to do it. You never were, you know. You weren't really carried away. You kept harping back to the witches."

It was true. He couldn't deny it. But he had been carried away by the idea of Lincoln Center.

"I didn't mean to tell you till after the Festival. If you hadn't been so unpleasant tonight. . . ."

Oliver leaned his head back exhaustedly. "If you'd been through eight solid hours of rehearsal, you'd sound unpleasant too."

Alicia, in one of her dizzying switches, said, "Poor lamb. It must have been horrible. And then I screamed at you too. I'm sorry. You may still sit with Willy and me at the opening if you like."

And catch your bouquets while you hog all the bows. He hated himself for saying yes. But it was important to meet Latham. And when Alicia was in a good mood, ask her to let him have an option on her witch story. Get her to put it in writing. That witches' quartet—do it in gibberish language— no real words—so the music would dominate. Witches chanting, howling incantations—storm, lightning. . . . Hadn't somebody done that storm bit with witches? No matter—he'd do it better. The storm music was rising so powerfully in his head that the first fierce roar of actual thunder seemed part of his own creation.

Alicia rushed to the window that took up the whole back wall. "Come look! It's spectacular." She was so incandescent with excitement, with the hurtled lightning as backdrop, that she looked to Oliver like a demon. The old childhood terrors yanked at him. He gripped the arms of his chair.

"You're afraid!" Alicia's peals of laughter mingled with the other hideous—to him—sound effects: crash, boom, rip, jag. He would no more have gone to the window than he'd have jumped through hoops of flame. He did think fleetingly of dashing out to roll up the windows of his new car, but dismissed the idea as madness. "Storms get on my nerves," he muttered.

"Why, you timid old maid." She flung this over her shoulder gaily. *C-r-r-a-c-k,* a new burst of thunder, with what seemed to Oliver closer stabs of lightning seeking their target. For the first time in weeks, he thought longingly of Cassie. As soon as the storm was over, he might go by her house and take her to the studio while he worked. He felt a great sense of relief then, as if he were already back in the safe, round circle of her love. He was so strengthened by the prospect that he went to the upright piano and crashed some trial chords to drown out the heavens and make his own disharmonies, for the new ending of "Liberty Pole."

"Stop that!" Alicia screamed. "I had that horrible noise dinning at me all afternoon from the music tent. Can't you even let me enjoy my beautiful storm in peace?"

Oliver said he had to finish the changes tonight. He sounded almost cocky, standing up to the storm and Alicia.

"Then go somewhere else to make your bloody racket."

The heat storm was over as soon as one of Alicia's tantrums. By the time Oliver went outside, the moon was already pushing through the blackness. Alicia turned off a porch light that revealed tiny crisscross lines under her eyes. "You *do* see it's best on the Benedict Arnold thing, don't you?"

Oliver said glumly he supposed so.

"I've just had a brain wave!" She clasped her hands, radiating delight. "You must do the incidental music for the play! We'll talk to Willy at the opening. I can hardly wait to see you in your new dinner jacket. Won't it be exciting?"

Oliver made suitable noises. But driving into Bevington, he thought of how shocked Cassie would be to hear Alicia had reneged on the opera. The thought of Cassie's warm indignation rather made up for the discomfort of sitting on a damp car seat.

He was more annoyed than disappointed to find the Murdoch house dark. He remembered, belatedly, that Prue Washburn had wanted him to come over. But if Cassie were there, she'd have called him herself. Skip that. Go to his room and get some dry pants, and something to cover the car seat. Maybe look in at the Stick Shift afterward on his way back to the studio . . . Cassie might be there with Lo.

He had barely got into his room at the staff dormitory when Lo burst in through the bathroom. "*Where* have you *been?* Didn't you get Prue's messages?"

Prue's upstairs guest room had sprigged wallpaper, white with blue, and a canopy sprigged to match over the four-poster bed. Cassie seemed part of the color scheme, lying there: white plaster cast supported down one side on a pillow, gauze swathing her head, and her eyes enormously blue. But her voice was reassuringly unsprigged: ". . . fractured my tennis wrist, damn it. You'll have to play me with one arm tied behind your back."

Chester, who had arrived five minutes before with a motorcycle escort laid on by Trumbine (courtesy of the Governor), was in a worse state of nerves than the patient. "I'm sorry you had such a scare," Cassie said. "But I'm really in much better shape than I look. I can take off this headgear by Friday. It's only a little cut. And the black-and-blue places won't show; they're mostly on my fanny. So if you don't mind a date with the walking wounded, I'm pretty sure I can manage opening night."

"You'll manage it if we have to carry you there on a stretcher," Chester said. He took her one good hand, conveniently the one on his side of the bed, and held it tightly. It felt firm and warm in his own, but tears slid down her cheeks. "Just invalid tears," she said cheerfully. "They don't mean a thing."

He felt a painful need to give her whatever she wanted no matter what it might cost him. "Does Yates know? Would you like me to find him?"

Cassie's bandaged head rolled back and forth on the pillow. "Prue tried to get hold of him earlier. I guess I asked her when I first came to. But now I've had time to think—I mean think straighter. And I'm glad it turned out this way. He and Alicia are—you knew, didn't you?"

Chester's silence answered her. "I just learned this afternoon. And I think I let myself fall because subconsciously I thought that was the easy way out. I'd have a miscarriage and that would get rid of all my problems."

"Anybody could fall down those crazy stairs," Chester said. "It doesn't need a push from your subconscious."

"But I think there was a second when I could have grabbed for the wall and caught myself. And I didn't. If it hadn't been for those quilts at the bottom. . . ."

"You might have broken your neck," he said roughly.

"I might never have been able to have another baby. Doctor Avery says I'm fine, and he should know. He's been my doctor since my first measle vaccination—he says I bit him. I told him about going to Sweden for the abortion, but he won't tell. I don't want Oliver to know. He'd blame himself and that wouldn't be fair. Because everybody has to do their own thing, and I tried to make him do mine instead. He never wanted a child."

It takes two to tango, Chester thought bitterly. He'd been afraid to smoke, in a daintily blue-sprigged bedroom without ashtrays, but now he lit a cigarette anyway and flicked ashes into a hand-painted pin tray.

"If I'd told Oliver the truth right along and he'd had time to think it over, he'd have married me even if he hated it. He's that way—he really is. But what would be the point? I don't think a slippery little foetus is anywhere near as important as people who are alive."

Chester must have looked startled, because she said, "I'm talking tough to myself because it's good therapy. And the funny thing is, I feel much more peaceful now than I did before this happened. Because there is no easy way out, is there? If I'd had the miscarriage, it wouldn't really have solved anything. I'd have been evading my responsibility and then I'd have felt guilty. I got myself into this and I have to get myself out of it in an honorable way."

222

For her to consider an abortion the only honorable way out moved him deeply. "You could marry me."

Cassie's eyes opened so wide the lashes stuck out like petals. "That's the dearest, most generous thing a friend ever offered to do for me."

"I'm not doing it to be noble. I like you."

"But what if you fell in love with somebody and wanted to get married before we had time to get a divorce?"

"There's no rush." Chester sat back in the antique lyre chair he'd been perching on; it creaked under his weight.

"But you can't tell when that sort of thing will hit you," she said. The bandages made everything sound weightier, more like a deathbed statement. "I was sort of engaged to a Harvard boy and we were going to Asia or some place, in the Peace Corps, and then I met Oliver. I'll never feel about anybody the way I've felt about Oliver."

Chester said carefully, "You shouldn't. With a different person, you have a different feeling. I'll never feel about anybody exactly the way I felt about my ex-wife, but the new thing might be even better."

"Do you really think so?" She appeared to chew on this and arrive at some pleasant conclusion, because she batted her lashes and smiled. Then she frowned. "But it wouldn't be if you married me just to have the baby. It's another of those easy-way-out things."

"It would be better than falling downstairs."

"Of course," she said warmly. "And I'm getting pretty fed up with boys my own age—they're so hell-bent on being unhappy. If something made you unhappy, you'd go out and *do* something about it—I mean, you wouldn't just rant on and blame everybody else."

Chester felt maturity sit lightly, becomingly, on his wide shoulders. There were certainly advantages to being over thirty.

"But what if the baby turned out to pound the piano day and night like his father? Would you like that?"

Chester, taken off guard, made an involuntary grimace.

223

"You see. It only works in soap operas."

Prue Washburn came in carrying a bowl of soup on a tray. "Oliver's downstairs," she said in a flat tone. "He insists he has to see you."

Cassie looked at Chester anxiously; it seemed to him pleadingly.

"I'm just leaving," he leaped up to stand on his own two feet like a martyr. Cassie raised her good arm and motioned him down. She said to Prue, "Tell Oliver I'm too sleepy from the codeine. Tell him I'm fine—and I'll be at the Festival yelling for encores."

Prue's bedside manner became a smidgin less brusque. "I'll go down and tell him right now. But somebody's got to stay here and feed you. I don't want you throwing this soup around left-handed on my best bedspread."

"Chet will feed me," Cassie said, "Hand up another bowl for him, and maybe some cheese and crackers. If you have any more of that wine cheddar in the brown crock. . . ."

Some time later she said, "Even if people don't go out and help each other plow any more, I think they're more concerned about other people than they used to be. Don't you think so?"

Chester said he did. He said it without thinking, simply to please her.

"Even businessmen," she said sleepily. "Look at the difference. They care more."

To his surprise, he realized she might have a point.

"The way the world is now," she said, "I don't think I could live with anybody who didn't want to help at least a little. Is that the way you feel too?"

This time, he didn't say yes to please her. He said it with sudden belief.

Oliver was wandering around the old cemetery. Although he hadn't gone there for morbid reasons, in his state of misery it seemed a suitable place to feel awful in. He was burning with a feverish need to do something to please Cassie, and she had asked him once to look at some old tombstone for the epitaph number. He knew her well enough to know she would never have refused to see him simply because she was sleepy. And although Prue Washburn had decently refrained from saying so, Oliver knew Chester Humboldt must be there because his car was out in front of the house. Faced with this threat of competition, Oliver was all the more determined to win Cassie back by glorious music. If she wanted an epitaph number, she would have an epitaph number—and only he, Oliver, could give it to her.

The moon was full enough by now to let him read inscriptions on some of the old tombstones, but he found them singularly lacking in material for a masterpiece. *Here lies buried the body of Thomas Klots.* . . . He thought irritably, What else did they think would be buried there—his money? The thought flitted through his mind that when he died, he'd leave instructions to have a few manuscript pages of his music buried with his ashes. The question of which composition he'd want to be buried with occupied him briefly. It was hard to tell, this early on; offhand he couldn't settle on any one piece.

He bent down to peer at another tombstone: *To the memory of Abigail Weatherby—Departed this life at the age of 9 weeks, 5 days.*

If Cassie had really been pregnant, instead of that false alarm, they'd have been married by now. . . . It was all Alicia's fault, holding out the opera as bait. I wanted to marry Cassie. . . . *But you wanted other things first.* When he barked his shin on a tombstone, after the first agonized yelp he took the pain stoically, as a manifestation of spiritual punishment. But he walked more warily then, trying to stay in bright moonlight and avoid the shadows thrown by cypress trees, shadows in which more tombstones lurked, waiting to trip him up. Why all the cypress trees? Did they grow better in cemeteries? Or were they considered a symbol of sorrow— gaunt, no reaching-out branches . . . ? Maybe a song in that

—I planted a cypress over you, and sat in the chill dark shade.
. . . Even in his grieving mood, this idea struck him as crap.
Too many sibilants anyway.

There was a large tombstone ahead, and he went toward it
hopefully to investigate what looked to be a carving above a
raised inscription. It turned out to be a skull and crossbones
leering over *Death Comes to All.* He beat a shuddering re-
treat. What if Cassie died? People didn't die of a fractured
wrist. She'd be fine in no time. She had to be. It was unthink-
able for her to be anything else. She belonged to him. She
loved him. She couldn't have stopped loving him. . . . Had
she found out about him and Alicia? He'd asked Lo and Lo
had said no, adding virtuously, "Cassie thought it was another
of my wild stories, so I let her think that."

Oliver couldn't help grinning as he remembered this. Like
the boy crying "Wolf." And since Oliver was the wolf in this
version, he was relieved Cassie hadn't believed a word.
Maybe he'd tell her himself after they were married. But first,
he'd better make up to her for all the weeks of neglect. . . .
Dedicate the new song to her. Maybe do two new songs—one
on the spirit of the settlers—she'd kept harping on that. . . .
But first the epitaphs. Where the hell was the Revolutionary
burial section she'd talked about? Young soldier died in the
Revolution—that's what she'd said. He went stumbling on,
searching. To strengthen his determination, he talked to himself out loud. "If she saw it, it's here. And if it's here, you'll
find it." He went on exhorting himself loudly as he walked
through an open gate that seemed to lead to a separate
section. Iron fence all around it. . . . "A guy could get im-
paled on those points," he said chattily, "Watch where you're
going, man." The echo of his voice seemed to bounce all
around him. But then a new echo came up from the ground.
And it wasn't saying what he'd said. It said, "Who's got the—
hey, what was that?"

He had never believed especially in ghosts, but since the
sound came from directly under him, there seemed no other
rational explanation; spirits of the dead conversing. He edged

to one side and was heading back for the gate at a pounding run when the earth gave way under him. He was catapulted through space till he landed feet first on a solid something. Flickering lights—small indistinct faces—dwarf spirits? he thought dazedly. And that odd smell, like. . . .

"Gee, it's Mr. Yates."

Oliver knew *that* spirit voice; it belonged to a student in his Harmony class. "Phillipson!" he said. "What are you doing in a tomb?"

"Gee, Mr. Yates," Phillipson said, "we were just smoking pot. We weren't desecrating or anything."

"You broke into a *tomb* to smoke pot?"

"We didn't break in, honest, Mr. Yates. There was a sort of a caved-in place, and when we were up here a while ago one of the guys found it. The watchman comes around every night, so we couldn't just sit up there in the open. This is more like a club."

As Oliver's eyes adjusted to the spotty candlelight, he saw that the place was really quite cozy, in a dank sort of way: a large vault, evidently a family vault because there were several coffins, currently serving as benches. There were also blankets, in the colors of Talladay School, blue and gold.

"Even in June it gets cold down here," Phillipson explained. "I sneaked the blankets out in my laundry bag. We meant to take them back before school was over, but we forgot."

As one of the shapes shifted position, Oliver caught sight of a new object in the center—a statue about four feet high, a small naked figure, a boy, in bronze greenish with age.

"That's part of our club initiation," a voice said. "We have to sort of salute him as the God of Pleasure. Then we squat around him in a circle before we get out the pot."

Oliver was trying to think where he'd seen. . . . In old Mrs. Troxell's garden!—Cassie had taken him there to tea.

"You won't squeal on us for smoking pot, will you, Mr. Yates?" Phillipson said.

Oliver hesitated. He had smoked marijuana himself a few times, although with no great enthusiasm. But he had never

227

broken into a family vault and sat on a coffin to do it. This seemed to him questionable behavior.

"Because Dr. Talladay wouldn't allow me back in school if you told."

Phillipson had been the most talented student in the Harmony class; Oliver was torn.

"And the other guys might get kicked out of Bevington Junior High. It's supposed to be illegal or something."

"Smoking pot is a stupid, dangerous habit," Oliver said in his most professorial voice. "And it can lead to much worse. Hashish, heroin—"

A new voice piped from the shadows, "There was an article in the New York *Times* last week said pot isn't harmful and it's not habit-forming neither—either."

"I won't report you this time," Oliver said. "If you give me your word of honor not to come here again."

This brought on a glib spate of "I promise." Oliver made a mental note to tell the night watchman to cement the place over.

"And you'll return that statue you stole—"

A voice cut in, "We just borrowed it."

"You take it back to Mrs. Troxell's garden—tonight."

"If we can't use this place as a clubhouse, we don't need the dumb old statue anyway."

Somehow this remark chilled Oliver far more than the marijuana. "It's bad enough to steal, but when you pick on helpless old ladies. . . ."

"That old dame has so much junk in her yard she'd never miss it."

Oliver remembered then what Cassie had told him ". . . bought it in Florence on their honeymoon sixty-six years ago. . . ." But what did sentimental value mean to these cold-war babies? "If it's not back there tomorrow, I'll report you to the police." Shocked murmurs. "Now clear up this mess and let's get out of here."

There was a bustle of activity. One club member bundled empty Coke bottles tidily into a blanket; another swept marijuana ashes off the stone floor with his handkerchief. Oliver and several of the other boys tackled the statue; getting it out presented a real problem. As one helper said complainingly, "It was much easier to get it down here than it is to lift it up." Eventually Oliver had to go topside and lie on his stomach on solider ground, to hoist the thing up. The last boy out smoothed the dirt back carefully.

"Who takes the pot?" somebody said. "We got seven left."

"Give it to Mr. Yates." That was Phillipson being the reformer. Oliver had the unworthy thought Phillipson would enjoy seeing a teacher get caught with the goods. He reminded himself to drop it in a trash can tonight. He wouldn't dare put it into the wastebasket in his room. . . .

"Do you come here often, Mr. Yates?" one of the boys asked politely.

Oliver explained what he was looking for, and why.

"You write *songs*," one boy said, "Wow, that's keen."

"You gotta go over to the other side. You came in the wrong entrance," another child said. They led him there, leapfrogging over tombstones, chattery as boys off on a hike with their new scoutmaster. "Here—see—it's a marker says 'Revolutionary War.' And then when you leave, you go out that entrance with the pillars." They waved cordial good-bys as they left him. "Good luck on your song . . . I hope you sell a million and get a gold platter."

It was oddly lonely without them. To keep from foundering again in his own worries, Oliver went doggedly from tombstone to tombstone. Most of them were too crumbly to read. Isolated fragments, parts of names, bits of inscription: *Wounded at battle of. . . . Capt. . . .* of something *Reg.* A shaft of moonlight picked out a stone lying on its side. The name was obliterated, but Oliver could make out the rest:

Died in his 18th year
He froze to death at Valley Forge

Grief pierced him like a small knife. He had a sorrowful sense of all the lives lost to save his world. And now that

world was going down the drain. Polluted by hate and violence. While the eighteen-year-olds still perished. And he had
never lifted a finger for any cause but his own. It was the
inviolate stand of the artist. He and Alicia had congratulated
each other on that total independence, that purity of purpose.
Yet when he thought about her, and himself, he wondered if
theirs was a kind of self-direction that might be finished
forever. He felt shaken, confused. The idea of being a do-
gooder repelled him; wasting precious work time yakking
about social justice when all he wanted to do, all he knew
how to do, was write music. And if he put chunks of propa-
ganda into his songs . . . what had Cassie said about "Will I
Trade My Lover for a Bag of Salt?" "Phony tearjerker."
Maybe she was right. He and Alicia had been standing aside,
spinning their talents, without getting to the heart of—of
what? The last thing he cared about was early settlers, the
whole patriot bit. And if he didn't feel concern, he thought
despairingly, how the hell could he show it in his music?

At some point he had sat down beside the tombstone of the
young soldier to light a cigarette and brood. He had left his
filter holder at Alicia's. Probably on the piano. And he thought
fretfully that sitting on the damp ground wasn't helping either. He'd get bronchitis and croak and cough and have to
suck lozenges all through his opening night.

In shifting his seat trying to find a dryer spot, he became
aware of the tombstone and read the inscription again. This
time if he felt any faint twinge of sorrow, it was instantly lost
in a cool rush of technical thinking. . . . Didn't fit the mood of
the others Lo and Miss Maulridge had dumped on him. The
first ones called for a kind of parody chant. If you mixed them
—Cassie was crazy, it couldn't be done—have to toss out one
lot or the other. This eighteen-year-old kid was more ballad
material. Soul stuff. Young farmer . . . liked planting corn and
wheat and making it grow. . . . Did they grow wheat in
Connecticut? . . . In love with a girl who could make the best
bread in the county, but she had a crazy habit of taking out
crusts to feed the birds even in four-foot snow . . . afraid

those mangy little sparrows would starve . . . she even wrote about the birds in her letters . . . and her soldier went on rereading the letters till his hands got too stiff to turn a page. . . . *Listen to the way I died.* . . .

The music was coming now. Making its own words. Oliver searched absently through his pockets for a scrap of paper. The only thing he could find was a receipt for the down payment on his new car. He spread it out on the tombstone and wrote. The stone was so full of pockmarks his pen kept jabbing holes.

Chapter
Eighteen

By Friday, the day of the opening, the road to the Festival was so jammed with cars that Oliver, coming from a last-minute run-through with the new male singer, had a queer hallucination: instead of people, machines were the patrons, four-wheeled robots spewing, honking, squawking their pleasure or fury. He had gone without sleep, except in half-hour snatches, for so many nights that these hallucinations were often more real than reality. He knew he must have eaten, off and on, all week long, but he couldn't have said what. Waxed containers, liquids, solids, whirling in chain smoke. Even faces were indistinct, although the sounds of singers' voices, of instruments, were clear and sharp as cut crystal. A frenzied music director had rushed in the new male singer, one of the most famous ballad-blues youngsters in the country, for "Listen to the Way I Died." The director had told Oliver, "That tape of yours slugged him. He practically fell on his knees when he heard it. He's doing it for free. His business manager'd kinda like to grab off a white Cadillac for a door prize, but the kid isn't having any."

Oliver liked to think he had done this song for Cassie. But in a way, even he knew he had done it out of that mindless passion that accounts for most acts of birth.

He still hadn't seen Cassie. Prue Washburn had stood guard like a stout little frizzle-tongued dragon. No visitors—doctor's orders. Oliver had left a note, not asking forgiveness but telling Cassie about the new song, because ever since he'd finished it he had been sure this was the one real atonement needed. "Wait'll you hear it," he wrote her. "The best thing in the show . . . it's what you wanted all the time. . . ." He had debated asking her to go to the opening with him, after all, but he was still scheduled to sit with Alicia and Latham, and it seemed safer to leave things that way. Although the cord binding him to Alicia was pretty much frayed, there was still enough tugging to keep him in line, a kind of emotional umbilical. He was a little scared to swing loose from her all that fast. Alicia as an ally was fine. Alicia inimical was more than he could face. Not that she had any reason to be mad at him, even if he added Cassie to the threesome for opening night. But he had learned that reason didn't prevail, with Alicia, except when she happened to need it. She had been in New York for several days; he suspected she was having talks with the playwright on Benedict Arnold. He had thought once or twice again, Have to get a written option on her witch story, for my opera; but he'd had no time, and no real urge, to do it. Songs were the thing for him now, the thing for the mood and the times. Cassie had been right about that. He would tell her; and he'd say he'd pulled out of the Benedict Arnold setup to concentrate on songs. It seemed to him more and more that this was the way it had happened. Maybe have a late date with Cassie tonight. . . . Try on the dinner jacket . . . where had he put those Tiffany cuff links? Alicia would notice right away if he wasn't wearing them. . . .

He was on his way to the parking lot behind the music tent when he remembered that he'd promised Mrs. Loomite to stop in at the Festival that afternoon. Something about his having to see the Blessing of the Animals. . . . Bagpipes, for God's sake. Last thing he needed was bagpipe music. . . . Was a one-string pickin' bow enough accompaniment for "The Leathery Man"? It hadn't worked out with full orchestra, but maybe one or two more instruments . . . a piano, guitar? Too late now for any more changes. As the finality of this surged over him, he was stunned and relieved all at once. Suddenly he couldn't stop yawning. He took the back road to the school, and nearly went to sleep at the wheel.

The Singspiel in the music tent was set for nine that night, but the Festival opened officially at noon. A ribbon had been strung across the main entrance between two liberty poles; Chester, armed with shears, tanned by a barber's sunlamp and looking much fitter than he felt, was to snip on the dot of twelve and say a few suitable words to the assemblage. These included a bosomy lot of Liberty Maidens, little girls costumed in pinafores, Dame Pilgrims (any female volunteer over forty; this arbitrary ruling of Lo's, on costumes, had occasioned some bitter feelings), Al Farwell in Town Crier garb, and several town selectmen in baggy wash-'n'-wear suits. Miss Maulridge, as senior Dame Pilgrim, stood next to Chester. In costume, with her broad hat tied under her chin, shadowing her bony old face, she looked oddly authentic—dignified and serene. And Chester, noticing this, had the last-second, generous impulse to mention her in his little speech: ". . . whose ancestors fought to make this a country where all men, of all creeds, colors and beliefs, might draw a free breath together." As Charles Wood said later, Miss Maulridge looked momentarily taken aback, as if this were the first time she'd realized what mischief her ancestors had had in mind. She recovered and nodded graciously to the head of the local N.A.A.C.P., who was also chauffeur for one of the town selectmen.

Cars were lined up at the entrance, waiting; two teen-age boys, wearing tasseled doublets and fringed, calf-length pants, stood at each side ready to direct incoming traffic as soon as the little ceremony was over. Unfortunately, Chester snipped the ribbon while he was still speaking, and the boys, in their eagerness, waved the first cars in so instantly Chester was almost run down. Further talk was unfeasible, like making a speech to stampeding tanks. But Trumbine said it didn't matter—he had already sent the speech to the papers. "And the reporters got notes on that extemporaneous bit about the old girl's ancestors. That was a nice touch."

The heat had lifted; it was the kind of blue-and-gold day every Festival committee prays for, but Trumbine was looking slightly sun-struck. As soon as he got Chester off alone, he said, "Allie's flying back for the opening tonight. Something tells me there may be fireworks when she sees Mama." He laughed hollowly. "Fireworks for the Fourth of July."

Chester wasn't in the least interested in this news. If Cassie was well enough to come to the opening, he didn't care who else showed up. The doctor had said, "It isn't just a broken wrist. She's had quite a shaking up."

Chester felt rather as if he'd fallen downstairs himself. He was still a bit shaky from Monday night's crisis and since then he had had only unsatisfactory ten-minute visits with Cassie, who seemed to him frighteningly subdued. "She's stuffed full of sedatives," Prue explained, in that portentous tone friends use outside a sickroom door. "And she was bound to have some delayed reaction."

But was it reaction against Chester? He couldn't tell. She smiled a lot whenever he came, but he didn't think she was happy. Prue, ushering him out after the second visit, muttered, "Oliver dedicated a new song to her. His letter churned her up again. I'd like to dedicate *him* to a fire sale." Chester had even more forcible ideas on the removal of Yates, but he couldn't express them aloud.

While he toured the Festival grounds with Charles Wood after the ribbon-cutting and an indigestible hot corn-ball lunch in the Food tent, this worry about Cassie lay so heavily it too felt leaden in his stomach. Wood, seeing Chester slip a TUMS into his mouth, said, "I'll send you one of our *Homely Herbal Remedy* booklets. There's a brew of dandelion tea and baking soda. . . ." Chester shuddered.

The *Homely Herbal Remedy* booklets were selling so fast Wood had already called the printer to rush up a new batch by truck. And Mrs. Tyndale reported that the Bevington Bosom Bottles were another sellout. "The girls are sticking them in the waistband of their pants-suits like flasks." Young males were lining up for spitboxes. More puzzlingly, they were spending four ninety-five apiece for replicas of a long-handled object like an old-fashioned corn-popper, the fire-carrier in which settlers had carried hot coals from a neighbor's. Mrs. Tyndale said, "I can't think what the kids want them for, unless it's arson."

The demonstration of how to make a spark with a tinderbox was so mobbed with male onlookers of all ages, watching openmouthed, that Wood said thoughtfully, "I wonder if we made a mistake, inventing electricity."

The stall directly across from this, the one emblazoned TAKE A TRIP ON SNUFF!, was doing a booming, or kerchooing, business. Chester, standing in the enthusiastic crowd of sneezers, thought wistfully, I never did tell her this idea was fun. He was haunted with a sense of things he'd forgotten to tell Cassie; almost every stall, every exhibit, reminded him of how she'd worked for this, how unselfishly and cheerfully she'd stretched herself between the young and the old, as loving liaison.

He and Wood were back in the section nearest the entrance when the first chartered busses (yellow school busses commandeered for the occasion) began dumping passengers. One was placarded: LOOKING FOR PARADISE? SEE DEVIN'S LOTS. ONLY $300 DOWN. Wood looked at this and swore. "Devin's idea of liberty is to make a fast buck." He beckoned to Al Farwell, bunchy and beaming in Town Crier's garb, who was shouting hoarsely, "Hear ye—hear ye! Vote 'Yes' on the new bond issue. Better education means better citizens. . . . There's a good game of Huzzlecap going in the Games section. All you need is pennies and luck. . . ."

"Al," Wood called, "When you have a minute. . . ." Chester shook himself out of his abstraction to join the parley on Devin's sneak coup. Al agreed it was unpatriotic. "If Devin pulls a trick like that, half the merchants in town are gonna say they oughta get free ads too." He sounded more wistful than censorious. "But what I figure is, Tom Devin did a great job of getting them liberty poles on every business property in this town, and he can stand just so much doin' good before he has to get somethin' out of it."

Chester detached himself to go and have a quiet talk with the driver of the bus, who agreed to remove the placard: "Just so's you square it with Tom." Chester promised, a bit grimly, to take care of Devin. When he rejoined the others, Wood was prescribing a nonherbal remedy—"Unless hops and barley are considered herbs"—for the Town Crier's hoarseness. "Tom's got his good side too," Al croaked. "He's relievin' me at two so's I can rest my voice."

Chester and Wood looked at each other. "That's out," Wood said. "Devin would be yelling, 'Keep America the way it was —for white Christians!'"

Chester went back to the Food and Souvenirs tent to consult Mrs. Hinck on a safer volunteer as relief man for Al. She had only women available. "The woman who teaches Dog Obedience has a good strong voice. And after all, there's no reason the Town Crier has to be a man." She looked at Chester severely. "That would be discrimination."

Chester had misgivings about letting the Dog Obedience woman take over; she might revert to form and shout, "To heel!" He said he and Wood would write out a small list of announcements for the new Town Cry-ess.

Mrs. Hinck's eyes brightened at the word "list." She herself had been in the midst of making lists of most wanted foods, to replenish stocks. "You'd think women just came to these affairs to buy homemade food," she said fretfully. "Cassie's pickled salmon sold out in a half hour, and of course I can't ask her to make any more, with that cast on. What a shame she can't be here. She kept us all going, that girl." Chester's opinion of Mrs. Hinck soared. "Isn't it nice she'll get to the opening tonight? I was just talking to Prue."

Chester hurried to the Crafts and Antiques tent and found Prue Washburn displaying a two-hundred-year-old gaming table to a bevy of visiting ladies from Ridgefield: "These holes in the four corners are for candlesticks," she chirped. "In case the gentlemen wanted to play late. And this leaf folds over so it looks like an ordinary table, and the cards were slipped into this secret drawer if the parson came to call unexpectedly. . . ."

Chester eased Prue away before she could explain the features of a pulpit lamp. She confirmed Cassie's improved condition. "She got your flowers—the sling—and it perked her up no end. I helped her wash her hair, and when I left she was setting it one-handed."

Chester had been married long enough to know what a good sign this was. He had consulted with his best designer on the flowers: "Something she can wear as a sling, but I don't want it to look like an over-the-shoulder funeral wreath." They had worked out a design in small yellow orchids with bright enamel butterflies; the designer himself had gone to supervise the florist. And hearing now that it was a success, that it had made Cassie want to set her hair, filled Chester with such elation he smiled warmly on every corseted antique lover in sight.

The Festival was suddenly festive, even for him. By then, the place was so crowded he let himself be carried along wherever the flow was strongest. In the Games section, he applauded heartily while contenders climbed the greased Liberty Pole and slid backwards. One boy had the cunning, or foresight, to wear flesh-colored rubber gloves, and these, with his rubber soles, took him to the top, where he clung like a monkey, grinning. Chester, with his aversion to heights, left hurriedly then, while other contenders were shouting "Foul."

Back in the center plaza, he caught the tail end of the teen-agers' fashion show. Lo, as master of ceremonies, was resplendent in his jackanapes suit of ribbon loops. "Notice the bull's-head curls and virago sleeves. . . . This head scarf was known as a clout. . . ." Lo interrupted his commentary to hiss at one youth, "Your steenkirk's undone." The boy looked down, horrified, yanking at his pants, while Lo hissed again, "Your neckpiece, stupid—not your codpiece."

The finale of the show had Fiera Young in cleavaged Liberty Maiden costume riding on a donkey, for reasons that may have been clear to Lo but not to anybody else. (One ingenious television commentator described her as "a camp follower.")

By the time Chester reached the Arts tent, twenty or so of the teen-agers, still in costume, were there examining Gail's poison-pokeberry painting with appreciative squeals. It was in a separate, darkened display cubicle lit only by strobe lights that cast a phosphorescent glow on the skull and crossbones. Whether it was or wasn't art, it was scary. Two middle-aged women, coming on it unawares, had fainted, and were being revived in another corner of the tent. Mrs. Loomite reported happily to Chester that *Arts Weekly* would feature it in the next issue. With catholic enthusiasm, she urged Chester to see the interfaith Blessing of the Animals in the plaza at three.

This event turned out to be a mixed blessing. Mrs. Loomite's Siamese cat, maddened by the water sprinkled on it during the ceremony, clawed at the nearest shinbones. A child's pet hamster bit the Catholic priest on the tender fleshy palm of the hand extended in blessing. The members of the Lions Club, dressed in Scottish kilts to supply bagpipe accompaniment, blew frenziedly, purple in the face, and most of the dogs gathered for the ceremony, hearing sounds not even a dog should hear, howled in agony.

Chester gave Cassie a faithful account of this before dinner at the Inn, while they were waiting for the Governor and other notables to arrive. The sound of her laughter stayed in his head even while he was listening to the Governor's cherries-jubilee oratory on the pioneer spirit. Cassie and the Governor got along famously; he had been in school with her father. Just once, the conversation threatened to get sticky. The Governor asked Cassie, "Where's Alicia Thorne? I thought she'd be here." Chester's breathing came shallow until he heard Cassie say, "I imagine she's having a facial and nap. After all, she needs her beauty sleep. She must be *much* older than you, Governor."

Cassie herself was looking enchanting, and using her flower

sling as if it were a fan, flirtily. Chester, seeing the Governor pat her pretty bare shoulder, thought, The old goat.

He was slightly ashamed of this later, when the Governor came over as Chester was helping Cassie into the car. "This girl of yours could get you a million or so votes on her own."

Cassie had looked up at Chester sweetly. "Governor, he doesn't need any help from me. He's terrific. He knows about housing and racial and labor problems, and tariffs, and algae —and women."

The shift in her mood came just before curtain time, when they were seated sixth row center. The orchestra was already on the overture; Alicia came down the aisle followed by three men. Chester, feeling Cassie stiffen, suffered for her even while he felt a disloyal surge of pleasure in Alicia's beauty. Her long white chiffon dress was rather Grecian in effect, and he thought he'd never seen her so beautiful. He had to admit, grudgingly, that Yates's dinner jacket fitted. He thought one of the other men was the Lincoln Center bigwig Alicia had joined for lunch in the Gray Humor Pub the day he and Trumbine were there. The third man was youngish, perhaps a few years older than Yates, with black-rimmed glasses and an insecure hairline.

Cassie, after one quick glance, opened her program and studied it busily while Alicia and her male entourage were seated across the aisle, one row ahead. To distract her, Chester said, "The Governor must be coming in now. Listen to the buzz."

It wasn't the Governor; it was Trumbine and . . . Chester stared, almost stupified with astonishment, at this other Alicia —a young version of Alicia with bronze hair streaming down, and a white mini-mini-sheath showing her marvelous legs. Not as beautiful as Alicia, perhaps, but so gloriously, carelessly young.

He murmured to Cassie, "That's Ross Trumbine's wife with him."

The expression on Cassie's face puzzled him; if he'd expected unholy glee, this was almost the opposite, more like compassion.

The buzz grew even louder as the girl was seated directly across the aisle from Alicia. Half the audience in the vicinity were creaking necks to watch. Alicia, perhaps expecting to see the Governor, leaned over to peer around Oliver, who was in the aisle seat. Her radiantly expectant smile froze.

"Hi, Mother," the girl called, in a clear, carrying tone. "What a long time it's been."

Chester, watching, had the curious impression he was seeing Alicia age before his eyes; her bones stuck out, and her cheeks had long hollows. Oliver looked as if he'd caught a slight case of lockjaw; Alicia recovered much faster. "Darling, how lovely," she called. She blew Trumbine a kiss. "Bless you for arranging this beautiful surprise."

Trumbine, caught between two fires, managed a two-way ploy. He took his wife's hand, and with his free hand he waved to his mother-in-law.

Almost nobody noticed the Governor come in. The curtain rose at that critical moment, on "Grow a Liberty Pole" and the audience insisted noisily on three encores, with a repeat of the pole-jabbing ballet before the "Him's a Trimmer" quartet could begin. But once on, the trimmers had to do four extra patter choruses with their soft-shoe routine. Cassie was giving off sounds of delight and beating her left hand on her cast to applaud. During the song of the Revolutionary plotters—"At the Tavern of the Headless Woman"—she let out a tiny moan, and Chester was anxiously solicitous. "Samuel Adams flatted his high note," she whispered. The next four numbers, including a charming duet, with pantomime, for "Me and Thee Here in the Stocks," went off without a sour note.

The last number in the first act—"Throwin' a Stone Bee"—began rather ominously. A group of farmers armed with large stones advanced on a lone man who was hoeing. It looked like one-sided mayhem, until the farmers sang lustily:

> "Don't go to your neighbor throwin' a stone
> Help him build a place to call his own.
> You do it for him, he'll do it for you,
> The Golden Rule brings profits too.

Got no room for bigotry
When we're throwin' a stone bee.

Perhaps partly out of relief to have so wholesome and happy an ending after the menacing start, the audience reacted with shouts of "Bravo." As the lights went up for intermission, a dozen or so people in the front rows raced to be the first to reach Alicia. Although they didn't actually carry her up the aisle on their shoulders, the effect was triumphal. "Oliver must have fixed up those lyrics," Cassie said. "Somehow they don't sound like Alicia." As Oliver was swept up the aisle in the tail end of admirers and people who just wanted to go out and smoke, Cassie waved and made a sign of victory. Oliver shouted, "Wait till you hear—" but was carried off before he could finish.

Trumbine, in the row ahead, turned to introduce his wife to Cassie and Chester. "What you're doing is so terribly important," Allie said intensely to Chester. "Ross has told me. You simply must run for Congress. We're desperate for someone like you."

Chester felt a splendid warmth invade his libido. She had golden-flecked eyes like her mother's. Nothing to look away from. "Promise me you will."

Cassie said firmly, "Chet can't promise yet. He has to decide where he can do the most good."

She sounded so wifely that Allie gave her a quick, direct look, evaluating, then tacitly acknowledging ownership. "You're right. Congress can be a quagmire. Oh, your poor arm. I broke mine water skiing. You must do exercises the minute you get out of the cast. The best one is to keep opening and closing your fist." She clenched and unclenched, demonstrating. "Why don't you two men go out and smoke? I'll stay here with Miss Murdoch. She shouldn't buck that mob."

Cassie agreed. The two women had established one of those instant, invisible enclaves any man would be a fool to try crashing. Chester and Trumbine went off meekly to have a cigarette outside the music tent.

A pantalooned youth was pushing through the crowd bawling, "Hot coffin pies at the refreshment stand. . . . Better than pizza for a late snack."

Alicia was holding court, but all Chester could see of her was the top of her head and occasional streaks of her white dress during the shiftings of courtiers and ladies-in-waiting.

The Governor left the group to come over to congratulate Chester and Trumbine, and he went back inside with them before the buzzer sounded, to meet Trumbine's wife. "I'd expect Alicia to have a daughter like you," he said to Allie. "In her day she broke more hearts than all the other women in Boston put together."

"I'm sure she did," Allie said coolly. "I was one of the victims. Governor, what are you going to do about Hartford's urban ghettos?"

The Governor, a custom-tailored sort who disliked the straight-off-the-rack approach, mumbled something about "appointed a distinguished committee" and retreated rather quickly. Trumbine said to Chester, "You can see she's the ideal mate for a public relations man."

"I'm trying to shame him into changing jobs," Allie said. "He has great potentialities, but he's still on the slick side." She asked Chester what *he* would do about black ghettos.

"He's already doing it," Cassie said. "He's too modest to tell you, but—"

"That's why he needs me," Trumbine cut in smoothly. "Brace yourself, baby. Here comes Medea-Mama."

Alicia was at her most charming. With the young playwright hovering behind her, she said to Allie, "Everybody is entranced with you, darling. And having you here has made this such a special night in my life. I do hope you'll stay in this country now, and not go kiting around living with Indians."

Listeners on the fringes could well have been convinced that Allie was a wild one who had defied the most loving parental guidance.

Allie gave her long hair a casual fling. "I'll stay here at least till I finish my novel."

"Lamb, how exciting," Alicia's voice was too shrill. "Let me send you to my publisher."

"I already have a publisher," Allie said. "I'll send you an autographed copy when it comes out. I think you'd be interested in the main character, Mother."

Alicia tried to laugh; it wasn't too successful. She clutched the arm of the young playwright as if it were a life line and went back to her seat. Cassie murmured to Chester, "And a mother can't sue a daughter for invasion of privacy. That would be like incest backwards." She glanced across the aisle. "I can't help feeling sorry for her. Go over and say something sickeningly flattering. She needs it."

"I love you," Chester said. It came out without volition, although it must have been there, formless, all along. He wasn't even sure Cassie heard him, because Oliver appeared suddenly, leaning over to blurt out, "The new song isn't in the program—they were already printed. And it can't be announced—we don't want the singer known ahead—you'll see why. Didn't you think 'Leathery Man' sounded much better done this way?"

Chester thought scornfully, He's like a child wanting to be told how good he is.

As the lights dimmed, Oliver was saying ". . . call you later tonight if I can duck out of Latham's party."

The curtain went up on the Illegitimate Mamas belting out the weaving song, "Thump the Batten." Chester, who felt like thumping something bigger than a batten, and reedier, was so frustrated he had a mean attack of indigestion.

It quieted during "Will I Trade My Lover for a Bag of Salt?" But he had a different kind of jabbing pain later when the younger members of the audience went wild over "Fiddle with a Horse's Tail" and stomped their approval in a rhythm of pounding. Yates was going to be famous; it hurt him to think that. Cassie said, "She's been good for his music. He's surer now." Chester felt even more inadequate.

For the last number, the stage was almost in darkness. It

took a while to make out the motionless forms of soldiers huddled on the ground. The light from a lantern picked up one boy in tattered uniform, who got to his feet slowly. The feet were wrapped in bloody rags. Softly, sorrowfully, the sweet young voice came reaching out: ". . . listen to the way I died."

At the finish, there was an almost total hush for several seconds, but as the lights came up, the audience—notably those under thirty—recognized their idol and exploded: cheers, whistles, jumping on seats to scream, "Again, Jimmy! Sing it again."

The singer shook his head smilingly and beckoned to Oliver, who got up from his seat looking rather stunned. Alicia gave him a little push. "Go on, darling. Go up there."

"You too," Oliver muttered, either out of professional courtesy or because he wanted support.

Once on-stage, Alicia stood between the two men, and since the star role came naturally to her—she not only looked the part but acted it, graciously accepting her due—she got a considerably bigger hand than Oliver. When she blew a kiss to the young singer, the crowd went wild. And on the last curtain call, it was she who graciously motioned the rest of the cast to come forward and share in her applause.

"She's hogging all the credit," Cassie said. When she turned, Chester saw she'd been crying. "I'm sorry. But I'm still in love with—"

He didn't give her a chance to finish. "You don't have to tell me you're sorry. You can still marry him."

"But I don't want to," Cassie said. "I just meant I'm still in love with his music. That's the best part of him." She hiccuped one more sob, and sniffled.

"You could use some powder on your nose." It had been his experience that women who put on a fresh face are more reluctant to cry.

Cassie looked at him, her lashes still wet with tears but her eyes very clear and blue. "Stand by for repairs. Will you hold up the mirror for me? I can't grasp it in my teeth." Chester held up her compact. The look on his own face, as he watched her dabbing left-handed, bordered on the fatuous.

"We'll skip Latham's party," he said. "You ought to be in bed. But before we go, let's catch Oliver and tell him it was great. Especially that last song."

In the lobby, Alicia kept saying to people with just the right degree of modest disclaimer, "I don't deserve this. It's really Oliver's song. Don't you love it? Isn't he talented? I spotted that the first day."

She went on saying this prettily, with variations, at Latham's party. Everybody (except Oliver) thought she was being madly generous.

The young playwright who was to work on Benedict Arnold was following her around with a dazed look on his face.